BLOODIED ICE

A KICKASS CASSIE NOVEL: BOOK FOUR

LEAH R CUTTER

KNOTTED ROAD PRESS

Bloodied Ice
A Kickass Cassie Novel: Book Four
Copyright © 2018 Leah Cutter
All rights reserved

Published 2018 by Knotted Road Press
www.KnottedRoadPress.com

ISBN: 978-1-943663-92-7

Cover art and design by Franzi Haase
https://99designs.com/profiles/rabbittm

Interior design copyright © 2018 Knotted Road Press
www.KnottedRoadPress.com

Come someplace new…
Are you a traveler? Do you enjoy exploring strange new worlds, new cultures, new people?

Journey into the various lands envisioned by Leah Cutter.

Sign up for my newsletter and I'll start you on your travels with a free copy of my book, *The Island Sampler.*

I will never spam you or use your email for nefarious purposes. You can also unsubscribe at any time.

http://www.LeahCutter.com/newsletter/

ALSO BY LEAH R CUTTER

The Cassie Stories

Poisoned Pearls

Tainted Waters

Spoiled Harvest

Bloodied Ice

Tanish Empire Trilogy

The Glass Magician

The Desert Heart

The Ghost Dog

The Shadow Wars Trilogy

The Raven and the Dancing Tiger

The Guardian Hound

War Among the Crocodiles

The Clockwork Fairy Kingdom Trilogy

The Clockwork Fairy Kingdom

The Maker, the Teacher, and the Monster

The Dwarven Wars

Seattle Trolls Trilogy

The Changeling Troll
The Princess Troll
The Fairy-Bridge Troll

The Chronicles of Franklin

The Popcorn Thief
The Soul Thief
The Child Thief

Contemporary Fantasy

Siren's Call
The Immortals' War

PROLOGUE

THE ANCIENT EGYPTIAN god Set stormed across the heart of the desert. Wind spun sand into great cyclones around him, towering whirlwinds that rose up to the blackened sky. Lightning crackled between the clouds, threatening to set the very heavens on fire. The smell of desiccated bodies and dark magic followed the god as he raced across the sands in his rage.

Set wore his Set-Animal form, which some stupid mortals likened to a pig because of his curved snout and square-ish ears. Others described him as a hound because of his dog-like body and thin tail. Any soul who dared to cross the border between their plane and this world of the Egyptian gods would quickly realize that Set was something much, *much* different than any of the traditional animals. He was unique in all the worlds.

He actually liked the term that one idiot human poet had used: Hell Hound. It held connotations of how Set would chase his prey to their deaths and beyond. Though he still wasn't a dog. Not like that dog-headed idiot Anubis.

Sure, men described Anubis as "jackal-headed" with all the

sinister implications implied therein. Had they never seen one of the pharaoh's dogs? Anubis was as faithful, and as dumb, as that purebred line, with all the brains purposefully bred out of them.

Stupid humans.

Set raced on, his burning red eyes seeing clearly through the haze of sand. Clawed feet found purchase over the shifting dunes. He was only the size of a lion, though he could grow much larger as need arose. He wore red fur today, the traditional color of death and destruction. His black forked tongue stuck out of the side of his mouth, panting in the great heat.

The god had been so sure that *this* time, man would actually destroy himself. Set didn't care enough to try to understand the science behind their toys. He just wanted the earth scrubbed clean of mankind's presence so the world (and the gods) could be born anew.

However, this time the birth of the world would be different. It wouldn't come into being through some dung beetle pushing the sun before him, a giant egg waiting to hatch. And it sure as hell wouldn't be the god Atum either, rising from the primeval waters and creating the first sacred mound.

No, Set himself would rise from the ashes of the world that had been, rebirthing the gods who'd been faithful to him, as well as creating a new race of men who displayed the proper amount of obedience and worship, instead of these godless heathens who steadfastly *refused* to do all the worlds a favor by blowing themselves to smithereens.

Damn them all! Set raged, hurling his winds and storms across the great desert, causing the few creatures who lived there to cower in their dens. The earth trembled with his passage. The sky bled gouts of fire like tears. Smoke and ash were all he breathed.

After what felt like an eternity, Set's anger blew itself out. The winds lessened, the clouds broke up, and the great domed sky cleared. Harsh sunlight shone down on the glistening sands. The smell of baked rocks and cool hidden oases rose up. Quiet reigned, the silence of the desert surrounding Set again.

Set looked around to see where he was, squinting in the bright sunlight. Same place he'd ended up last time, on the far southern border of the desert, near the mountains and the coast. He smelled the wet of the ocean, still leagues and leagues away, but insinuating itself into the desert air. The finest grain grew in the valley between the sands and the rocks, from which Set brewed the sweetest beer.

Maybe he should go check on his crops. He shook himself and transformed into a more human-like form. He wore the traditional braided beard of the pharaohs, though he kept his head shaved clean. He had no crown or headpiece, and woe be to the one who suggested his naked skull looked barren. Black kohl outlined his dark eyes. A proud nose stood out from his face, hanging above thin, cruel lips. His skin had the golden hue of the first morning sunlight.

He wore a white robe that went down to his calves and was tied around his waist with a brilliant red belt. A rainbow colored necklace of precious stones hung down to the middle of his emaciated chest. Set had lived too long in chaos and the desert for his body to ever "plump up" again.

A giant staff rose out of the ground for Set to walk with. It was forged out of black iron with bronze rings decorating it. A sharp, hooked *khopesh* rose out of the top of the staff, towering above Set's head. Traditionally, only the outer curve of the blade would be sharpened, but Set had made both edges deadly.

Set walked slowly across the fierce desert sands. What would he do after he visited these fields? There was nowhere else for him to go but back to his palace, to visit his wife Nephthys and enjoy the fruits of the labors of his *shabits*, the clay golems who worked the fields, baked his bread, and made his beer.

Suddenly, the ground underneath Set's sandals trembled. The

air in front of him grew hazy. Set stopped walking and willed the mirage before him into being.

That stupid, *prideful* Norse god Loki rose up. He was as white as a maggot who gnawed on corpses and not much more intelligent than one as well.

Set barely managed to stop himself from cutting the idiot in two.

Loki wore his blond-white hair loose down to his shoulders like a woman. Scars traversed his face like a river delta, caused by some poison, probably also from a woman, knowing him. He only had one eye this time that blazed as blue as the sky, who was also a woman. As for the gaping black hole…must have given the other eye to a woman.

"Finished with our tantrum, finally?" Loki said. "Ready to talk like a civil being?"

Set pressed his lips together so that he would not blast this disrespectful "god" to pieces.

The last time he'd done that, Loki had had the gall to laugh, *laugh* at Set. And complain how his mistreatment had *tickled*.

"Seems we both have the same problem," Loki continued. "Mankind."

Set refused to be interested in what this trickster had to say. In Set's day, he'd also been known as a trickster. As the modern saying went, *it takes one to know one*, so Set had a deep aversion to Loki and mistrusted every word that tumbled from his spoiled lips.

Set started walking again, striding across the desert. Anything would be better than to dally and exchange words with this one.

"Don't you gods have the ability to be re-birthed?" Loki asked, falling in beside Set, easily keeping up with him.

Set always forgot that the damned god was part giant and so could match him stride for stride, even though Loki only rose up to Set's chest at this point.

"We have myths of being reborn as well," Loki said after Set didn't reply. "Stronger and better than we had been."

"What, do you want me to come and kill all of the Norse gods? So that you might be reborn?" Set asked, sneering.

"You know, that might not be a bad idea," Loki said, sounding as if he'd never had such a thought before.

Set snorted in derision. Despite how "spontaneous" Loki acted, Set knew everything Loki said had been rehearsed many times.

"Right," Set said. "I suppose you'll kill us first, then promise to bring us back. Seems I've heard that myth before." He knew of other gods who'd fallen for such a trick.

Not Set.

"No, I think you should raise an army and come storm Valhalla," Loki replied.

"And get slaughtered," Set replied dryly.

"I'd get you across the Bifrost bridge," Loki said. "After that, yeah, you'd be on your own. But you'd cross the first hurdle without a scratch. Besides, wouldn't you want to put your greatest enemies up front? So that if some did get killed, the faithful would still be surrounding you?"

Set considered the Norse god's proposal. The first task was indeed getting to the land of any other gods. Set was never sure how Loki managed it without getting permanently killed. (Though Set had killed the other god a number of times over the centuries just because Loki was such an annoying shit.)

"I need to consider this idea of yours," Set said slowly. He didn't trust this Loki.

"Better hurry," Loki said. "My plans are already starting to take shape. And I could use a mighty warrior like you on my side."

Set knew better than to believe the praise, though he still found himself puffing up. "I will judge the worthiness of your suggestion in the fullness of time," Set said.

"Of course, you will," Loki said.

Really, did Loki need to sound so snide? Especially since *he* had come *here*, to Set's desert, to essentially ask a favor?

"You may go now," Set said, well aware of just how pompous he sounded.

That was one of the good parts of being a god. He really didn't have to care what he sounded like, or how others saw him.

Set merely *was*. He lived, despite the centuries. That was all that mattered.

"Fine, fine, I can take a hint," Loki said. "But at some point, you need to introduce me to that sexy wife of yours. Or is it your sister?"

Set shrugged. Such relationships tended to be fluid as well.

"Bother me later, little man," Set said as he strode off, using his desert power to push himself along faster than the other god could have walked.

"I'm counting the minutes until you call!" Loki cheekily replied.

Set took a deep breath as he felt the peace of the desert return. Loki was such a disturbing force.

However, he had a point.

Instead of focusing on men and getting them to destroy themselves, maybe he should turn his brilliant, burning gaze on the other gods. Get them to kill each other off.

Who would support him in this grand scheme? Which idiots, besides Isis, Osiris, and Horus, along with the dumb dog Anubus, would oppose him?

And how could he turn this plan to his advantage before Loki changed the rules and made him lose?

HUNTER SAT at the back of the church meeting hall with all the other addicts who'd decided AA was the place for them. Two dozen men and women filled the uncomfortable, gray plastic chairs. Many of the people there were anxious or scared, but none of them were actually dangerous, not like Hunter, who'd assessed the threat level in the room as fairly low.

He sat perfectly still in his chair, unlike everyone else who shifted restlessly and muttered. A wooden podium had been set up at the front of the room, which could easily double as a pulpit. The tall, skinny man standing behind it looked like a scrawny English professor, like Hunter's dad. He had thinning hair around the fringes of his balding skull and an extremely long, pale face. His Adam's apple bobbed rhythmically with his nervous swallowing. Watery gray eyes looked out through thick, wire-rimmed glasses.

He was still going on and on about his addiction to pain killers and how he'd started circling the drain.

Hunter let his attention drift, recounting the number of escape routes that already existed, as well as the ones he could create, punching through walls or jumping through windows. He hated it when the meetings were held in places like this—underground, without enough proper exits. At least the far end of the hall was all windows, along with a sliding glass door, all of which were currently covered with snow. However, no matter how brightly the long neon lights shone down on him, shadows lurked in the corners.

The room smelled of fake sugar and bitter coffee. Seemed that most addicts exchanged one addiction for another: instead of booze, they now drank gallons of the blackest coffee they could find. They'd probably shoot up the stuff if they thought it would do any good.

The cheap linoleum floor had a pattern on it at one point, but years of careful scrubbing had removed it, so now it was just a dingy yellow instead of white with gold squares.

The door leading up the stairs and out of the hall was directly to Hunter's left. He'd had to stare down some punk who'd thought that *she* belonged in the spot closest to the door. However, that was Hunter's place. Though it wasn't as if he couldn't *move* faster than any of them, or even possibly than all of them, their speed added together.

Hunter still wore his coat in case he did need to leave quickly, though he'd had to unbutton it in the warm basement. Cassie, his boss, had bought it for him the previous fall, a nice dark brown wool jacket that hung down to his knees and kept him warm through the Minnesota winter. Of course, he had on his old combat boots, so his feet stayed dry and would be well protected in a fight. He also wore tough jeans, not those pre-faded ones that tore easily, or even, heaven forbid, the ones that came already ripped. His only concession to "looking nice" was a clean white shirt.

A long plastic table stood beside the door, pushed against the wall. It held a huge coffee urn, bottles of water, and the cheap, store-bought cookies that Hunter had come to expect at these meetings. A squat wooden basket sat next to the "goodies," empty except for the helpful note explaining that all donations were welcome.

Hunter recognized the gait of the person coming down the stairs before he turned his head to let his eyes verify.

Yes, that was Mac, his sponsor. Bald guy, short and round. His ruddy cheeks burned bright red in the warmth of the hall after the brutal winds and cold of Minneapolis in February. Mac wore his usual khaki army jacket, combat boots, and jeans. No hat or scarf—he agreed with Hunter those "accessories" were too easy for an opponent to use against the wearer in a fight.

"Sorry I'm late," Mac said. He slid into the row and sat next to Hunter, leaving Hunter in the spot closest to the door. "Traffic."

Hunter nodded, though he didn't drive and was only ever aware of the number of cars on the roads as possible threats. Cassie had been on his ass about that lately, letting him know how *useful* it might be if he'd grow the fuck up and take on a few more responsibilities for the business.

She didn't mean it in a cruel way. Her heart was in the right place. But their business was, well, busier than before, and she was stressed.

He suspected she was also stressed because Cassie's girlfriend—Theresa, also known as Dr. T—had been hinting about making their arrangement more permanent. And Valentine's Day was just around the corner.

Maybe someday Hunter would renew his driver's license. Let the government have yet one more way of tracking him. Hell, he might even just use his real name on it—Robert.

Except that wasn't his real name. That was just the name he'd been born with. Maybe it would be better to use that one on all his official paperwork, though he hadn't been called Robert by anyone other than his parents for years.

"This guy got anything useful to say?" Mac whispered, nudging Hunter and directing his attention toward the front of the room.

Hunter shrugged but didn't apologize for his wandering thoughts. He didn't come here for the confessions of other addicts.

"I was at the very bottom of my rope," the man behind the podium up front was currently saying. His voice sounded hoarse, as if he'd been screaming for the last twenty minutes.

Hunter wished he could fast-forward through the guy's speech instead of having to go through the agony of his growing addiction. He wanted to hear how the guy *stayed* sober.

No luck there, though. He ended with how he'd started to come to meetings, and how god had saved his life.

Hunter wasn't about to roll his eyes over that. He'd hurt something. Gods were too involved with their own petty lives to actually try to help humanity. He knew. He'd met more than one.

As the others applauded the guy behind the podium, Mac raised an expectant eyebrow at Hunter.

Hunter just shook his head.

He wasn't ready to tell his story. He might never be. How could he trust a group of mostly strangers (as the people who came to these meetings shifted constantly) enough to tell them his story? How could he speak of being purposefully addicted by the government and then deliberately kept in that state, first by Jacobsen Consortium, then by a drug dealer?

It had been hard enough for him to learn to trust Mac. But Mac had a built-in advantage: He was also a veteran and lived in the same shared housing as Hunter. Hunter had been able to watch Mac for more than a month, work beside him in the kitchen and out in the yard, spot each other doing weights while grousing about the washing machines they all used.

Hunter had come to trust Mac as much as he trusted anyone. Hunter trusted Cassie more, but she was his true blood brother, a concept that he didn't even bother trying to explain to anyone else. They'd honed their hunting skills together over the past year and a half since Hunter had gotten out of jail, working in tandem as a pre- and post-cog, their strange powers complementing each other.

"You know, people might be able to learn from your story," Mac said as the meeting ended and people started getting ready to go.

"Naw," Hunter said, trying to sound casual. He was aware that for the others, the story of overcoming addition was cathartic for them. For him, he needed the tips and tricks more. He'd learned to distract himself so he wouldn't go searching for more drugs. He'd also been figuring out how to engage his senses in *this* world to block the cravings for the *other*. He'd had to trust Cassie as well as himself that his *area of knowing* was large enough that he didn't need the drugs to expand it to more than a couple of city blocks.

Hunter still wasn't sure how to get the ghosts and various bored gods to stop pestering him. They wanted him to take the drugs so he could interact with them better. Over the past year, they'd shifted their focus to Cassie, since she still took the *poisoned pearls* on a quarterly basis.

However, she wasn't addicted to them, not like he'd been.

For Hunter, coming to the meetings wasn't a matter of

transforming and becoming sober and clean. It was how to *stay* sober and clean.

"Maybe someday you'll share your story," Mac said.

"Someday," Hunter agreed. After all, he would never have expected to be clean as long as he'd managed. He'd been addicted for more than a decade, and only off the drugs for one year and five months. (He didn't count the time he'd spent detoxing and getting clean while he'd been in jail. The sober time for him didn't start until he was out and had a choice in the matter.)

Hunter wasn't sure what Mac meant by the look he shot him. Hunter hadn't told Mac the full story, though Mac had enough of the pieces that he could probably put together a map of Hunter's journey. Did Mac want Hunter to talk in front of the group in order to hear more?

"Dinner?" Mac asked as they stood up and got ready to go.

"Uhm," Hunter said, pausing. "I, uhm, have a date."

Mac stood stock still and stared intently at Hunter. "Okay, who are you and what have you done with the real Hunter?"

"It's not my first date ever, you know," Hunter said. He didn't want to show Mac how bothered he was, but he suspected his tone gave away how hurt he felt. Hunter was trying so hard to pass and learn how to at least appear normal.

"Right on!" Mac said. "You get 'em, tiger."

Hunter rolled his eyes. This was just another date with Audrey. He wasn't actually her boyfriend or anything. Audrey had been very clear about that. This was just their fifth evening out together. They weren't officially dating. Might not ever.

Maybe Hunter could finally kiss her tonight, though he didn't know if she'd allow that yet. She, too, had issues with people getting too close, having been in the Army. However, she was mostly normal, or at least more normal than Hunter. She didn't have psychic abilities, wasn't one of the *blessed*.

"Where are you taking her?" Mac asked as they both buttoned

up their jackets and started up the stairs, bracing themselves for the cold winter night outside.

Hunter gave Mac a grin. "Double date. Hockey game with Cassie and her main squeeze."

"You dog! Styling with three ladies," Mac said, laughing.

Hunter just shook his head. Like the rest of the guys, Mac had no idea how Cassie would hand him his balls if he made a move on her or Theresa. They just didn't get the concept of *lesbian*. They all figured that she'd just never met the right guy. They were wrong.

A long black town car slid up to the curb as soon as they stepped outside. It gave Hunter such a sense of satisfaction seeing how well Hakeem had integrated into the business. No matter what Cassie might say about Hakeem being a double-agent, their tiny Ethiopian driver had learned their patterns very well.

"You need a ride?" Hunter asked Mac as Hakeem got out and came around to open up the back door. He wore his usual spiffy black jacket, warm argyle vest, white shirt, and running shoes. He came up to about the middle of Hunter's chest.

"I got my car," Mac said. He put his hand out to make Hunter pause, though he didn't actually touch Hunter. He knew better. An unexpected touch, even from a friend, might have left Mac with a broken hand or wrist.

"Someday, kid, I do want all the stories," Mac said seriously. "You and Cassie, this crazy job, your driver, everything."

Hunter shrugged. "Maybe someday," he said. He wasn't about to promise anything.

As Hakeem pulled smoothly into traffic, Hunter tried to figure out why Mac wanted those stories. Was it just human nature and curiosity? Or was it something else?

Cassie would scold Hunter for questioning Mac, someone who'd been nothing but a friend to Hunter for months now.

But it was in Hunter's nature to question. Even his friends.

Maybe especially his friends.

1

I swore that if one more weird thing happened tonight, I was declaring the start of the apocalypse.

First of all, Hunter had shown up with a girl. *A girl. A DATE.*

When Hunter had asked if it was all right to bring someone along to the game, I'd figured he'd bring Mac. As far as I knew, Mac was Hunter's only friend, a guy he'd do things with outside of the vet housing they both lived in.

I sure as hell wasn't expecting this girl named Audrey. Freckles covered her pale nose and cheeks. She had huge green eyes and long, black, wavy hair that went midway down her back. She wasn't much taller than Hakeem, which meant that Theresa, me, and Hunter all towered over her.

"So, where did you two meet?" I finally asked after introductions had been made. We stood in line outside the arena, waiting to get in. At least it was a fast line. It was still February in Minnesota and the winds whipping around us were cold enough to instantly freeze any exposed body parts. The air smelled clean, though, and no storm was coming.

I was wearing my usual black leather jacket, even though it wasn't completely appropriate for this weather as it only came down to my waist and it left my butt exposed to the freezing winds. However, I had a fantastic ass, one of my best *assets*. Tight blue jeans covered it, tucked into my twenty ring docs. Underneath my jacket, I wore a subdued (for me) green sweater over a white shirt, also tight enough to show off my curves.

Theresa wore a brown leather jacket that went down to mid-thigh. It was butter soft. Wrapped tightly around her neck she wore a gold and maroon scarf (the colors of the Golden Gophers, her team). Under her jacket she had on a matching jersey with a huge M—the team's emblem—in the center of it, obscuring her great rack. She'd listened to me bitch about it but then went ahead and wore it anyway. That tended to be our pattern. At least she'd worn a really nice set of jeans that showed off her own assets. Her hair was wavy, down to her shoulders, and so soft that I always wanted to touch it. She'd added a subtle streak of maroon to the front piece, close to her face.

"Audrey and I met at the VA hospital," Hunter told us after glancing at Audrey for a moment. He stood close to his date. I bet he wanted to hold hands with her. Though possibly he might have just wanted to share some body heat.

That had been another sign of the apocalypse: Theresa had actually taken *my* hand while we were in public! While I was no prude and a little PSA never bothered me, Theresa was a bit skittish about these sorts of things. In many ways, I was her first girlfriend —though she had dated a girl for a brief time in college, that was over a decade ago.

Unlike my former girlfriend Sam, Theresa never hid her relationship with me. Hell, I'd been introduced to her parents during our first month of officially dating, which had been weird enough on its own. Now, we went over for Sunday dinner once a month. Not anything I'd ever expected in my life.

"Are you a doctor?" I asked Audrey as we moved closer to the door. Heat blasted out of the stadium, though I knew better than to hope that we'd get really warm in there. Plus, I was certain that Theresa had gotten us seats close to the ice.

My question earned me a quick smile from Audrey. I figured that was because I'd asked if she was a doctor and not a nurse. A man would have assumed she held a lesser position.

"No, I don't work at the VA," Audrey replied in a surprisingly deep, firm voice. "I'm a vet. Hunter and I met because I'm also getting my head shrunk there."

Though I'd never, *ever* imagined that Hunter would start dating, it made sense that he'd pick someone who was not only a veteran, but kind of screwed up as well. Hunter would be the screwier of the two, but a woman who'd gone through basic training wouldn't put up with his shit, which would be something he needed.

We made it to the door before I had to engage in any more awkward social commentary. Theresa knew the layout of the stadium and led us proudly to our seats, which, as I'd guessed, were close to the ice, right near the center, front row behind the visitor's penalty box, so we could see everything.

I kept an eye on Hunter as we made our way down the steep stairs. He'd had his throat cut by Loki in a sports arena, though not this one.

However, he didn't appear to be worried or having any flashbacks. He and Audrey both still darted their eyes everywhere, counting exits as well as doing a general threat assessment. I figured that the guys who'd be the most dangerous were the drunken frat boys sitting a few rows up and back. Hockey fans were rowdy, but generally not destructive, at least in my experience so far.

I wasn't worried about our safety. Hunter would *flatten* anyone who threatened us, and I pretty much assumed that Audrey would do the same.

Which led to the third sign of the apocalypse: Not only did

Hunter volunteer to pay for our hotdogs, cheese curds, and beer, he volunteered to traipse through the crowds on his own to go get them.

"Are you sure?" I asked him after he'd taken all our orders. His hands would be full on the way back. Of course, he'd drop everything if someone came after him. For all I knew, he'd been practicing killing someone by spearing them with a hotdog.

"I'm fine, Cassie," he said with a smile that appeared a hell of a lot calmer than I expected.

"You go, then," I told him with an imperial wave of my hand, just to fuck with him.

Which left Theresa, me, and Audrey all sitting together waiting for the show to start.

"You ever been to a hockey game before?" I asked Audrey. Which was kind of another sign of the apocalypse. This wasn't my first game. Not by a long shot. I wasn't a fan, not like Theresa. But an evening of watching pretty boys skate around and damage each other wasn't a horrible date for us.

Of course, I'd rather be someplace private where I could do naughty things to Theresa, but then, that was my default state.

"Not college," Audrey admitted. "Saw the Wild play once."

I didn't have to look over at Theresa to see how hard she was rolling her eyes. She had a deep abiding disgust for the NHL and all the teams who played in it. The North Stars leaving Minnesota hadn't killed her interest in the sport, as she'd been too young when it had happened. But the strikes had. She'd never forgiven the millionaires (the players) fighting with the billionaires (the owners). She'd sworn off hockey for a season but found she'd really missed it, and so had switched her allegiance to the University of Minnesota team instead.

"So, Hunter works for you?" Audrey asked into the ensuing silence.

"Yeah," I said proudly. It was kind of awesome that I was finally making enough to keep Hunter employed. I couldn't hire Hakeem full time, not yet. I'd actually listened to Chinaman Joe's advice and had made the decision not to bring on Hakeem until after I had a full year of his salary in the bank. "The business had been doing great this last year," I added. "Hunter's a big part of that."

"He told me that he works as a pre-cog for you, while you're a post-cog," Audrey said. She sounded proud of him and his abilities.

That made me like her a whole bunch more. "Are you a PA?" I asked. Officially, PA stood for *paranormal abilities*. Before I'd found my powers, I'd called them *Pain in the Ass* instead of what they called themselves—the *blessed*.

"Nope, one hundred percent normal here," Audrey said. Then she shrugged. "Sort of."

I nodded but didn't push. I knew what she meant. She'd already admitted to seeing a therapist at the VA. Hunter went regularly, as was required for what he called his *wergild*, the blood money the government paid him for having gotten him addicted in the first place to the *poisoned pearls*.

The therapy had done him a lot of good, honestly. So had the AA meetings, as much as he'd deny it.

"Where do you work?" I asked her politely. I figured she'd be in an office or something white collar.

"I run a carwash, downtown," Audrey said. "The Pink Hippo."

That surprised me. I knew the spot. It took up a little triangle of space where three streets merged. It had a huge pink-and-white neon sign above the building that showed a gigantic hippopotamus dancing in the rain. I wouldn't have taken any bets on how long the carwash would survive there, given how hard the area was gentrifying.

Then again, if Audrey ran the place well, and if she owned the building, a developer would have to add a few zeroes to whatever offer they made her. Audrey wasn't one to be pushed around.

"I hire a lot of vets and homeless people," Audrey continued.

"Since I'm enrolled in the city Fresh Start programs, the carwash has become something of an institution."

"Speaking as a formerly homeless person, I thank you," I told her sincerely. I didn't know where I would have ended up if Chinaman Joe hadn't taken pity on me and decided to hire me despite not having a lot of job experience.

Audrey nodded and said, "You're welcome. I hear that a lot."

"I suppose that Hakeem has already talked with you about a discount," I asked. I still took on far too many of his "relatives'" cases. Fortunately, a few of them actually paid money, not just in barter or food.

That made Audrey laugh. "Hakeem is quite charming," she said. "But charm won't pay the bills. I take on too many charity cases as it is."

"Good," I told her, though I was kind of in awe. I mean, I wasn't a pushover by any stretch of the imagination, but Hakeem had wormed his way into my good graces, even though he worked as a double-agent and reported on us to Jacobsen Consortium.

I was doubly impressed that Audrey had managed to stand up to him.

Hunter came back, his hands full of goodies. I passed things along to Theresa. When Hunter looked over at me, apparently checking in with how things had gone, I gave him a thumbs up.

Audrey had passed with flying colors.

Hopefully Hunter wouldn't do anything to screw their relationship up.

THE CROWD WAS a bit riled for this game. The team was playing an arch rival—the Badgers from Wisconsin. Too many fans wore black and red, the team's colors. Those were also Loki's colors. It made me uncomfortable. Plus, I hadn't been bothered by the smart-mouthed god in a few months, which meant that he was up to no good.

Fortunately, the Gophers were ahead by the end of the first period. The Zamboni skated slowly around the rink while people sang to old-school rock and roll. I suppose hip hop just didn't do it for hard-core fans like Theresa, though I'd seen her shake that very fine ass of hers to some pretty funky music more than once.

Audrey talked with Hunter quietly, asking about the game. Wasn't sure what he was telling her, since he had even less of a clue about what was going on than I did. Theresa was the expert by far.

As the players skated onto the rink at the start of the second period, I noticed Hunter had grown still, as frozen as the ice for at least a minute.

Then he swung his head around, looking in all directions, eyes darting to the far corners of the arena.

"Hunter?" I asked, ignoring how Theresa continued to cheer on the players skating onto the ice.

He nodded. "Something's coming, boss."

I'd almost gotten used to him calling me boss, though I suspected he still did it, in part, to mess with me.

"Any idea what?" I asked.

Audrey waved her hand and used her finger to indicate that we should switch seats.

I gladly let her climb under me to sit next to Theresa, who'd finally noticed that something was going on.

"Don't know," Hunter said. He scratched at the back of his neck, then rolled his head from side to side. "It's got my spidey-sense tingling, though."

I'd explained the reference to Hunter once, and he'd run with it ever since. Between us, it meant that something other than a usual crime was about to occur. A regular murder, stabbing, or hell, even a common robbery didn't make Hunter's "spidey-sense" react.

Nope. This was something major. Probably dealing with a god, a ghost, or some other weird supernatural being that Jacobsen Consortium continued to deny the existence of.

"Crap," was all I could answer to Hunter's assessment. "We safe?"

I wasn't about to stick around if it meant putting Theresa into danger. Audrey and Hunter could take care of themselves, I was certain. Beyond a little self-defense, I wasn't trained, not like they were. However, when push came to shove, I was meaner than all of them put together, and that went a long ways in a fight.

Theresa, though, worked in a lab. Hockey was about as dangerous as she got.

"We're safe enough," Hunter said, shrugging. "Threat isn't against us."

"You let me know if we need to boogie," I told him. "First sign of danger, you get Theresa out of here. You hear me?"

Hunter paused, glancing over at her, then at Audrey. Finally, he nodded. I knew that he'd come to the same conclusion I had: Audrey was a trained vet and could fight her way out if necessary. Theresa couldn't.

Audrey and I switched places again and I explained to Theresa that shit was probably going to get hinky in a bit.

She bit her lips together and nodded, though I knew she really wanted to comment on how she hoped the weirdness wouldn't occur until after the third period was over. She really wanted her team to win.

I kept looking around the stadium, trying to see if I could spot where something, anything, was going wrong. However, as a post-cog, I was never invited to the party until well after it was rolling.

None of us expected a body to come plummeting from the ceiling, landing with a hard splat in the center of the ring just as the first goal of the period was made.

I'll SAY this for hockey fans: There were minimum shrieks and screams when the body came down. They did surge to their feet and start searching the catwalks above them to see if any more bodies were about to fall.

They didn't see anything, of course. No one *normal* would.

This was when my post-cog abilities tapped in. The place on the ceiling where the guy had fallen from (and don't ask me how I knew it was a guy, but I did) was lit up like a damned Pride parade float. I'd never seen such a rainbow of colors around anything.

I actually think Timothy, the gay guy who worked for Chinaman Joe, would have been jealous of how bright and sparkly it was.

The area was shaped like an oval, with a black swirly bit in the center. It looked like all the Hollywood interpretations of a portal that I'd ever seen.

"Do you see that?" I asked, pointing up at the spot.

Theresa shook her head, as did Audrey and Hunter.

"Show me," Hunter said, reaching across Audrey and holding out his hand.

We'd "shared" our hunting space before. My *area of knowing* was different than most psychics. Instead of straight lines and a square, the timelines spread out in a fan-shape. Hunter's area overlaid mine in an interesting pattern. Where the lines intersected, we could generally find the most useful information.

I took his hand and tried to "share" what I saw, or had seen, rather. The phenomenon had already disappeared.

I took Hunter's surprisingly warm hand in mine, closed my eyes, and sought out my *area of knowing*. The shape and blue lines formed quickly. (Though my fan-shape was different, all psychics used the exact same color blue.) I quickly chased along the strongest line, sliding back to what had happened *before* the body had fallen.

However, I was out of luck. The rainbow portal appeared, the body fell through it, and then the portal disappeared.

Fuck.

Though I could show Hunter, no one else was going to believe me, particularly not the cops. Only a psychic who saw *weird shit* would get a glimpse of the portal, and those types of psychics weren't regularly employed by the police department.

My parents had named me Cassandra after one of their favorite aunts. However, I'd learned the hard way that my name was too appropriate most days.

***

Theresa was as disappointed as the rest of her team's fans that the game was cancelled. I'm sure she was just kidding when she pointed out that the Zamboni could easily clean the bloodied ice once they moved the body.

While most of the fans shuffled out of the arena, the four of us stayed. As part of my agreement with the city, as the only privately-licensed psychic investigator operating in Minneapolis, I was required to give my statement and any psychic findings to the police who responded. In addition, they could request my help on the case and I would have to give it for free.

Fortunately, no one on the police force would voluntarily work with me. Hopefully nothing would require them to call me later.

But that was why I specifically did *not* try to focus on the body and follow his timeline back to see how he was killed and by whom. I only had to talk about what I'd seen at the hockey arena. I also didn't tag the area so I could revisit the timeline later, call it up in precise detail. Giving my help away for free didn't mean I had to voluntarily go that extra mile.

I gave Theresa a quick hug and a grope goodbye. She volunteered to take Audrey home as well, while Hunter and I stayed behind.

I didn't see if Hunter gave Audrey a kiss goodbye or not. I

assume he didn't. Audrey wasn't the kind of woman to do a PDA. Hopefully they didn't just shake hands, though.

Hunter and I got our PA badges out and headed down the stairs while everyone else made their way up. We aimed toward the far end of the oval, where the entrance onto the ice was.

The arena security guards had already set themselves up as bouncers so people wouldn't spill onto the ice, trying to get a closer look at what had happened. I was sure that pictures were already up on all the major social media sites.

However, the guards let us onto the ice after looking at our badges. Sometimes being officially licensed had its perks.

Of course, I nearly fell on my ass with my first step on the ice. Hunter reached out, lightning quick, and grabbed my arm.

Now, I'd grown up in Minnesota. I was used to ice. But this ice was fucking smooth as glass. I suppose they kept it that way for the game.

I tried to take another step and nearly fell again. When Hunter held out his arm for me to take, like an old-fashioned gentleman, I did. I'd rather have the help than make a total fool of myself. Most of the time.

The guy lay crumpled on the floor. He wasn't spread-eagle out but lay on his left side, one knee bent up and the other leg straight out. His left arm stuck out, the palm up, while his right arm lay by his side.

He looked loose, almost as if he were asleep. I thought back to how he'd fallen. He hadn't been struggling or anything. Had he been dead before he'd hit the portal?

He had brown skin and black hair, but he looked more middle-eastern than Hispanic. He wore a plain brown suit with a cream-colored shirt.

I'd never seen him before. Neither had Hunter.

It was only when we got up close that I realized his left eye was missing. That was where all the blood spreading across the ice had been coming from. I didn't see any other wounds.

This guy wasn't some creepy follower of Odin, was he?

"Stand back," came an officious voice from over my left shoulder. I deliberately stayed exactly where I was standing and just turned my head. I sure as fuck didn't want to fall on my ass in front of these cops.

The officer in charge looked vaguely familiar. It took me a couple moments to recognize Ferguson, the detective who'd been in charge of the investigation when Loki had killed Kyle, one of my best friends.

I was sure he probably still felt that I was guilty of that as well as any number of other indecencies.

Ferguson wore a thick down jacket that made him look rounder than he already was. He certainly hadn't lost any weight over the last few years. He still had a thick set of dark brown curls that ranged wildly over his head, and piercing brown eyes set wide in his pale face.

"What are *you* doing here?" Ferguson asked, clearly disgusted.

I didn't flip him off. I did show him my PA badge, as did Hunter.

"I've heard about you," Ferguson said slowly. "Finally got yourself tested, but it was drugs that made your abilities bloom, right?"

"That's correct, officer," I told him eagerly. "I've used drugs in my past."

That didn't get as much of a rise out of him as I'd hoped, probably because he was a seasoned cop. I'd have to work harder to get his goat.

Challenge accepted.

"I'm required by law to tell you what I've seen. We both are. Then we'll get out of your way," I explained.

"Yeah, yeah, I know the drill. What the hell happened?" Ferguson asked.

"A portal of unknown origin opened, right up there," I told him honestly. "The body dropped through. The end."

"Are you kidding me?" Ferguson said.

I hadn't seen a cop look that disgusted at one of my statements before. Obviously, the others hadn't been trying. Or I was going to have to up my game.

"What do you mean, 'a portal opened up'?" Ferguson asked.

"Right up there," I told him, pointing directly above us.

He looked up, then looked back down at me, scowling. "All right, since you're refusing to cooperate—"

"I *am* cooperating," I growled at him. "I am telling you the truth. You won't believe me, of course. But any of your pet psychics can verify it. Happy to share the area with them."

Ferguson got a canny look on his face. "Oh, really?" he asked. "Suppose I just might do that."

I didn't like how that sounded. I hadn't heard of any new procedure that the cops had started that would be as painful as the look that Ferguson gave me promised.

A short Asian man came walking up. He looked like a supervisor at a munitions factory, the kind of guy who enjoyed blowing things up. His black hair was cut short but stylish. He slinked as he moved, though it took me a moment to realize that wasn't his natural gait but rather how he walked and managed to stay upright on the ice. He wore a camel hair coat that screamed money, along with a dark brown three-piece suit.

Hakeem would have approved of his boots. They looked expensive, yet at the same time, durable. This guy could just as easily run in them as go dancing.

"Mr. Chao," Ferguson said, turning to the man. "This *post-cog* was present at the time of the event. She suggests you *share* the area."

My palm itched when I saw Mr. Chao's smarmy smile. I had the urge to slap it from his face.

"Thank you," he said, his voice just as smooth as I'd figured it would be. "But let me try first."

I nodded and stepped back, letting him do his thing. It was always fascinating for me to watch another post-cog at work.

Mr. Chao folded himself down on the ice as neatly as one of those tables from Ikea. I was surprised that he didn't get out a hanky and wipe the spot off first. He didn't shake or moan, like psychics do on those stupid shows on TV. His eyes did roll back in his head until just the whites showed, which I'd seen a couple of psychics do before.

How much of the sparkling rainbow lights would he see? Normally, I'd say he wouldn't see anything out of the ordinary, except the guy falling from the ceiling.

However, by the way Mr. Chao's eyes came back and he shot to his feet, I'd bet he'd actually seen a whole lot.

"Show me," he demanded, sending his hand angrily my way.

Hunter was suddenly by my side, looming.

Mr. Chao didn't seem impressed.

Idiot.

"It's okay," I told Hunter.

That finally got Mr. Chao to look up and notice the pissed off non-civilian glowering at him. "Please," he finally added.

His hand was hot, as I'd expected it to be. Psychic work tended to warm me up too, both physically and emotionally. I was looking forward to possibly seeing Theresa later on that night, if she'd have me.

Because of all the work I'd done with Hunter, it was fairly easy for me to set up my *area of knowing*, then shove it at Mr. Chao.

"What is this?" he angrily demanded. He dropped my hand as if I'd stung him.

"As I told the officer, a portal of unknown origin opened up in the ceiling and the body fell through," I said cheekily.

Mr. Chao shook his head. "This is not possible." He paused, fuming.

Hey, at least it wasn't *me* that had gotten him so pissed off, though I knew he was blaming me for everything at this point.

"I saw lights. Like a rainbow," Mr. Chao said. "That—that is what you saw, too?"

I nodded and beamed at him, like a star pupil about to earn his first A.

"But it couldn't have been a portal," he complained. "Such things only exist in fairytales."

I bit my lips together so I didn't blurt out, *Bub, do I have some stories for* you.

Mr. Chao looked at Ferguson, who glared at the pair of us equally. "What, are you both broken or something? Give me something useful here," the cop snarled.

"I'm sorry," Mr. Chao said.

The fucker actually did sound sorry. I wished I could have recorded it for posterity as I was fairly certain it happened so rarely.

"I must recuse myself from this case," Mr. Chao continued. "Something, or some*one*, must have messed with the timelines."

Now, I was on the receiving end of both Mr. Chao's as well as Ferguson's anger.

"I did *not* mess with the timelines," I told them both. Thankfully I had Hunter right there, backing me up, so no "accident" could happen to me. "It isn't possible for a human to screw up the timelines. That takes a god."

Shit. Now I was in it. They were both going to try to put me away for believing in gods and the other beings that I'd actually seen and interacted with. Seeing things that no one else did meant a short trip to a rubber room with only an unsympathetic ear to whine to.

"Or so I've heard," I told them, trying to back my way out of it.

"When was your last evaluation?" Ferguson asked smoothly.

"Last month," I said. Dennis, the asshole inspector the government had assigned me, had been playing games the entire time, trying to get me to agree to a shorter time between visits, as well as to pay extra "fees" that were unnecessary.

Luckily, Hunter had showed up and distracted Dennis, despite knowing that Dennis could *influence* Hunter, make him feel and say things that he hadn't planned on.

Hunter looked at it as a challenge: How long could he hold out before Dennis started influencing his thoughts, and how long before Hunter realized it and left?

Or as Hunter had put it, "How can you recognize or defeat your enemy if you don't engage him?" Or some Sun Tzu shit.

Ferguson just grunted at my reply. I was sure he'd look up my record with Dennis, as well as see that I always passed. Not with flying colors, of course, because Dennis was an asshole that way. But I still passed.

"I'm sane," I said bluntly. I knew that was a problem for some of the *blessed*, and one of the reasons why they called themselves as such. Their basic training was hell. Frequently, they didn't survive the first few years after their powers had manifested. They needed to hold themselves up as better than everyone else, particularly since so many looked down on them or were afraid.

I still thought of them mainly as a *Pain in the Ass*, even though I'd joined their ranks.

"And you're still sane," I said, pointing at Mr. Chao. "What you saw was real."

He got a very stoic look on his face, as if stone were more expressive than he was.

"Bring in anyone you like," I told Ferguson. "What just happened, happened." Though I had no idea if any other post-cog would see the same portal as Mr. Chao and I did, or if he was just extra sensitive.

"Are you still at the same address?" Ferguson said after a few moments.

"I am," I said. I wasn't about to tell him that I spent at least half my time at Theresa's, now. That was none of his business.

"We'll be in touch," Ferguson promised. "Don't leave town."

"Sure," I told him.

I had no idea if I was lying or not. That portal and the sparkly light worried me. What the hell did it actually mean? And why the fuck could some other post-cog see it? Normally, the freaky shit only happened to me or Hunter, or the types of psychics that Jacobsen Consortium tried hard to deny. Was this Mr. Chao just special? Or was it something else? Maybe one of the gods messing with something he or she shouldn't have?

Or was this really the start of the apocalypse?

2

____

UNFORTUNATELY, Theresa texted me back that she wasn't good company right now and that I shouldn't come over. She was still too pissed off about the game.

I'd given my chances about fifty-fifty. While my sweetie was certainly appreciative of the attentions I plied her with, she wasn't as interested in sex as I was. Not many women were. Supposedly guys were, but I was a gold-star lesbian and had never been with a man.

Technically, that made me a virgin, as Loki had once pointed out.

Asshole.

So Hunter and I left the arena together. Camera crews were already set up, looking to get some "insight" into the mysteriously falling man.

"Should we go give an interview?" I asked Hunter as the reporters started calling to us, trying to get us to walk toward them.

I kind of adored the horrified look on his face. He would never voluntarily step into the spotlight. A couple of times I'd pushed him gently toward it, but I knew he wasn't ready for it. Not yet, possibly not ever.

"Why would we go give them an interview?" Hunter asked, sounding as terrified as he looked.

"Good for business," I told him. We couldn't give any useful information to the press. This was still an active investigation, and the best I could probably say would be, "No comment."

Though I'd love to say something about a portal of unknown origins opening up, or hell, even the sparkly lights. If I did, my phone would be ringing off the hook in the morning and my website would have crashed from the number of weirdos looking me up.

The thing was, though ninety-nine percent of the cases that kind of publicity would bring in would be nutters, the one percent that weren't were generally gold.

I could tell Hunter was torn. He remembered how, even as much as a year ago, we were struggling to make ends meet. However, we'd had a surge of good paying clients soon after that. Word of mouth had finally started to build up. Hell, even my mom's lawyer, Michael John Adams, Esq., had sent us some cases, clients who had paid *very* well.

"Don't worry, we don't have to talk to the press," I reassured Hunter as I led him toward where the cops had set up. They let us pass and we made it out to the street beyond without being hounded.

Though it wasn't more than a few miles to my shithole apartment from the arena, it was too fucking cold to walk. It had been a nasty winter, and early February was just getting painful at this point. The wind chill was stupid at this time of night, particularly as the winds blew through the icy corridors formed by the tall buildings downtown.

Unfortunately, Hakeem was taking Audrey home, so he couldn't fetch us. "Bus?" I asked Hunter, pulling out my phone and opening the app that would tell us when the next bus would show up at the nearest corner.

Hunter nodded and huddled further into his jacket. I was damned glad I'd bought that for him, and that he'd wear it. The freak looked good in it, actually. It showed that Hunter had muscles across his chest and tapered down to his waist. But he wouldn't wear a scarf or hat, convinced that those would impede him in a fight.

Idiot.

We'd made it to the bus stop and were waiting the promised eight minutes when a navy blue BMW pulled up. The passenger window rolled down. "Want a ride?"

It was too cold for my jaw to hit the curb and my mouth to stay open. However, it was Mr. Chao making the offer.

I glanced at Hunter to see what his read on this guy was. However, Hunter looked too miserable to do a proper threat assessment.

"Sure," I said, reaching forward and opening the front door. Hunter slid into the back a moment later.

I mean, if you don't engage your enemy regularly, how can you hope to defeat them?

THE CAR WAS BLESSEDLY WARM, and like Hakeem's town car, had butt warmers built into the seats. It smelled of expensive leather and fancy men's cologne, the kind that subtly sang of masculinity.

"I'm Phil, by the way," Mr. Chao said as he pulled away from the curb, after I'd given him my address and he'd plugged it into his fancy GPS.

"Cassie," I told him. "And Hunter, back there. Why'd you stop to pick us up?" I asked. I figured I might as well get the awkwardness out of the way first.

But Phil just laughed. "I heard from Ferguson that you were into 'weird shit'," he said.

"That about sums it up," I said. Didn't surprise me that Ferguson had described us that way. The tapes of Hunter fighting those followers of Cthulhu had never made the official news channels; however, I'd heard from other cops that they'd been incorporated into some of their specialized training programs.

I knew no one normal would be able to stop Hunter if he was *moving*. Probably all their "special training" involved was learning how to shoot targets like him. They couldn't hope to take them down any other way.

"So where do you think that portal came from?" Phil asked. He sounded curious, not judgmental.

"I wish I knew," I said.

"Did it come from the gods?" Phil said, trying to sound casual.

"It might have," I told him seriously. "But it also might have just been some other weird shit." I mean, that Cthulhu group had been trying to raise a fucking *island* in the middle of Lake Calhoun. What other sort of dumb stuff could someone really powerful be pulling off?

"How will you find out?" Phil said. "Where would you start, uhm, investigating such a thing?"

That made me grin. "So you've decided to stick with the case?" I asked.

He nodded. "I am too curious not to," he admitted. "Plus..." he paused, then continued, not looking my way at all, "I can't track the timeline back to find out how the victim was killed or by who. It's just a black hole. So where would *you* look to find information about the death?"

It took me a moment to answer, but I decided to tell him everything. On the one hand, too many cooks in the kitchen could burn the broth. On the other hand, more investigators chasing leads might actually scrounge up something.

"The victim has one eye gouged out, right?" I asked Phil. He nodded. "That would make me start looking into his background. See if there was some connection with Norse mythology as well as Odin."

Phil looked thoughtful for a moment. "The victim, Aqil Hamada, was Egyptian. We found his passport in his jacket. So wouldn't you look at the Egyptian mythos as well?"

"Yeah, I would," I said. "The amount of research I end up doing for these kinds of cases gets silly sometimes."

"I would look at myths of the god Horus, then," Phil said. "He also was frequently portrayed as a one-eyed god. Plus, after his eye was taken, it went and had adventures on its own."

"Swell. More one-eyed gods to deal with," I said, shaking my head. That was the last thing I needed. "Does Horus have anything to do with rainbows?"

Phil thought for a moment. "I don't think so. I think that was a different god—goddess, maybe—the one who brought moisture to the river valley."

"How do you know all this?" I asked. Given his ethnicity, I would have expected him to know Asian myths, not Egyptian.

Phil gave me a true smile. "Got a seven-year-old boy who's into mummies and everything Egyptian. I've been learning all sorts of new things. Between them and the dinosaurs, it's been quite an education."

Well, shit. That made me almost feel empathy for the man. But just almost. I still had a gut feeling that he was the enemy and would quickly turn against us.

"I'd look into the guy's religious affiliations," I told Phil. "See if he goes to a mosque or temple that's a bit different." Like Deacon, who'd been a monk of a slightly twisted organization.

"That might be difficult," Phil said. "We don't want this turning into some kind of religious affair."

I snorted at him. "I hate to tell you, but most of the weird shit I deal with is the result of gods. Trust me, I've met my fair share." Though to be honest, I'd only met a few at this point. Poseidon, Odin, the Ahura Mazdâ, and of course, Loki.

Phil gave me a disbelieving sideways glance. "Come on. You're not really telling me the gods are real, are you? All the gods?"

"You can pull up here," I told Phil. As the car stopped, I turned in my seat to look at Phil fully. The streetlight outside shone through the front window, lighting his face. He appeared to be listening to me.

"The gods are real," I said. I knew he wouldn't believe me, but I had to try. "Possibly, *all* the gods are real. Generally, they only bother me or Hunter, or psychics like us, people who are used to dealing with cases outside the norm. Honestly, what worries me more than the dead body was that *you* saw the portal when you went looking through the timelines. I would have lost good money betting that you wouldn't have seen anything but a guy falling to his death."

I'd give this to Phil—he had a great poker face. "I'm not sure I believe you," he said slowly. "However, *you* believe you're telling the truth. And that worries me."

I fished a business card out of my wallet and handed it to him. "Feel free to call if more weird shit happens," I told him. "Hopefully it won't. But this kind of thing never goes away on its own."

"Needs an inoculation?" he said, aiming for teasing. "Something to stop the rash?"

"Antibiotics that worked would be better than an apocalypse," I said as I slid out of the car. Hunter stood beside me on the curb. I knew better than to have insisted Phil drive up north to where Hunter stayed. It wasn't that late, and there was a direct bus that Hunter could take home.

"Think what's happening is that bad?" Hunter asked as Phil drove off. "Bad enough to bring in strangers?"

I didn't tell Hunter that I'd been thinking about the apocalypse for most of the night. But I had. Even in a joking manner, it probably meant something was up. Theresa always worried that I dove too far into the timelines. Plus, whatever case I was investigating took over parts of me and I wasn't aware that it was even happening.

"Whatever's happening might be that bad," I said. "And you know what we're doing tomorrow, right?"

"Research?" Hunter asked perking up.

"Research."

I knew that Hunter enjoyed the research angle of things. He'd gotten good at "hunting" for information. He preferred doing physical work, but in this weather, I figured even he wouldn't object to spending half a day at the library, where it was warm and out of the winds.

We said goodbye and I headed up to my empty apartment and lonely bed.

Hopefully Theresa would be better company tomorrow. Particularly if there was a real threat to the world once again, and I was about to get swallowed by my job.

The real kicker? Preventing the apocalypse didn't pay worth shit.

I SLEPT POORLY THAT NIGHT, no surprise there. I woke up staring out the window right above my bed. The sky was overcast; however, I knew better than to assume the weather had warmed up. It was still probably ten below. Or worse.

Nothing had changed in my shithole apartment overnight, which made me glad. Waking up to find Loki making me breakfast wouldn't have been all that weird today, even for me. My place was a studio, though the slumlords who owned my building had supposedly "renovated" all the units so they could call them "lofts" instead, as well as charge slobbering amounts of money to the yuppies and hipsters.

To my immediate right stood a purple loveseat with a coffee table in front of it. A large flat screen TV hung off the wall. Just beyond that, a one-butt kitchen took up the far corner, the counter clean only because I cooked so rarely.

Fortunately, my shithole apartment still had the best hot water supply. When I had the time, I'd take long hot soaks in the claw-foot tub, but I knew I had to get going that morning. Plus, given how little sleep I'd had, I was afraid I'd relax too much and drown. Of course, I could call Theresa and make her come and "rescue" me. That had been fun, the one time I'd done that.

But I really didn't have time for that, either. I was meeting Hunter at eleven at the main public library. I'd slept late in an attempt to at least get a few good hours of sleep.

While others claimed that breakfast was the most important thing of the day, they were wrong. Having that first sweet cigarette of the day was really what it took for me to get things going. I made my morning coffee, sat myself down on the soft purple loveseat, then broke out my first cancer stick.

I knew that Theresa didn't like the fact that I smoked. But she never ragged on me about it. She wouldn't kiss me if I'd been smoking a lot, would make me go and brush my teeth first. I'd cut back tremendously since we'd started going out. I was down from three packs a day to about one pack a week.

I could break the habit. I just hadn't wanted to yet.

I drew in that sweet smoke and drank my bitter coffee, waking up and thinking about my day. However, the smoke wasn't as sweet as it once had been. Instead, it was a reminder that I was alone. Many of the mornings when I was with Theresa, I wouldn't have that first cigarette until mid-day or later.

The coffee, however, did turn out to be smooth. I'd gotten it in barter from one of Hakeem's "relatives" who'd wanted me to find out who'd been stealing eggs from their chicken coop in the back of their house. (Turned out one of the hens had gone walkabout. The hen was missing, not the eggs.)

My life had changed so much in the last year. Mostly for the better.

The question was: How much did I want it to change?

Theresa hadn't been subtle at all in her hints about us moving in together. Or some huge declaration, a change in our relationship status, as it was nearly Valentine's Day.

There was an old joke about the lesbian who showed up on her second date with a U-Haul, ready to move in. However, Theresa and I had been together for over a year, coming up on a year and a half. And it had been good—Hell, great—so far.

Was it time for me to give up what had once been my sanctuary? To move into her house? Or, god forbid, for us to buy a house together?

I couldn't even think beyond that. Didn't want to think about the logical next step of our relationship: getting married. True, I'd never wanted to live with anyone other than Theresa. I adored her. I felt much better about our chances of "making it" than I had with anyone, even my old girlfriend Sam.

But moving in with Theresa meant becoming someone different than who I was. I would become someone who no longer smoked, who went to the farmer's market in St. Paul on Saturday mornings to get fresh eggs, who grilled in the backyard during the summer.

Mind you, I already did all those things. Moving in with Theresa, though, would make it official.

It meant I was growing up and having a normal life.

Shit.

I'd always be getting involved with weird crap through my job. That was the nature of my business, something Theresa would never ask me to give up.

The other thing that stopped me was that Theresa was still Dr.

T in *her* other life. She still worked as a researcher for Jacobsen Consortium. We'd come to an uneasy peace about her occupation: She didn't talk about it and I didn't ask.

However, like my smoking, it stood as a barrier between us.

I couldn't ask her to give up her job. No one would hire her as an independent researcher. No one but Jacobsen Consortium did the kind of research she was trained to do.

Which was why, in part, I figured she couldn't ask me to give up the cancer sticks.

Would we both like who we'd become? If we became other people?

Psychic abilities or not, I couldn't answer that question.

RESEARCH at the library didn't turn out to be a bust so much as opening a tangled can of worms. There were far too many Egyptian myths. And the gods had changed so much over time. Hell, even the god Set was considered a good guy in some of the tales. While the simplified pantheon involved primarily Osiris, Horus, Isis, Anubis, and Set, the true number of gods was rather impressive.

Plus, the Egyptians never met an animal that they didn't transform into a god, so that made not just the number of gods, but the forms they'd assume extra confusing.

I took some notes of the major players so I would at the very least be able to identify whichever asshole came to visit me. Knowing my luck, someone like Tefnet would appear, wearing the form of a lioness.

Hunter didn't find a lot more than I did. No gods were associated with rainbows that he could find. He did find a lot of references to water and moisture, as well as the sun and the desert.

That led me back to the Norse gods, Odin and Heimdall, and that damned rainbow bridge of theirs. I had no idea why an

Egyptian man would be associated with Norse gods. Maybe he'd married a Scandinavian ice queen, like my mother.

I wasn't surprised to find out that the victim, Aqil Hamada, was a poet, with several self-published chapbooks. He wrote a lot of epic fantasy poetry, so I was certain he was familiar with the Norse Eddas.

Hunter did find Aqil's visa application (and no, I did *not* want to speculate just how illegal that was) as well as the address of his hotel, which was out by the airport.

Did I want to call Hakeem to drive us out there? Of course.

Did I trust that Hakeem would only tell Jacobsen Consortium what I wanted him to?

Hell, no. Hakeem had family, both in this country and still back in Ethiopia. He was too vulnerable. He had too many weak points that an unscrupulous person could apply pressure to.

However, I'd gotten into the habit of calling Hakeem anyway.

I wasn't sure what, if anything, we'd find in the victim's hotel room. If the police caught us breaking in there, we'd both get thrown into jail. Ferguson would probably make certain that the paperwork would go missing and we'd be stuck there for days, if not weeks.

I did have an ace up my sleeve. Michael John Adams, Esq., my mother's lawyer, would probably be able to apply the appropriate pressure to get us out quickly. He wouldn't stoop to bribes, though he could certainly afford them.

"We really want to do this?" I asked Hunter as we waited inside the entrance of the library for our driver to show up. Hakeem had been "in the neighborhood" and would arrive quickly, which could mean five minutes or thirty minutes. While he could see patterns and drove better than anyone I'd ever met, he often exaggerated his timeliness.

Hunter shrugged. "Just another adventure," he said. "Unless you want to go call on Odin."

I cursed silently. I did *not* want to have to call that asshole. Chances were, even if I did invoke him, he wouldn't tell me anything useful either.

I knew I was grasping at straws, though, by going out to Aqil Hamada's hotel room.

In the end, I was going to have to deal with the gods again.

———

THE OH-SO-FRENCH BOUTIQUE hotel out near the airport kind of freaked me out. The entrance led to a huge atrium. All the floors of rooms shot up from there, overlooking the idyllic fountain in the center. The splashing noise carried loudly throughout the open space. Just a little sharper and I would have likened it to gunshot, the *crack-bang* being similar. Yellow and white marble covered the floor and rose about half way up the walls. I suspected the architects were trying to soften the huge space with the softer color, but they'd failed miserably.

Reception was off to the left, a long desk built in under the first floor, almost looking like a bar with the dark wood and shiny brass. The back of reception was painted a lovely green and looked much more comfortable than any of the fussy chairs and glass tables that filled the lobby.

Elevators were straight ahead, past the lobby and the reception area. Hunter and I made a beeline for them, acting as if we belonged there. That was at least half of all surveillance: Don't look guilty and act like you belong there.

We didn't know what floor we were looking for. However, we'd done this before. Either Hunter or I would get a premonition, or a post-monition, giving us a hint about where to go next.

Normal humans called it *following their gut* or *relying on instinct* or some such nonsense. Hunter and I had an advantage of having trained our "instincts" to be efficient.

However, when I stepped into the small elevator box, none of the numbers on the panel jumped out at me or demanded that I should press them first.

"Hunter?" I asked as he studied the numbers, peering at them curiously as if he'd never seen them before.

He nodded, then pressed the 11. "Not sure," he said quietly.

I'd take Hunter's uncertainty over some asshole's absoluteness any day of the week.

The elevator was made out of the same dark wood as reception. The Muzak they played made it certain that no one would stay in the tiny box for long. Ads for live jazz at the hotel restaurant had me rolling my eyes. Who went to a hotel to listen to music?

Nothing jumped out at either of us when the doors opened onto the eleventh floor. A huge pot with white calla lilies stood opposite the elevator. While the flowers were fake, someone had still liberally applied some sort of perfume to the hallway to make up for it. I sneezed after just three steps onto the funky green and red carpet.

I didn't know who designed hotel carpets, but they all followed the same school of thought. This rug was particularly obnoxious, made with a background that was almost Kelly green then had large red swoops and white squiggles running through it.

Luckily, neither Hunter or I were high, or we might have spent hours being distracted by the patterns.

We stood in the area in front of the elevators and looked first down one hallway, then the other. The hotel was set up in a square, so walking long enough in either direction would bring us back to here.

My nose kept twitching, though, leading my head to swivel back to the right. "This way?" I asked Hunter, indicating that direction.

"Suits me," he said, though he still seemed to be searching for his prey.

The doors all looked the same, plain beige set into the wall. Along the first hallway, there were rooms on both sides, while on the second, they were only on the outside wall, away from the atrium.

We passed all the way down the second hallway before Hunter and I both stopped and turned back at the same time.

Something was there, some great event with a lot of emotional power. And it wasn't a fresh incident, either. It had happened a while ago.

If I'd been on my own, I would have had to walk each and every floor until I reached this one. I don't know what led Hunter to choose this floor, except it was his senses working the same as mine.

Was something else about to happen here? Was this the site where he and I would be caught by the police, which was how he knew to come here?

We walked back down the hallway slowly, then stopped at room 1157. Hopefully there wasn't a magical significance to that number, though I was certain it would come up and bite me in the ass if there was.

"I'm going in," I told Hunter. "You stay by the stairs. You see anyone coming, anyone official, you *run*. You got me?"

"Not abandoning you, boss," Hunter said.

By the stubborn line I saw in his jaw, I knew he meant it.

"Look, despite how your record is now mostly clean, the cops still have a hold on you. They've got nothing on me. I'm a good, upstanding, tax-paying citizen. Plus, it would be way easier on Michael John to just have to get one of us out of jail," I explained. "If someone catches me, you go see him *first*. Don't try to rescue me or break me out of wherever they'd holding me. He can do that legally."

"Even if they take you to the prison beneath Jacobsen Consortium?"

I took a deep breath. I did *not* want to get into that argument again. There was no "prison"—it was just Hunter's overly-active paranoia.

"Especially there," I said. "I'm a known person. Jacobsen Consortium can't *vanish* me like some illegal alien. Michael John will be able to get me out."

I could see Hunter wavering.

"Besides, you don't want me to have to call Audrey to come and fetch you from jail, do you? Because I would."

I knew that was a low blow, but it worked. Hunter didn't want to go to jail and have his new girlfriend see him that way. Despite the fact that he insisted they weren't dating, at least according to Audrey. They were, instead, "activity partners," whatever the hell that meant.

"Fine," Hunter said with a sigh. "But not until we clear the room first."

I took a deep breath, then let it out slowly. "All right," I said slowly. "But you get out of there immediately afterward. You got me?" I knew I was being selfish by letting him come into the room. However, if there was a boogie man still in there, I'd much rather that he try to get through Hunter first before coming after me.

Hunter drew what looked like a blank hotel room key from his wallet. Then he pulled out a small electronic device from his front pocket. It looked like a key fob for a car, only with twice as many buttons on it. A curly yellow wire connected the key fob to the room key, the end of the wire sliding into a tiny socket on the side.

It took three swipes for the card to "learn" the codes for the door and open it. I suspected it probably messed with the existing lock as well. Whoever stayed in this room would have to get their key reprogrammed at the front desk. But that happened all the time. Nothing sinister about that, right?

As Hunter slid the door open, I sneezed again. He glared at me over his shoulder for daring to make noise. I just shrugged. Anyone paying attention in the room would have heard the door click open already.

But that damned perfumed smell permeated the hallway now. I tried to stifle it but I still sneezed again. Damn it!

Hunter gave up trying to be sneaky and *flowed* into the room. I couldn't even follow him with my eyes, though I knew where he was going.

I stopped in the hallway just inside the hotel room door. The carpet at least had been toned down to a dark brown. To the right stood a huge mirrored closet door. To the left, the door to the bathroom and shower stood open. The lights were off. I was tempted to turn the fan on, at the very least, to get rid of some of the stench.

When I looked forward again, I realized that Hunter had come to a standstill. Something about Hunter's posture concerned me.

I rushed toward him. I instantly wished I hadn't.

Another body lay on the bed, twisted in death. One eye had been gouged out. However, she'd been dressed in a white toga. Dark eyeliner surrounded the one piercing blue eye that was still open, like she was in shock. Golden blonde hair spilled around her head like a halo.

At her feet I saw what looked like white fairy wings, the kind that little girls wore, or even big girls when going to a costume party.

She'd been dead for a while, I'd bet. The perfume had been liberally applied to mask the smell of the decomposition.

Hunter and I looked at each other.

"Well, shit," I told him.

We were going to have to report this, do our good deed for the day. And probably get thrown in jail for breaking and entering at the same time.

3

———

ODIN SHIVERED as a cold wind suddenly blew down the length of his long hall. He sat on his great chair at the far end, opposite the doors which remained tightly shut. Fires burned in the pits that ran down the center of the room, the sparks dancing up toward the towering, peaked ceiling. Snakes decorated the many pillars dividing the room. They stirred sluggishly, the sound as ominous as sand blown against an empty ship's hull. Tapestries detailing Odin's many victories in battle lifted off the pine-timbered walls, waving as if in a sail-filled breeze.

What ill omen was this? Odin's ravens, Hugin and Munin, perched on the back of Odin's chair, shuffled their feet uneasily and squawked. Odin peered out into the darkness that seemed to fill his hall, but his single eye couldn't pierce the gathering shadows.

The wind blew again, hard enough this time to stir Odin's long gray robe. He pulled on the stiff, heavily embroidered white cuffs, trying to fend off the chill air. Chicken flesh rose across his shoulders and along his neck under the standing white collar. The dark scent of dried blood filled the air: Not the invigorating smell of the battlefield but the stench of the graveyard.

"Enough!" Odin declared. His great staff flew to his hand and he pounded it against the stone floor. A loud *crack* filled the air. Silver and gold sparks arced up and away. The ravens croaked and complained.

The air cleared. Odin still saw nothing.

"Is that you, Loki? Skulking around like some sort of damned dwarf?"

The insult didn't draw a figure out of the air. Odin pushed himself out of his chair and strode down the length of his hall. The fires leaped up as he passed, the bright light eating at the encroaching shadows.

As far as Odin could see, he was alone in his hall. However, he still couldn't shake the sense that someone, or some*thing*, was still present.

With a wave of his hand, the far doors flung open, revealing the dark, star-filled night outside. Odin stepped out of his hall and paused, unsure where to go next. The rich scent of peat fires filled the air, along with the rhythmic chanting of his warriors drinking in their hall. Softer winds blew here, bringing cool, clear thought from the snow-covered mountains above.

Suddenly, the All Worlds trembled under Odin's feet. It was only a slight tremor, not as great as the shaking that occurred from the writhing of the Midgard Serpent or even Loki in his agony. He could never tell if the troubles were from the future or the past.

Yet another sign that something was amiss. But what?

Odin lifted his head into the air, casting for the scent. He must be missing something. Was Loki causing problems again?

Then he shook his head. Of course, Loki was causing trouble. That was his nature. He caused fewer problems now that Odin had trapped much of Loki's essence on a different plane. The All-Father had been driven to that extreme when Loki had tried to swap fates with Odin so that Loki would survive Ragnarok.

However, banishing Loki had the unintended consequence of making it easier for the trickster to visit other planes, such as those where foreign gods lived, or even the human worlds.

What was Loki doing this time? Odin cast around for a clue. He didn't want to drag Mim, the seer, out of her apple barrel again. She wouldn't tell him anything useful. She'd grown sullen and uncooperative. Maybe Odin shouldn't have blasted her with ice the last time he'd forced her to talk.

Who else could Odin seek? Who was clear sighted enough to see what lay ahead?

He thought for a moment about returning to his home and asking Frigg's advice. However, he had enough difficulty with her as it was. Asking her advice about something as nebulous as the future trouble that Loki might cause might risk her questioning his manhood. Again.

There had to be someone else, though…

A bright light skimmed through the sky, the start of the evening dance of the Borealis. Beautiful green sheets of light fell, waving through the air. A hint of other colors lined the edges—red, orange, blue, and white. Almost like a rainbow.

Would Heimdall be able to help Odin? He did guard the bridge to the land of the gods. Sure, Loki, Odin, and the others could come and go as they pleased. But for beings other than the Norse gods, they had to cross the Bifrost bridge. Plus, Heimdall had the knack of foretelling. He wasn't as consistent or accurate as some of the other gods, but perhaps he could shed some light on what Odin was currently feeling.

With long strides, Odin began crossing the beautiful mountain valley. He hummed a war song as he marched, the low notes echoing off the great cliffs. Merry rivers ran under the many bridges he crossed on his way. Snow covered the fields, the fertile earth patiently waiting for spring. The Borealis continued its dance above him.

Odin kept his long gray robe tightly tied around his waist, though the air here felt different than the winds that had infested his hall—a clean, honest chill rather than one that infected his body and sank into his bones.

Mountains marched closer and closer along with Odin, the valley of the gods narrowing to a single point. A magnificent bridge stood there, hewn out of blocks of solid ice. Spikes of ice made up the balustrades on either side of the meter-wide surface. Icicles on the ropes strung between the spikes tinkled softly as the wind blew. Vertical cliffs rose up on both sides of the bridge, and an endless gorge dropped below. Shifting fog gathered at the far end of the bridge, hiding its location. An army could only gain entrance to the land of the gods by crossing the Bifrost bridge.

Heimdall stood guard outside. Generally, he spent much of his time inside the house beside the bridge, a beautiful long building full of delightful wood carvings, many of them made by Heimdall himself.

However, Heimdall always knew when someone approached the bridge, and so awaited for them outside.

"Greetings, oh pale one!" Odin called out to the bridge keeper. Heimdall was the whitest of all the gods. His eyes were the palest gray, and in the right light, the iris would disappear altogether. He wore his blonde hair tied into a long braid that flowed down to his waist. Odin had seen that braid transform into a tail as Heimdall changed shape and became a seal.

Heimdall wore a long, brown leather cloak trimmed in bright red fox fur. Underneath, he had on a silver tunic decorated with brown braid around the edges. Warm woolen pants covered his legs, the calves wrapped in leather strips, with heavy ankle boots covering his feet. More than one sword was tied to the great belt wrapped around his center. A special holder for his bow and arrows sat at the end of the bridge, in close reach.

Heimdall's mighty horn hung from a bright gold chain strapped across his chest like a sash. The horn was made out of a twisted ram's horn, striped in muted white and black, with gold bands decorating it, along with gold trim on both ends.

When Odin looked at the horn, a ghost of an echo blasted forth. He stopped and shook his head, knowing that what he'd just heard was a possible future slipping into the now.

Would Heimdall be blowing his horn soon? Was the twilight of the gods actually drawing near?

Heimdall waited until Odin had stepped closer before he said, "Greetings, Val-Father."

Odin couldn't help but shiver at Heimdall's deep tone. Were the bridge keeper's choice of words prophetic, choosing the title *father of death* among Odin's many names? Or was the bridge keeper just being formal and respectful?

"What have you seen?" Odin asked Heimdall.

The keeper of the bridge turned and looked out into the nothingness across the far edge of the bridge. Cold winds gusted up from the icy crevasse it crossed, making Odin shiver.

"I see trouble, my lord," Heimdall admitted. "Trouble under a foreign sun, where sand spills across the land like snow across the mountain tops."

"What kind of trouble?" Odin said. His back straightened and his hand gripped his staff more tightly, as if readying to go to war.

Heimdall shook his head. "Weird animals. Strange tongues and words casting evil magic." He paused, then added, "And today, foreign hawks flew above the bridge. Strange white vultures as well. They attacked the bridge, drawing out chunks of ice with their huge claws."

"They did what?" Odin asked, worry chasing through him. How could a foreign bird attack the bridge? Were they from some other god? Did they hope to destroy the bridge and to isolate Odin and his ilk?

"I've never seen anything like them," Heimdall said. "I was planning on calling you to the bridge come morning. The hawks arrived first in a small flock, maybe six or seven. Their coloring was that of drying blood, and black tipped the ends of their feathers and their beaks."

Odin had never heard of such birds, even in his wide travels. He couldn't even guess where they came from.

"The hawks made strafing runs at the bridge, as if they couldn't quite get close enough at the beginning," Heimdall continued. "The piercing calls they made echoed strangely as well. Then one finally made contact with the ice. It died instantly, as if the bridge made it freeze solid. The next attacker did as well. But eventually, one snagged a claw full of ice and flew off. After a few hours, a second group appeared, doing the same thing. Then a third. And so on, throughout the day."

"But why?" Odin asked. What could these strange birds use the ice of the Bifrost bridge for? He didn't think the ice itself was magical. The bridge, yes. But surely the ice lost its rainbow color and any abilities it might have once it had been pulled away from the bridge?

"Have you shot down any of the birds?" Odin asked Heimdall.

The bridge keeper nodded. "Many of them. I've driven off more attacks than have gotten through. But the birds I shoot disappear into the mist. Their bodies never make it onto this plane."

"Have you shot the ones holding the ice?" Odin said.

Heimdall shrugged. "Sometimes, yes. Sometimes I've missed. But I still don't understand why they're coming, or what they're doing with the ice."

"I don't know either," Odin said. "But I have a feeling it's nothing good."

Heimdall nodded, looking grim. "I will keep constant watch," he assured Odin. "And I'll try to kill all who approach."

"Thank you," Odin said. "Be steadfast and true."

Heimdall picked up his bow and arrow and stepped to the foot of the bridge. "Aye, Val-Father," he intoned.

Odin shivered again as he walked away. Death father. Was that what Heimdall foresaw?

And whose death this time? Odin's? Or all of the gods?

***

SAM CAREFULLY INCHED her car up the icy hill. The streets here, just north and west of Lake of the Isles, were narrow and twisting. Throw in some ice and reduce the width of the street with huge snow banks on either side, and Sam wasn't sure she could get through without scratching up her new BMW or banging up against the other, equally expensive parked cars.

The houses in this neighborhood were beautiful old mansions, sitting back from the street, staring out at a lofty height. She would have to remember to come back and walk through here when spring finally arrived. The Christmas lights had all been put away—just snow and ice wreathed the houses and the street. Old trees still arched overhead, their bare bones stark against the clouds.

Sam drew a deep breath when she found the address she was looking for. After carefully parking her car, drawing as close to the huge snow bank on her right as possible, she sat for a moment, trying to shake off the adrenaline. She was not looking forward to the drive back home.

Though Sam braced herself for the biting cold, she still couldn't help but shiver as she climbed out of her car and the winds attacked. It had been twenty below for the past few days and the weather report had predicted more of the same for at least another week.

Sam walked carefully across the icy street and between the huge mounds of snow that marked the entrance to the sidewalk. In addition to the cold, they'd had a snowy winter. The banks rose up almost to her shoulder. They seemed like pillars she had to pass between on her way to the grand palace.

Shaking her head, Sam tried to clear her thoughts. Normally, she wasn't that fanciful. However, a huge ice palace had been built that winter as part of the Winter Carnival celebration in St. Paul. It had been modeled off old English castles, with many round towers wearing witch-hat roofs, crenulated walls, and huge arched doorways. Pink, red, blue, and green lights lit up the ice, like a fairy rainbow.

Though generally the ice palace would be dismantled after just a few weeks, this year it had been left up due to the extreme cold.

The house Sam was looking for was just a short ways up the very well-shoveled sidewalk. A short cinderblock wall rose up next to the walkway. Yew trees grew up above the wall, extending it far above Sam's head. Ice clung to the flat needles, giving her, again, the impression of an ice palace.

A small black intercom perched on the wall beside the trees, looking as though it had been grown there as well. The gate itself was made of solid black iron. Razor wire topped the gate. It looked impassable. A scrolled pattern of diamond shapes was done in *bas relief* on the front of the gate, though none of it stood out far enough for even a professional cat burglar to get a toe-hold.

No instructions were printed on the intercom, nothing to help the uninformed gain access to the mansion. Luckily, Sam had been given a one-time access code to use for calling the main house.

She punched in the number, then waited. A smooth man's voice came out of the speaker after a few moments. "Hello?" he asked.

"My name is Samantha Monroe. I have an appointment with Mr. Jacobsen at ten o'clock," Sam stated.

"You're early," the man said, sounding greatly put out. "Someone will be there shortly."

Sam pulled her phone out of purse and looked at the time. It was 9:55. She wasn't *that* early. Did they expect her to punch in the number exactly at ten o'clock?

Of course, they did. They were busy people and probably had some small country to buy before her appointment.

Sam bit her lips together so she wouldn't giggle. Though she didn't often think of Cassie, not anymore, not like she once had, she still felt Cassie's influence now and again.

Usually, now it was for the better.

A young man hauled the door open. He wore an expensive camel hair coat that came down to his knees, along with finely-stitched black leather gloves and a dashing red scarf. He looked at Sam, then looked at the sheet of paper in his hand. He had bright green eyes set into a dark-skinned face, along with straight black hair that hung partially into his eyes. If Sam had to bet, she'd say either his mother or his father had come from India.

"State your name," the man said. He peered at the paper again.

Was that a picture of her? To make sure she was who she said she was? "Samantha Monroe," she said.

"Can I see your ID, please?" the man asked.

Sam dug out her wallet and showed the man first her driver's license, then her PA badge to prove that she was one of the *blessed*.

Were people that angry at Jacobsen Consortium that a former board member and great-great grandson of the founder needed this much security? Was he just being paranoid? Or was it a little of both?

Finally, the man nodded. "Follow me," he said, indicating that she should step inside the grand gate. He pushed it shut with some effort. It closed with a loud *clang*. Sam chided herself when her first thought was of prisons and dungeons.

Wouldn't it be easier to have an electronic gate? Then again, anything automated could be spoofed.

Directly in front of the gate stood more walls with more yew trees. Stairs led up to the left. They were immaculately clean, as if someone came by with a broom every hour to brush away any snow that dared to fall.

At the top of the stairs, the path curved back to the right and Sam caught her first glimpse of the house. It was made out of brown-painted timber and had the look of a Swiss Chalet. Delicately carved wood dripped down from the eaves. Large windows opened up onto the street, and she'd bet from that high vantage point there would be views of Lake of the Isles. The peaked roof held no snow. Balconies extended the house on the right side, as well as out front.

As Sam walked up the sidewalk, she got a better impression of just how *big* this house was. It was three stories tall, and the property was at least half a block deep. Yet, as far as she knew, just Mr. Jacobsen lived there, his wife having died a few years before. All their children were grown and lived elsewhere, none of them taking up the family trade.

A palm lock waited above a normal deadbolt on the door to the house. The door itself was solid wood, and Sam would bet that it was reinforced with steel. She stepped across the threshold and felt herself instantly relax in the warmth, despite an underlying fear of having stepped into the bear's den.

The front hallway was the same brown color as the house, though it was mostly made of natural wood, not painted. It looked both formal as well as homey at the same time.

The young man reached out his hand for Sam's coat. "It will be right here," he told her, indicating the empty closet that stood next to the door.

She pulled her peach-colored sweater down further over her wrists, then brushed down her black slacks. Normally she'd wear a skirt for an interview, but it was too cold. Her shoes were sensible as well, with a closed toe and a good waffle-grip pattern on the soles.

"This way," the young man said, not deigning to take off his jacket.

They went to the right, through a living room that had statues of African art in the corners, brightly woven baskets sitting on glass-and-stainless-steel coffee tables, an uncomfortable-looking white sofa and matching love seat, and brown-and-gold African rugs over the bleached hardwood floor.

The room was a showplace, not somewhere people actually lived.

As they passed through the room, the smell of rich coffee and blueberry waffles reached Sam's nose. Her stomach suddenly growled. She glanced up, hoping the young man hadn't heard it. She hadn't eaten breakfast that morning, too nervous about her upcoming interview.

The young man led Sam back through a formal dining room with places for twelve, all the chairs carved out of black wood with tall, straight backs. No pictures or statues were in here, though the walls were covered in old-fashioned wallpaper, from the 1950s, a sage green with golden sheaves of wheat.

Finally, they reached the back of the house. A man sat at the far end of a small table. It was the first room that looked comfortable, like a breakfast nook. The table and chairs took up much of the room. Windows looked out on a snowy landscape on two sides. The smell of rich buttered bread filled the air. A modern steel lamp hung down over the table like a witch's hat. The table itself was probably an antique, made of blond wood and scarred.

The man who sat at the far edge of the table looked like his photos. Aaron Jacobsen, a former board member of Jacobsen Consortium. He had no psychic ability himself, but his wife had been reported to be a very strong telepath.

He was in his eighties, though he could possibly still pass for sixty. His bald head shone in the harsh light. Dark eyes peered out intently from flabby, ruddy cheeks. He had thin lips that Sam would bet rarely smiled with joy. His age showed mainly in his neck, which had thinned like an old man's so that his Adam's apple became more prominent. She was surprised that he wore not only a very well-tailored gray suit, but a brown and red tie as well. He looked as though he was off to a meeting with his banker.

"Mr. Jacobsen?" Sam asked, just to make sure.

The man slowly put down the tablet he'd been reading. "Yes," he said. "And if that busybody Debra Lewis hadn't insisted that I see you, you'd already have been shown the door."

Sam nodded. Mrs. Lewis—Debra, Cassie's mother—could be quite convincing when she needed to be. Sam still wasn't sure what her grand scheme was. Sam had put together some of the pieces, but she knew she was missing major parts. Mrs. Lewis was as deep as an ocean. Sam couldn't swim in the same waters without being torn apart by sharks. Still, she'd managed to scavenge some clues.

Sam still worked for Mrs. Lewis, running errands and such, despite how much Sam distrusted the woman.

One day, Sam expected she'd turn against Mrs. Lewis, when Mrs. Lewis' true plans came forth. For now, her influence had been essential for furthering Sam's own plans.

"Mr. Jacobsen, I'd like to ask you a few questions about Jacobsen Consortium. Not the current operations," Sam hastened to add. "But what happened in the past. Before 1972."

Mr. Jacobsen peered at Sam as if trying to read her. Did he have some ability? It did run in families. Samuel Jacobsen had founded Jacobsen Consortium back in 1910, and he'd been a powerful pre-cog. (Though back at the beginning, the company had just been called Jacobsen and Sons.)

"There isn't much I can tell you," Mr. Jacobsen said slowly. "Non-disclosure agreements and whatnot. But ask the right questions and I'll give you what I can. Please, sit. Would you like coffee?"

"Please," Sam said, trying not to sound smug. She'd done enough research into Jacobsen Consortium, reading through the annual reports, that she'd pinpointed 1972 as the turning point for the group. Aaron Jacobsen had been a member of the board from the time he'd turned twenty five; however, he'd left (voluntarily?) the following year.

Mr. Jacobsen poured coffee out of an etched-glass French press into a plain white cup. He passed it to Sam, along with the cream and sugar that matched the press.

Sam had learned to drink coffee black and didn't want to dilute the heavenly beverage that Mr. Jacobsen provided. She had no idea where the beans were from. Judging how smooth the coffee was and how many layers it had, she would bet that even she would hesitate before socking in a month's supply.

Mr. Jacobsen appeared to be waiting for Sam, so she took another sip then reluctantly put the cup down. "Lovely," she had to say.

He merely nodded. No smile.

"Prior to 1972, the composition of the board was roughly equally divided between those with abilities and those without," Sam stated. That hadn't been that easy to figure out as PAs weren't required to be registered in those days. "After 1972, no PAs sat on the board ever again."

"That is correct," Mr. Jacobsen said. "There's nothing in the company charter requiring that the *blessed* be on the board."

"Had it always just been assumed that there would be *blessed* on the board?" Sam asked. "At least by the PA community?"

Mr. Jacobsen shrugged. "The business was formed in 1910, incorporated in the 1930s," he said. "There had been plans after that to replace the bylaws, but it would have meant losing some of the advantages the corporation had grandfathered in. Then wars got in the way."

Sam had read about that, how Samuel Jacobsen had wanted to set up training centers around the world. When WWI had broken out, he'd scuttled those plans and concentrated on training as many psychics as he could to help the war effort.

Though the years between the wars had been peaceful enough, after Samuel died, no one pushed for international status until after WWII.

"It was a different country back then, after World War Two," Mr. Jacobsen said. "Time of the Communist scare, with plenty of fear washing over onto the *blessed* as well. That was part of the driving force to become an international corporation. Things could have gotten ugly. Well, more ugly. It was important to not put all our eggs in one basket."

Sam took another sip of her divine coffee before asking, "But now, only lawyers and bankers make up the board. What happened in 1972?" Sam knew she'd made a mistake by the sour look that crossed the man's face.

"Non-disclosure agreements mean that I can't actually talk about what happened, or even if anything happened," he snapped.

"Your wife was a powerful telepath, right?" Sam asked, trying a different tact.

Finally, she got a smile out of the man sitting across from her. "Helen was as powerful as she was beautiful," he said softly. "Smart, too. But she could never have sat on the board."

"Because of her abilities?" Sam asked. She would imagine it would be difficult to trust a telepath in a room full of powerful men with secrets.

Mr. Jacobsen gave a harsh laugh. "No, because she was a woman. That was just the start of woman's lib. While spoiled college brats protested and burned their bras, nothing changed in the halls of power. It still hasn't."

Sam blinked, surprised. She hadn't considered that women would be barred from holding a position on the board. Then she stopped and counted. Of the nine board members, only one was a woman currently. Previous boards hadn't had a much better ratio.

"I see," Sam said. She didn't run into a lot of prejudice herself, so it hadn't occurred to her to look beyond what had been presented as "normal".

"Were there other telepaths on the board in 1972?" Sam asked after a moment.

"Can't say I remember," Mr. Jacobsen said blandly. "It was over fifty years ago. I was a young man, in my thirties at the time."

"But something caused the nature of the board, as well as the direction of the consortium, to change," Sam insisted. "I'm not asking for particulars," she assured Mr. Jacobsen. "Just general trends. You tell me yes or no."

"All right," Mr. Jacobsen said slowly, though Sam could tell he thought this was a stupid idea.

"Before the seventies, the focus of the consortium was on finding eligible candidates and training them," Sam said. This much she was fairly certain of, given the literature and marketing materials she'd found in the library, ads in old papers and magazines. Plus, that was what she'd been told during her own training. In fact, it had been stressed over and over again that the primary charter of Jacobsen Consortium was to train those with psychic abilities.

"That's true," Mr. Jacobsen said. "We developed several strategies for third-world countries that didn't rely on electricity. Here, we have fancy computer simulations and recording devices that we use for testing. We couldn't do that in a village that had no power."

Sam vaguely recalled reading about the different testing strategies used outside the U.S. She'd never paid that much attention to it. She wondered if the African art she'd seen in the front room had been acquired while the Jacobsen's had been visiting Africa.

"During the seventies, the consortium narrowed the definition of what it meant to have psychic abilities," Sam guessed. It wasn't apparent in the literature, but that was the sense she had.

"All companies need a consistent brand," Mr. Jacobsen said. He sounded as though he was teaching a business course. "They need an identity that the general public can easily recognize as well as identify with. Many businesses go through a focusing phase when they determine what they are as well as what they are not. Who is their audience? What does that audience need? What do they love? What do they fear?"

Sam blinked. She'd never had any business training. She'd never thought of Jacobsen Consortium actually *marketing* to anyone. They were merely there to serve the *blessed* community. Right?

She put her thoughts together slowly. "And what if there are two audiences?" she asked. "Both the general public as well as the *blessed?*"

"Any business would look at that and ask itself which audience had more influence, as well as more money," Mr. Jacobsen said. He still sounded as if he were giving a lecture.

Sam couldn't help her shiver. She knew the answer. *They do.* The general public had a lot more money and influence than the significantly smaller population of the *blessed.*

She could see it now, how the consortium had turned away from serving its primary audience to focusing on everyone else.

"It was the end of the seventies when Jacobsen Consortium started to register PAs with the government. The process wasn't codified until the mid-eighties," Sam said as she continued to mull over her thoughts.

She couldn't afford to get angry at how Jacobsen Consortium had lied to her community. How they'd stopped being there to merely train her kind. Not yet.

"True, registration wasn't required for quite some time," Mr. Jacobsen said. "And the ACLU and the other bleeding hearts didn't have enough power to challenge those rulings at that time. The public needed to be protected at all costs."

Sam gave a sigh. And now, in these days of terrorists and mad bombers, of fear mongers and few sane voices, the public needed to be *protected* more than ever.

"Is there a way to bring the focus of Jacobsen Consortium back to its original constituency?" Sam said. She was afraid she knew the answer, but she still had to ask.

"Only if the *blessed* can learn to frighten the people in power, more so than a mob of the Average Joe," Mr. Jacobsen said. "Otherwise, you're a lost cause. Look for railroad cars soon."

Sam shivered. It wasn't that bad, was it? Then again, there was that new bill being considered in Congress that would ban the *blessed* from certain public buildings, like government offices. She knew there were laws already in place about PAs and the military.

Would they be banned from schools and churches next? Not allowed to get a job in the public sector? Required to work as slaves for Jacobsen Consortium? She'd been shocked when she'd realized that the wages of PAs were going down. The kids just starting out were making half what Sam had made when she'd been their age.

"Thank you for your time," Sam said as Mr. Jacobsen stood, indicating that the interview was over.

"You're quite welcome. And tell that harridan you work for that I won't listen to her blackmail a second time. She'll deal with my lawyers or not at all."

Mr. Jacobsen sounded friendly enough as he gave his warning. Still, Sam took it to heart. "I'll let her know," she said. Though Mrs. Lewis was likely to just laugh at Sam's news and call Mr. Jacobsen an old scoundrel.

On her way back to her car, Sam pondered the way Jacobsen Consortium had changed over the years, but at the same time, had remained the same. They still tested people. Laws now required that everyone must be tested by the time they turned eighteen, both in the United States and in many other countries. A person couldn't get employment without a testing certificate. Sure, some skipped it, like Cassie. But it was harder to do so now, more difficult to get around the testing.

Jacobsen Consortium were determined to sweep up every PA into their net, despite the fact that they wouldn't necessarily recognize all the talents a PA had.

But why were they so determined to have such a large base? What were they planning on doing with all those folks?

And what could Sam do to stop them?

4

____

I wish I could have protected Hunter from the shit that was about to hit the fan, from discovering a crime after breaking into a hotel room. However, any post-cog worth their salt would have seen that it was Hunter who broke into the room, not me. I was just collateral damage. Nor could I just leave, because I would have been in the viewing as well.

So we stood outside the hotel room with the hippy-dippy carpet and waited for the cops to show up. I moved us down the hallway to get out of the stench of the body and the stupid perfume that they'd used to cover up the smell. I'd already tried calling up my *area of knowing* to see if I could follow the body back up its timeline, to see where and when she'd been killed. But as Mr. Chao had said, the portal messed that up, so I couldn't follow her anywhere. I did tag the area so I could come back later if I needed to recheck details.

"Why do you think the room wasn't cleaned?" I asked Hunter to try and get him to stop freaking out about how the cops would soon be there to take us away. Hotel security had already locked down the elevators, not allowing anyone else onto the floor.

He shrugged. "Lots of ways to do that," he said. "Room might be marked as 'in maintenance' on the housekeeping charts. The maids wouldn't come in and clean until it was back in rotation."

That made sense to me, more sense than someone coming and hanging a "do not disturb" sign on the room every morning, just to remove it after the maids had finished that floor. "But someone had to be coming by regularly because of the perfume," I said. "Someone who knew the body was in there, rotting."

Hunter shook his head. "I can't smell it. I didn't smell the perfume earlier, either. I think it's an aftereffect. Possibly no one sprayed anything."

"That can't be true," I said. The stench of the perfume had been awful, like one of those men's body washes that boys bathed in sometimes, strong enough to choke a horse and sweet enough to put someone into a diabetic coma. "Post-cog is *sight*, remember? Not smells." I think I'd be grossed out if I started to include smell in my *area of knowing*.

"Smell-o-vision?" Hunter asked with a small smile. "Like those movies?"

I wasn't sure if he was teasing me or not. When had he learned to be so calm? That wasn't like him at all. Then again, if I watched carefully, I could see his hands twitching now and again as if they wanted to hit something. Was his calm only surface deep?

I gave him the benefit of the doubt and tried to relax as well. "Smell along with sight would be awful," I assured him. "Worse than those stupid movies."

Hunter nodded, then asked quietly, "Why are you smelling things, then? Is it this case?"

Now it was my turn to shrug. I told him about how I'd been thinking about the apocalypse. At this point, I assumed it was related to the case.

"It sounds like whatever this case is, you're getting in too deep," Hunter warned.

"If you want to say something useful, tell me how to not do that," I said hotly. I wasn't really angry at him. To be honest, I might have been a touch scared.

"Have you talked with Theresa?" Hunter stubbornly said. "Asked her about not diving head first into this?"

I sighed. "I haven't."

He gave me a look.

"Fine, fine, I will," I promised. Since when had Hunter become the more sensible of us two?

"Still thinking the dead bodies may be connected to Odin?" Hunter said after a few more minutes.

"Yeah," I said. The elevator doors binged. I pushed myself off the wall and started walking toward them. "And you know what that means."

"An invocation," Hunter said. "After we get out of jail."

"How do you think Odin would react if I called him from inside a jail cell?" I mused.

Hunter snorted. "Probably accuse you of trying to trap him with mortal bars and would laugh at your puny efforts."

"Think he'd break me out?"

"Nope. He'd let you sit there and rot," Hunter said.

He was probably right. Fortunately, I was hoping Michael John Adams would break me out long before I resorted to calling on the gods.

SOMEONE AT DISPATCH had been paying attention when the call came in, as Ferguson, along with his sidekick Mr. Chao, stepped out of the elevator.

I didn't expect either of them to acknowledge us as they strode from the elevator and up the hallway to the dead girl's room. I was not disappointed in them or their manners, as both of them merely sneered at us before continuing on.

I shrugged at Hunter and went back to leaning against the wall, content to wait. I was curious if Mr. Chao, in his fancy brown jacket, would see a rainbow portal like we had.

I was convinced that both bodies had been killed elsewhere, then just dumped through the portals. But where had they died? And why? Had someone just run out of eye of newt and so was using people's eyes instead?

Mr. Chao stormed back down the hallway toward us after a short time. "Do you have any idea why the body dropped from a rainbow portal?" he asked, fuming.

On the one hand, I was happy that he'd seen the same thing I had. On the other hand, I think he wanted to lock us up himself and torture us until we confessed.

"I don't know why bodies keep being dropped from portals," I told him. "I wish I did. But I'm still thinking Odin, not Horus."

The glare that statement got me warmed my heart. I couldn't help but smile at the poor man. It was the little things that made my day, such as sincerely irritating cops.

"We'll need to see you down at the station," Ferguson said as he came walking up. Really, that man needed to see a stylist or something. That round look from the puffy down jacket wasn't doing him any favors. "We'll need to get your full statements. Including why, and how, you entered that room."

"We were following a lead," I told him honestly. "Though I couldn't tell you *why* we went to that particular room. Other than it was a hunch. It just felt like the right room. You know?"

"No, I do not know," Mr. Chao said sharply.

"Poor boy," I said. Maybe that was pushing it. But he needed to realize that Jacobsen Consortium had drawn a tight box around him and his abilities. He could break out of his training, if he worked at it.

"The *blessed* were taught to ignore their hunches and feelings because they might not be right," I recited, as if reading from company propaganda posters. "If you can't predict something with one hundred percent accuracy, it can't be real. That's what Jacobsen Consortium would have you believe. And we all know they *never* lie."

Mr. Chao narrowed his eyes at me, but he didn't reply. Too bad. I would have loved to continue his education.

"Come along, boys and girls," Ferguson said, earning a glare as well from Mr. Chao. "We can argue training and abilities on our way down to the station. You two are coming with us."

"Don't you have to do stuff here? Like questioning the staff, seeing if there are any witnesses—you know, police stuff?" I asked, confused. I'd worked with the cops before. Nothing ever moved this fast. A scene was never cleared as quickly as a TV show portrayed.

"That's what junior detectives are for," Ferguson told me smugly. "They know what to look for and when to call me back to the scene. But I've seen enough here. And the coroner will be sending video of her findings shortly."

I was impressed. Generally, the cops used still photographs. Obviously, someone's budget had been increased, probably to deal with the constant protesters since the elections.

We stepped out of the hotel and into the fucking freezing wind. God, would it never let up? Just thinking about stopping to have a cigarette in this weather made me shiver harder.

Good way to quit, though, particularly if I told myself that I could only smoke outside my apartment and not inside.

Hunter was watching me, curious. He didn't seem to be as affected by the weather as I was. Freak.

Then again, neither of the cops were either.

Ah, shit.

I really was getting drawn too far down into whatever the hell was going on.

Hopefully Theresa would have some strategies for drawing me out before it was too late.

MICHAEL JOHN ADAMS was waiting for us at the police station. I didn't know if he had some sort of police scanner so he could listen to their chatter or if he just had an informant in the department, telling him which station to meet us at. Probably both, as I hadn't been able to give him any more details other than the fact we were about to be arrested.

The lawyer looked immaculate as always in his dark brown three-piece suit with matching gloves and scarf. Instead of fancy loafers with no socks, he wore sensible boots. He and Mr. Chao probably went to the same cobbler.

The police station itself seemed like a busy office building. Mind you, everyone there was armed. Still, it had that feeling, particularly given the layout of the room. A counter ran the length of the room, just inside the door. Behind it, clerks and cops worked at desks and computers. Long, beige filing cabinets lined the back wall under the glazed windows that let in light but nothing else. The smell of cheap coffee and overly-sweet pastries underlay everything.

"Where are you taking my clients?" Michael John asked as soon as we were led through the door, before we could be hustled into the back, away from all watchful eyes.

The sigh Ferguson gave was truly impressive. I think teenagers could have learned from him how to sound put out. "They are witnesses to an ongoing investigation and need to be questioned," he said.

"Only with their lawyer present," Michael John said, smiling.

I nodded when Ferguson looked at me. We weren't under arrest yet. And we had the right to have an attorney present.

"Fine, you can tag along," Ferguson said. Then he gave an evil smile. "Though questioning them one at a time is going to take a *lot* longer."

"Go with Hunter," I said immediately. I was a big girl. I could take care of myself.

"I'd rather you waited," Michael John said.

I shrugged. I'd been through this before. They'd probably bring in some heavy hitting telepaths to question me, as they'd done before. I'd driven them crazy by thinking about smoking. Hopefully whoever they brought in would be just as susceptible.

Michael John clearly didn't like it. But I'd dealt with telepathic assholes who questioned the public before. "I'll be fine," I assured him.

Really, how bad could it be?

OF COURSE, the fuckers kept the room they brought me to for questioning ice cold. I was glad I was still in my leather jacket, though I wished I had yet another pair of heavy wool socks on. My twenty-ring Docs kept my legs warm enough, as did the fleece-lined leggings I was wearing.

I glanced down at my outfit. Hadn't changed from my normal clothes at least, despite diving too far into this case. Maybe this apocalypse would be gaily colored. I wore a fuchsia-colored camisole under a lavender-colored, long-sleeved shirt, with a gray-and-black striped vest over it all. Anything to layer up and stay warm. No, really. I wasn't wearing the vest because of how tight it was or how the top of it came to just under my tits and gave them a nice lift.

The two across the table didn't seem impressed, though. Then again, there was no guarantee that I was the right gender for either of them, let alone the correct species. They both looked like your typical office geek, wearing cheap white shirts and knock-off power ties. The black guy on the left wore thick glasses that made his eyes seem huge in his gaunt face. The white guy on the right had the acne of a teenager, probably from too many donuts.

The room itself was pretty bland, with gray walls, no windows, and a plain wooden table. The wall just past the two guys was a one-way mirror, distorted and dark. A single, uncomfortable looking metal chair waited for me on the other side of the table.

I nearly swore when I sat down on the chair. Damn, that was cold. I was looking forward to riding in Michael John's car after this was all over, just for the butt warmers.

We started with the usual routine—full name, date of birth, home address, where I worked, and so on. I didn't let myself be lulled by the process, though. In between every question I kept up my mantra: *one times two equals two, two times two equals four, three times two equals six.*

I didn't think that would throw off a professional telepath. But I had to try something to keep these two assholes out of my head.

"Tell us what happened this morning in your own words," the black guy, Theodore, started off with.

I explained how Hunter and I had a hunch about the hotel (which we did, though I didn't get into the specifics of the previous victim's visa). Going to the right floor had been just a matter of feeling around for it. We'd played yet another hunch pushing that button.

That seemed to put the white guy, Fredrick, on edge. He didn't like dealing with such imprecision. "What do you mean," he asked, staring hard at me. "Hunches?"

"You know. Those little feelings you get about a case?" I asked innocently enough.

"You weren't trained at Jacobsen Consortium," Fredrick sneered.

"That's right," I told him. "I got real training, out in the street, instead of cleaned-up school lessons."

Fredrick didn't like that one little bit. But Theodore wasn't about to let the interrogation be derailed.

"What happened after you reached the correct floor?" Theodore asked.

This was where it was going to get tricky. I needed to gloss over the breaking and entering in order to get them to the body. "I smelled some god-awful perfume when we got off the elevator. Like someone was trying to cover something nasty up."

The two looked at each other. I figured that whatever preliminary report they'd received from Ferguson's minions hadn't included that tasty tidbit. Despite the fact that Hunter said he hadn't smelled anything. Surely someone else had.

"You know that overly sweet men's body wash? Like that," I said. I tried to recall the scent as clearly as I could to give these assholes a taste of it. That would also help me judge just how strong of a reading they were giving me.

Theodore stiffened, while Fredrick didn't. Interesting. So Theodore was the stronger telepath of the two?

I told them about walking past the door, then walking back to it. "It was one of those *feelings*, you know?" I said, smiling sweetly at Fredrick. He bristled, but I kept going. "Once we got into the room, there was that *smell* again." Just to keep Theodore involved, and possibly to distract him. "And the body."

"Tell us how you got into the room," Theodore said, his eyes drilling into me.

"You wouldn't understand how hard it is to ignore some of those *feelings*," I told them. "Like that craving for the first morning cigarette. You *need* that hit, that sweet nicotine flowing into your lungs. We *had* to get into that room."

I surprised myself with how truthful my description was. I

hadn't realized it at the time how much I really had needed to get into that room.

I didn't want to admit it to myself, but that really wasn't a good sign.

"So how did you get into the room?" Theodore pressed.

"Magic," I said. "Hunter did something. I'm not sure what." All of which was technically true. I had no idea how Hunter's device worked.

Theodore and Fredrick both kept pressing me about how we'd managed to break in. I continued to disavow any knowledge of it. Hunter had done something. Hell, for all I knew, the door hadn't even been locked.

Eventually, Fredrick and Theodore moved on, asking about the body on the bed, how it had gotten there. The sparkliness of the portal didn't impress either of them as much as it should have. No accounting for taste.

I told the truth as much as I could, sticking to it literally. They couldn't really sweat me, that room was too damned cold for that.

Finally, they seemed to run out of things to question me about. I wouldn't turn on Hunter, nor would I back down from the rainbow portal. Hell, I bet even Fredrick caught a glimpse of it when I talked about it, not that he'd admit to that.

They had no idea how much *weird shit* was actually true outside of their personal white-picket-fence philosophies.

After the usual warnings about not to get in the way of an active investigation, as well as to stay in town, Fredrick asked, "If this were your case, what would you do next?"

I wasn't sure what he was looking for, if he thought I'd give him some sort of incriminating evidence by answering that question.

So I told him the truth.

"Go summon a god."

HUNTER LOOKED a little worse for wear when he came out of the interrogation room with Michael John. However, he was still a free man. The cops hadn't arrested him. I was so happy that Michael John had been there for him. If I ever got really rich, I was going to put him on a personal retainer instead of having to rely on my mom.

It was close to dinnertime and quite frankly, I was starving. Dealing with assholes burned a lot of calories. I asked Theresa to join us, though Michael John declined, so Hunter and I ended up meeting Theresa at a small diner in downtown St. Paul.

The restaurant had been built back in the 1950s and had been a diner the entire time. An old-fashioned cash register still reigned on the display case just inside the door. A big, hand-written sign in red marker was posted on it: *Cash Only!!!*

Beside the register, a stainless steel counter stretched all the way to the end of the room. Round, red-padded bar stools that swiveled were anchored in place in front of it. Behind the counter, a large rectangular window opened up onto the kitchen.

A narrow aisle separated the counter and stools from the ten booths that lined the windows. Kitschy lights hung over each table, with white-frosted glass shades. They looked like they were from when the place had first been built. The tables had been updated, probably in the '70s, with cheap plywood that matched the wood paneling that lined the walls under the windows.

The place smelled of heavenly fried food and cheap meat, plus the apple and blueberry pies I saw in the display case.

Theresa had arrived before Hunter and I, and waved at us from a table close to the far end.

God, she looked great. Her soft brown hair curled just under the ends on her shoulders. She wore her black leather jacket over a maroon sweater that made her look as delicious as anything that would come out of this kitchen. A light pink tinted her lips, and her eyes sparkled with joy.

I knew I was in love. I'd even told her that I loved her regularly. But seeing her like this just made me want her more.

"Hey sweetie," I said as I slid into the booth next to her, sneaking a kiss.

She smiled at me, then pointedly turned her attention to Hunter. "How are you doing?" she asked, obviously as worried about him as I was.

Fortunately, I didn't have to be jealous that her attention wasn't on me. She'd pressed her warm thigh against mine on the seat, reminding me of just how cold I still was.

Was that because of the current case? I mean, it was Minnesota and we were having a nasty February freeze. However, I wasn't normally this cold.

"I'm fine," Hunter reassured us both. "But food will help," he admitted as he pulled one of the menus toward him.

"My treat," Theresa announced. "So get whatever you like."

I raised an eyebrow at her. She seemed a touch happier than usual.

"I got a raise," she told me proudly.

"Good for you!" I said. I was happy for her, happy for us. Not that we were having problems making ends meet, but she deserved to be paid a hell of a lot more than she was.

At the same time, the reminder that she was still working for the enemy stung. If I didn't love her so much, that would have broken us up a long time before.

I told Theresa about our current case, how we'd found a second body. "Have you ever heard of bodies being dumped through a rainbow portal before?" I asked.

Theresa shook her head. "There's so much general unrest, it's hard for any of the pre-cogs to get a good read on something specific happening." She glanced at Hunter, who nodded in agreement. "Some pre-cogs *are* predicting the end of the world, but it's all the usual stuff—civil unrest, nuclear war, zombie apocalypse."

I nodded. Theresa had talked before about this group of pre-cogs who were convinced the zombie apocalypse was just one mad science experiment away. They had no idea about the other weird shit that was actually going on.

Or maybe they did, and I was the one who was out of touch. Which would keep me up at night if I let myself think about it. Like, did Odin have a secret zombie fetish? Was that the actual reason he'd created Valhalla, in order to create his own zombie army?

We ordered dinner from our harried waitress and mulled over what we knew, what we needed to learn. Theresa didn't seem surprised that I was planning on invoking Odin. Though she didn't experience the gods or the other strange stuff that I did, she believed me when I talked about it.

As far as I knew, she hadn't met anyone during the course of her work who talked with the gods once, let alone regularly. Then again, we never really discussed her work.

Theresa asked, "Are you sure you need Odin? Or do you need to chat with Loki, instead?"

"I'd thought about that, since he's frequently one-eyed now. But I think I need to speak with the original god, not his copycat." Plus, if I really wanted to talk with Loki, he'd probably not appear, just to piss me off. Loki would come and visit me himself if he really wanted to talk to me. Or tease me. Or lead me down the wrong path.

Loki had *plans* for me, or so he'd mentioned previously, and more than once. I wasn't about to try to contact him and possibly further those plans.

"How will you summon him?" Theresa asked.

"Last time, I used a paper 'henge'," I explained. "It had been an art installation. Kind of like Stonehenge, only with great paper shapes made to look like stones."

"Cool," Theresa said. I could tell that she wished she'd been there to see it. "What will you use this time?"

Before I could reply, Hunter said, "Could I make a suggestion?"

"Sure," I said, curious.

"Since we're dealing with rainbows and possibly the Bifrost bridge, why don't you use an ice bridge instead of a henge?" he said.

I couldn't help but sigh. "Ice bridge, huh?" I asked. "Where would I find one of those?" I was going to freeze to death on this case, I just knew it.

"Minnehaha Falls has completely frozen over this year," Hunter explained. "You could stand either at the top of the falls or underneath them."

Figured. This was going to call for many, many layers of warm clothing, a huge thermos of hot chocolate, and maybe some rainbow sparkles as well.

Because rainbow sparkles, duh.

I mean, if I was going to summon a god, might as well do it right.

5

———

After dinner, Theresa invited me back to her place. We talked of ordinary things in her warm car, the kind of everyday things that make up a life, like whether or not she should stop and get gas (we did) and if we had enough coffee for the weekend (we didn't, and I volunteered to pick some up).

Her house felt like home in more ways than one. My jacket went into the closet next to my other coats. I could take off my boots here and not have to worry about whether or not I'd have to put them back on in a hurry as I tried to flee. The novel I was slowly making my way through sat on one of the wooden end tables beside the couch. (What? I couldn't help that I'd much rather make out with my girlfriend than read.)

The only light in the living room made the room seem soft as opposed to casting black shadows in the corners. Curtains that we'd picked out together covered the front window that looked out on the street. They were a beautiful gold-and-black brocade pattern that my friend Tess had sewn up for us.

I followed Theresa into the kitchen for our usual ritual of hot chocolate before going to bed. After she'd measured out the milk and put it onto the stove to warm up she finally turned to me and said, "Okay. Out with it."

"Out with what?" I asked, trying to sound completely wounded, though I had a feeling I knew what she was talking about.

"Hunter said you had something to ask me," she said, sounding stern as she turned back to the milk on the stove and stirred.

"Damned busybody!" I said. "Where's this whole 'blood brother' allegiance he was talking about before?"

Theresa smiled but didn't turn to face me. "He's worried about you."

I sighed and gave in. "I know. I'm worried as well. I'm getting drawn too far into this case." The unspoken words *as usual* that followed that statement hung in the air between us.

"Have you kept up your meditating?" Theresa asked, frowning.

"No," I said. "It didn't seem to be helping." At Theresa's glare, I added, "I know, I know. I'm supposed to meditate so that I don't end up in the position I'm in. I'll get back to it. I promise."

Theresa pressed her lips together and nodded, obviously unwilling to say anything more for fear that she'd snap at me for being an idiot.

That was okay. I would berate myself later for being stupid on her behalf. "So what can I do now? To draw me back out of the case?"

Theresa shook her head. "I'm not sure."

I pushed myself off the kitchen counter I'd been leaning against and tucked myself in behind her, wrapping her firmly in my arms and nuzzling behind her ear before giving the soft skin there a kiss. "I know something that would ensure my attention was in the here and now."

I felt more than heard her snort of derision. "I'm sure," she said dryly. "But we can't be having sex all the time."

Before I could respond, she raised her hand to stop me. "And no, that isn't a challenge." She leaned back against me, solid and warm in my arms as she whisked the cocoa powder into the heated milk. "While I like sex, and I'm glad that will help, you need something else to root you." She paused, then added, "I hate to suggest it, but you should look into an amulet or some other jewelry that you can wear that would remind you of the present."

I couldn't help but stiffen. I hated that I couldn't hide it from her, that she knew how tense she'd just made me. "Like a ring, perhaps? To remind me not just of the present but of good times to come?" I tried to keep my voice soft but I sounded harsh even to my own ears.

Theresa sighed. It had been a thing between us now for the last couple of months, this whole specter of getting married.

It was currently legal. We both were afraid that it would become illegal again, given the general political climate.

"That wasn't what I meant," Theresa said. "I really meant an amulet. Maybe a necklace that you'd never take off."

"You just don't want me to get totally naked with you," I said, aiming for a teasing tone, trying to make the conversation lighter again.

Theresa smiled, seeming to appreciate my effort. "No, not really," she said. She paused, considering. "Ask Hakeem," she said after a moment.

I rolled my eyes. "You know if I mention something like that, one of his relatives will *make* me something out of chicken feet and burlap."

"Are you just afraid of being unfashionable?" Theresa teased as she poured the steaming hot chocolate into the two mugs I'd gotten out.

"Oh honey, I can make anything look good," I reassured her.

We didn't talk about it more. But later that night, my girl made damned sure that I was firmly rooted in the here and now, at least for a little while.

I TEXTED Hakeem to have him come and pick me up from Theresa's place the next morning. It didn't surprise me at all that he immediately replied and said he'd be there in five minutes.

Hakeem saw patterns. It allowed him to anticipate where he needed to go to next.

I figure he'd seen some pattern and knew that I'd need him this morning. And where.

At least it meant I didn't have to wait long at the corner. I was still wearing my shorter black leather jacket, though I'd switched to heavier jeans that morning. I'd chosen the brightest shirt I had hanging in Theresa's closet, white with red hibiscus flowers on it, over a searing pink camisole.

"So how goes the life of a spy?" I asked as I slid into the front seat of the black town car. While Hakeem continued to sort of work with Hunter and I, I never let him forget that he was a double agent, also reporting our actions to Jacobsen Consortium.

The car smelled faintly of the lavender satchel that Hakeem hung from his rearview mirror. He'd already turned on the seat warmer and the car felt toasty. Despite the cold, Hakeem was merely wearing his usual argyle sweater vest, no jacket in sight.

Hakeem seemed to understand my reluctance to trust him. Hell, Hunter still trusted Hakeem more than I did. Hakeem always sent his reports to me before he sent it into Josh, his contact. I took the time to read them carefully, though I never censored them. I figured if I couldn't censor myself, I didn't deserve to be called an adult.

"Josh—presses me for more information," Hakeem admitted.

That surprised me. Hakeem usually just laughed and teased me back about reporting how often I was making out with Theresa in the backseat. (It had only been that one time. Okay, maybe more than once. But it wasn't like it happened every time Hakeem drove us somewhere! Just almost every time.)

"What are you going to do?" I asked Hakeem. There wasn't really anything I could do to help him. I was the one he was reporting on, after all.

Hakeem shrugged. "I try to tell him about other PAs," he admitted. "But Josh really only ever wants to hear about you and Hunter."

"Hunter hasn't been breaking his restraining order, has he?" I asked. Hunter still sometimes felt the need to go spook Josh by placing himself just outside the radius of the court decree and staring intently at the man.

"I don't think so," Hakeem said. "You should talk to Hunter. Make sure. Josh needs to stay calm."

"Why?" I asked, surprised. Hakeem had never expressed an interest in keeping Josh calm before.

Hakeem's shrug didn't surprise me in the least. I knew it was just a *feeling* he had, some pattern that would remain nebulous until it came closer.

I talked a little with Hakeem about the latest case. As it was an active investigation, I couldn't say that much. I certainly didn't want Josh to get the idea that I was breaking police procedure. If I screwed up, he'd gladly squeal on me to get my license pulled.

"But I seem to be getting too involved again," I admitted as I finished up. "Smelling things that aren't there. Feeling…well, jittery. Or maybe I just had too much coffee this morning, I don't know." I had to add that, though I'd had tea that morning. I needed to give myself an out in the report Hakeem was already writing in his head.

"What are you looking for?" Hakeem asked as he slid the car easily in and out of traffic. We were heading up north to pick up Hunter before going to the falls.

"A token. Maybe an amulet," I said. I couldn't tell him that Theresa had suggested it. She was off limits when it came to any of my conversations with Hakeem. I couldn't afford to get her into trouble with her company.

Though sometimes it felt like I was dancing on knife points, between Hakeem and Theresa both working for the evil empire.

"I see," Hakeem said, nodding. "I think I know what you need. After the falls, I take you there."

It surprised me that Hakeem wouldn't announce that he had a relative who made the perfect thing. That was his usual reply.

Though chances were, he was taking me to a relative's shop.

We didn't talk much for the rest of the ride up to the northern part of Minneapolis. He had traffic to deal with, and I had a poem that I was still preparing.

I mean, how else do you summon a god?

HUNTER STOOD OUTSIDE THE VETERANS' shared housing. Freak. It was at least fifteen below. Then again, he was dressed for the weather, with his long brown coat firmly buttoned all the way up. If only I could get him to wear a hat. Then again, his brown hair generally frizzed out around his face like an electrified halo. Hunter with hat-head wouldn't be the same.

We got to the falls just before noon. I didn't know if a particular time would mean anything to the invocation or not. I wanted to start at twelve o'clock, though. I wasn't worried about anyone being able to see us: Odin had hidden his presence from Sam the last time I'd called on him.

Hard-packed snow covered the stairs leading from the parking lot down to the bottom of the falls. The handrail was covered in a sheet of ice. Bare branches lined the path, and the trees shivered in the wind. At least the sky had stayed overcast, keeping in some of the heat, otherwise it probably would have been another ten degrees colder.

Despite the many landings and switchbacks, my knees were starting to hate me by the time we reached the last stair. I'd caught glimpses of the falls through the trees as we'd walked down, but it wasn't until I turned and started up the path that I got a good look.

I must admit, the sight took my breath away. The water had frozen mid-fall. Huge spikes of yellow and white ice looked suspended in the air. The wind blowing off the frozen waterfall was seventh-circle-of-hell cold. However, I still wondered if maybe I could bring Theresa back with me sometime. She'd love seeing this.

I risked frostbite by taking off my gloves and snapping a few pictures with my phone, just to show her.

Warnings about dangerous ice and falling rocks blocked the path leading closer to the falls. Hunter ignored them and I followed right behind. I didn't think that Odin would be a complete asshole and suddenly unfreeze the falls and drown us. Plus, Hunter could dodge any rocks the god threw at us, all while dragging my ass to safety.

When we drew close to the falls, Hunter swerved to the left, following some trail that only he saw. I was happy for my tall boots. The snow got fucking deep here off the beaten-down path.

Fortunately, Hunter knew where he was going. Huge boulders blocked off what looked like the regular trail. Hunter led me around them, then along another hidden path that dipped under the frozen waterfall.

"It's not quite a bridge," I told Hunter as I looked around.

A frozen rock wall rose up on our left, while the solid sheet of ice was on the right. The light coming through the ice was dim, but it also had a soft glow to it. The air felt still, as if it had been frozen, too. I couldn't smell anything, not even the scent of water. Only muffled sounds came through the ice and the rock.

He shrugged. "It's isolated and it has the essence of a bridge, being neither here or there," he said.

His voice echoed weirdly in the small space. I didn't think it was something he was doing consciously, however.

"All righty, then," I said. The last time I'd called Odin I'd marched around one of the large paper pillars that made up the "henge." There really wasn't space here for me to do much marching. I could spin in a circle, but I felt as though I was already doing that too much on this case.

I sure as Hell wasn't about to kneel. Still, I needed to do something to "sanctify" the space, to mark it as separate from the mundane. Cutting myself and drawing a circle of blood in the ice was out of the question, though I'm sure that would have pleased just about any of the gods I called.

Hunter looked at me quizzically as I hesitated.

"I need to mark off the space, somehow," I told him. "Separate it." I couldn't explain more than that.

Damn it! Was I losing my words because I had such a strong *feeling* about this?

I was really going to need that amulet, sooner rather than later.

Hunter nodded and slowly pulled a woman's shawl out of his pocket. It was made out of a beautiful purple-and-white paisley silk.

"Where did you get this?" I asked as I took it from his outstretched hand. It felt warm against my fingers, lightweight and soft.

"It's a *pashmina*," Hunter replied. He seemed intent on studying the toes of his boots and not looking up at me.

"It's Audrey's, isn't it?" I asked. I could smell her faint perfume on it, though before just now I wouldn't have been able to even tell you that she wore perfume.

Hunter nodded, his fair skin showing his blush.

"You go," I said, not asking how Hunter managed to be in possession of an item of his girlfriend's clothing.

I was also *not* going to start thinking about how odd it was for Hunter to even *have* a girlfriend.

I took two ends of the pashmina and twirled the cloth together, tightening the shawl into a long scarf. Then I laid it down on the ground, separating Hunter and I from the rock wall, while leaving the ice in front of us.

"Ready?" I asked Hunter. "Though you may not be able to see anything." I'd already warned him about that, but I thought I'd mention it again.

He nodded. "It's okay. I've seen other gods."

And that was the real kicker, wasn't it? That invoking a god was kind of just part of our job, and not even the weirdest part, some days.

I just wished it paid better.

"Odin, Val-Father, I call on you!
I call on the wielder of the spear Gungnir!
I call on Hugin and Munin, thought and memory,
I call on the great puzzler to see wisdom in these strange deeds!
Share your wisdom! Come to my side!"

Winds whistled by us, pushing along the short tunnel between ice and rock. Hunter stood stock still, his jaw tightened, his eyes wide. I knew he'd stayed clean and didn't take the *poisoned pearls* drug anymore.

Was he regretting that now? Did he need to see more, so he could protect us?

"I invoke thee, O Slayer of Ymir, who died and lived again
At the end of all time, the end of the twilight war
Who teacheth the importance of sight above all things!
Loan me your visions! Come to my side!"

Yellowish light poured out of the ice wall in front of us. Cold air pressed against me, freezing me to my very bones. I thought I heard the sound of a group of men chanting along with me. The smell of snow and long, frozen nights filled my nose.

Damn it! Why wasn't that enough? Stupid god probably needed to be flattered more.

"O great rider of Slepnir,
O gray one, O weary traveler,
O husband of Frigg, hear my call!
Rest your feet at my hearth! Come to my side!"

Instead of the god fully manifesting, a vision of Odin appeared in the clear ice, like the best of the Hollywood movie effects, showing someone looking out through a mirror. He wore a gray robe, long and full. A blood-red belt, about the width of my outstretched hand, cinched it closed. A great leather cloak lined with thick white fur hung around his shoulders, a golden rope holding it in place.

Odin's face seemed more pale than usual, but maybe that was the ice. He wore a black patch over the one eye, though I would have sworn he could still see through it. He was taller than Hunter or I, with broad shoulders and wide features. He had a large nose that looked as if it had been broken more than once. Silver hair crept up from his temples, highlighting the dark brown. His beard, too, had silver edging it.

"Ah, Cassandra, good," Odin said. "I was planning on speaking with you."

"Really?" I asked. "Then why make me go through the whole incantation thing?" It just proved my point that being a god didn't make you special or different, it just meant that you were more of an asshole than everyone else.

I glanced over at Hunter who appeared to be following the conversation. Good. I didn't think that Odin had forgotten Hunter or had tried to freeze him and failed. Maybe he thought that Hunter had something useful to say.

Oh no, wait. This was a damned *god* we were talking to. Odin probably hadn't frozen Hunter so that he could praise Odin as well.

"Because it amused me to watch you strain yourself casting such a verse," Odin said as if there was nothing wrong with that statement.

Asshole. I didn't say that out loud, but I sure thought it. Hopefully, Odin had enough of the whole god-like abilities that he caught it like a good telepath would.

"Why did you want to see me?" I asked Odin. I figured I should at least try to get information out of him first before he disappeared on me. Gods were annoying that way.

"I'm assuming that you called me because something odd was occurring," Odin said, instead of answering my question. "What is it?"

Fine. I'd go first. "Why would someone kill a person, then gouge out their eye?" I said. I watched Odin carefully, wanting to see if this was a sore subject for him or not.

However, Odin gave a very casual shrug. It didn't even looked practiced, but natural. Stupid god. "I tied myself to the tree of life and hung there, suffering, for a week while seeking knowledge," Odin said. The words sounded rote, as if he'd given this speech many times before. "I gouged out my own eye in order to gain wisdom, to see, to try to prevent the twilight of the gods."

"Jeez," I said softly. "Do you think these people were convinced, somehow, to remove their own eye? So they could also see?" Just the thought made my stomach roll.

"It's possible," Hunter said. "We'll have to wait for the coroner's reports. Unless you can tell us?" he continued, asking Odin.

"I'll see what I can find out," Odin said. He sounded as smooth as any politician making a promise he never intended to keep. "What else? Why else are you calling on me?"

"You having any problems with the Bifrost bridge lately?" I asked, aiming for casual.

Bingo. Not even a god could hide that tell. Something was rotten in Valhalla.

"Maybe," Odin said slowly. He didn't want to give me any more, but he had to ask. "Why?"

"Bodies keep falling out of portals that are lit up like rainbows," I told him, watching him like a hawk. How was he going to try to get out of this one?

However, Odin surprised me. "Damn it!" he said. He blinked and looked thoughtful for a moment. "I didn't believe that the ice of the bridge could be used for anything magical. Blood-colored hawks and death-white vultures have been breaking off chunks of the ice," he continued. "We didn't know why."

"Don't give me that look," I warned him when he glanced hopefully at me. "I have no idea how they're doing it. Or even what they're doing."

"You mean, what Loki is doing," Odin said.

"Is it Loki? Or someone else?" I asked. "There's that god Horus, you know."

"Who?" Odin asked, sounding as haughty as an old white lady being asked to seat a black man at her table.

"Egyptian god who also has one eye. Though his eye went off and had its own adventures after he plucked it out," I said. Okay, so maybe I was trying to get under Odin's skin a little. That was second nature to me.

"I see," Odin said frostily. Then he shook his head. "It's too difficult for the gods to cross from one plane to another."

"Loki does it," I pointed out.

"Loki's a special case," Odin said. "Which is partially your fault."

"What did I do?" I asked. "Oh, right, I was just the one who saved your ass the last time he tried to bring about Ragnarok."

Odin rolled his eyes at me. "Fine. Though I have already paid you back for that favor," he said.

"But what is Loki up to this time?" I asked. It was a fair question, now that I knew that Odin wasn't actually behind the disfigured bodies as well as the rainbow portals.

Odin sighed. "He is a usurper. Even if he was living in the perfect circumstances, with the perfect life, he'd still start agitating and trying to change things. That is his nature."

"Is he trying to overthrow you?" I said.

"No," Odin said slowly. "This feels much bigger."

That worried me. "Bigger than casting you aside?"

"Loki's always dreamed big," Odin said dryly. "Why not try to take over all the worlds on all the planes?"

I had no answer to that one. It sounded about Loki's speed, though.

"What else can you tell me about the bodies? Or the portals?" Odin asked.

"Generally, I'm the only one who deals with the weird shit. Seems that other PAs can also see the rainbow sparkles," I said.

Odin narrowed his eye at me, though again, I had the feeling that the hidden eye was making the exact same gesture. "Interesting," he said. He paused, then added, "Thank you."

I didn't have time to recover from my shock of actually being *thanked* by a god before Odin disappeared, taking his cold winds and ice with him.

I glanced at Hunter. I couldn't say it. But I knew we were both thinking it.

Gods thanking humans? Yet another sure sign of the apocalypse.

I'd never seen Hunter be…well, tender for lack of a better word. But that was the best way to describe how he picked up that pashmina and shook it out. It was almost as if he was making love to the scarf. It gave me the willies, quite frankly, how he stroked the cloth, running his fingers along it and smoothing out the wrinkles.

But damned if I was going to say anything. Hunter had a girlfriend. What happened between two consenting, screwed-up adults was none of my business.

Finally, he finished carefully folding up the pashmina and put it back into his pocket. Then he looked up at me, startled, as if he'd forgotten I was standing there.

It must have been some night for him to block out not only the cold and the ice, but someone else in his space.

Hunter gave me a sheepish grin. "Ready, boss?"

Cocky bastard. As if I hadn't been waiting all this time for him. "Sure," I said. I turned to go out the same way we came in.

"Just a sec," Hunter said. When I looked over my shoulder, he was headed out the other direction.

Why the hell did he want to go traipsing around in the cold? Or was there something else there? I followed him reluctantly out the other side.

Hunter stood a few feet away, looking up. He had that faraway look in his eyes that meant trouble. I'd worked with him enough to know that even without going into his *area of knowing*, Hunter's spidey sense was working overtime.

"Incoming, boss," was all he managed to say before I heard a soft *whump* behind me.

Goddamn it. There was another body. An older man this time. Asian, with a bald head and a long, skinny white beard. He wasn't dressed for this weather, wearing a ratty old T-shirt depicting the Great Wall of China, shorts, and sandals.

Like the others, he had one eye gouged out. Blood spilled from it, turning the ice bloody. The way the body had landed at the foot of the falls made for an artistic picture. That is, if the painting had been done by a sadistic lunatic.

I didn't know for certain, but I'd bet that this guy had been killed much more recently than the other two bodies.

Then that stupid smell wafted over me, that same goddamned perfume I'd smelled in the hotel. However, this time, the smell seemed fresher. Instead of reminding me of boy's body wash, it had deeper, richer undertones. More like incense than perfume.

I closed my eyes and tagged the area so I could revisit it later. I didn't know if the tag would carry the scent or not. But my friend Tess worked in a hippy store that sold tarot cards, statues of gods like Ganesh and Guan Lin, offering bowls and altar kits, as well as incense. Maybe she could help me identify the type of incense and give me a hint about the god who enjoyed it.

When I opened my eyes again, Hunter shook his head at me. "Ferguson is not going to like this."

"Fuck Ferguson," I told him. "We're going to have to stand here in the goddamned cold until he gets his ass here." My toes were already starting to grow numb.

Hunter's lips twitched as if he wanted to laugh at me. However, he knew better.

So I made the call and we walked back up the staircase. I could already hear the accusations that Ferguson would throw at us, about how bodies seemed to be following us around.

I wouldn't be able to deny that. Three bodies in a row was just too much of a coincidence. We were being targeted.

But by whom? And why?

6

——————

DEBRA LEWIS contentedly sipped her morning coffee. The news played on the radio in the background, a soft murmur that she didn't really pay attention to. Her tablet showing the local Twin City's newspaper sat on the kitchen table beside the remains of her eggs benedict. She really was going to have to compliment her chef Henré on the hollandaise sauce—it had had the perfect amount of tartness yet had been creamy as well.

Despite how much Debra packed into every waking minute of every day, she always took this time in the morning to have her breakfast and coffee, to read the paper, and to center herself. It was an old-fashioned concept, not only that breakfast was the most important time of the day but that she needed this time alone with her thoughts. The days when she was forced to take a breakfast meeting always left her feeling unfocused. Almost resentful.

Right now, she couldn't afford to let her attention stray one single iota—not when everything she'd wanted and had worked for was so very close.

Jacobsen Consortium had continued to shift its position over the past eighteen months. They'd restructured their internal departments, isolating some while exposing others. In terms of war, they were retreating and were leaving behind the units that weren't vital to the company.

Those sectors would either be killed off deliberately or just left to die, sacrificial limbs while the main core thrived.

However, Debra had been paying very careful attention for years, particularly since her daughter, Cassandra, had turned out to have powers. Executing her plan had taken longer than Debra would have expected, but Jacobsen Consortium was still privately held. There was only so much that was publicly reported. However, she had her internal sources and knew how to read between the lines much better than most.

Jacobsen Consortium merely had to blink at this point, and Debra would have them. It had taken time and money, but she was gradually learning where all the bodies were buried. Then using that knowledge to her advantage.

Blackmail was such an ugly term. She preferred to think of it as influence, pressure points designed to make a body lean one way or the other.

The board was on the ropes, whether they realized it or not.

Samantha, Cassie's old girlfriend, had been useful in that regard. Not that Sam had been able to ferret out any new tidbits of knowledge that Debra hadn't already found on her own. It was rare when Sam gave Debra something she didn't already know.

More importantly, Sam had been open to the education that Debra had been providing. Sam no longer trusted Jacobsen Consortium, which was a huge step for most of the *blessed*. Sam had volunteered to learn more about the consortium's actual history, looking behind the propaganda that she'd been taught. Debra had been thrilled when Sam had asked about interviewing old board members.

It had taken every bit of Debra's fortitude for her not to laugh at Sam's outrage that Jacobsen Consortium, this pseudo-parent of hers, had ulterior motives. But the *blessed* were deliberately indoctrinated not to question the business, as well as to trust that the corporation had their best interests at heart. After all, the corporation not only trained them but provided most of their jobs as well.

Debra wouldn't call the *blessed* slaves, necessarily. They were more like sharecroppers who could never buy the land they worked on.

And who, for the most part, didn't even realize that there was a way out of their chains.

In addition, Sam had been educating others in her community, something that Debra couldn't do. The *blessed* were fairly close-knit, and Debra would always be an outsider. There was no possible way for her to fake having powers and worm her way in there, though she'd considered it more than once.

Sam's true use was as an agitator in her community. Her constant questioning had put additional pressure on Jacobsen Consortium and highlighted more of the cracks in the company's façade.

Debra took another sip of her excellent coffee. She was going to have to remember to recommend this brand to Cassandra at their next mother-daughter lunch.

If only Cassandra had come into her powers the normal way! She would have made a much better leader for the *blessed* than Sam. Cassandra would already be calling for action against Jacobsen Consortium.

Or possibly for blood, given the nature of her daughter.

Though if Debra was being truthful, Cassandra would probably anger as many of the *blessed* as she engaged. That was also the nature of her daughter, to be willfully obstructive in every way possible.

However, Mother knew best.

Debra was firmly convinced of that fact. She'd known it from the start, since she'd first held Cassandra in her arms, all wrinkly with her eyes shut tightly and her fists flailing.

Once Debra controlled Jacobsen Consortium, she'd be able to prove that to Cassandra.

Mother *always* knew what was best for her daughter. And soon, she'd be able to make Cassandra follow where Debra led.

LOKI RODE his eight-legged horse along the long end of the battlefield that still burned in places, foul black smoke rising and mixing with the night sky. The horse wasn't *Sleipnir*. No, that would cause more unease through the All-Worlds and Odin already suspected something. Loki's horse was an amalgamation of creatures from Norse mythos as well as others—a huge black monster with burning red eyes, an emaciated chest, and a spiky short mane. Sparks flew from his hooves when he ran, causing whatever he flew past to catch fire.

Recently slain gods laid strewn across the fighting plane: that crazy old goddess who sometimes manifested as a spider; an ancient iguana god, who Loki swore had been partially made out of smoke; even a feathered serpent who now lay in tattered pieces.

The smell of gore mingled with the sweet smell of the burning corn. Loki's horse delicately stepped around a patch of blood and continued on.

They wouldn't stay dead, of course. They were gods.

The only two of the Mayan heavenly court who remained alive at this time were the monkey twins. They sat in a nearby tree, recording the last moments of the Mayan gods and the glorious battle they'd all just died in.

Past the burning field, Loki's army of demons (most of whom had been raised by Set) marched on, searching out all the other gods who lived on this plane and subjecting them to a similar fate. A purpled night sky hung over them, the stars shining dimly through the smoke.

Behind Loki stood the remains of the great pyramid temple. Set had taken particular joy in destroying it. He'd even pried huge boulders out and thrown them into the battle, crushing those who didn't move out of the way fast enough or who had grown too weak to block them.

Loki stopped his horse when they reached the leading end of the field and the beginning of the jungle. He had no desire to travel under those trees. Vines reached between the massive trunks and made slithering noises, like snakes. The chorus of cicadas was deafening. Birds called out harshly, their songs full of dismay. Huge buzzing clouds of flies and gnats hovered, waiting to descend on the corpses. The insects didn't care that at one point the bodies they feasted on had once been gods.

It was awfully hard to permanently kill a god. Loki had no illusions that the Mayan gods would actually *stay* dead. They had strong myths about rebirth, as did most gods born of agricultural societies. Their main god "died" and was reborn regularly, usually coming back at the start of the growing season.

When morning came, Loki would bet that the Mayan gods would waken and rise. Some might not come back until nightfall. He didn't know their myths well enough to predict when they would be reborn, and he didn't care.

While temporarily slaying the Mayan gods had been a goal, it certainly hadn't been Loki's *only* goal.

Loki turned his horse around to ride the edge of the battlefield again. He would have to leave soon, before the dawn. The Mayan gods might actually be reborn stronger than they had been.

Again, not the point.

What Set and the others didn't realize was that by destroying the temple, they'd weakened the portal that these gods had to the human plane.

No matter how often the gods rebuilt the portals, they'd be permanently weakened.

In a week or so, Loki would come back and attack the Mayan gods again. Then come back again. He would destroy every access point to the human planes that the Mayan gods had, thereby forcing them to make a decision.

Did the gods stay here, isolated on this plane, for the rest of their immortal existence?

Or did they travel to the human planes and make new lives for themselves there?

The twilight of the Norse gods had never treated Loki well. Plus, he was rather fond of the world as it existed. He'd thought more than once about going back to shake the hand of the man who'd invented pizza. As well as fresh potato chips. Coffee he didn't care that much for, but chocolate was pretty high on his list.

Oops. These were the people who'd brought chocolate to the world.

His bad. Maybe he'd focus more on the temple and fields and not the gods next time.

Then again, maybe not.

The Mayans weren't the only gods Loki had targeted with the help of the Egyptian gods: the Chinese pantheon had put up quite a fight, as had the Koreans and the Japanese. Some of the African tribes as well.

Technically, Loki was interested in bringing about the apocalypse, though not in the sense that he wanted to destroy all the worlds as well as all the lives in them.

Instead, he was more interested in forcing the gods to descend on the human plane.

If humankind was suddenly inundated with gods, they'd start to worship them again. They'd have to. The gods would be right there among them, doing godly things. Being their usual, punk selves.

Loki was certain that he'd win a large contingency of followers through guile as well as through charm, while that fellow Set might only have a few. He was just too different, too chaotic, as well as too bloody.

Set was also an idiot to think that all they were doing was killing gods on the various planes. No, Loki had *plans*.

Soon enough, Loki would return to the human plane to start his reign.

He'd already chosen the human goddess to rule at his side. She'd just have to give up her girlfriend for godhood.

Say what you would about Cassie, even she wasn't that stubborn.

THE GODDESS SEKHMET sang hymns and danced sacred steps around the body lying on the sand-covered floor of her temple. She wore the head of a lioness, proud and fierce. Her human body easily supported it as she danced, waving her arms in complicated patterns that had been lost for too long. Green paint streaked the sides of her muzzle, showing that she was also a goddess of healing. A blood-red robe, tied around her waist with a gold belt, covered her torso. On her feet, she had war sandals that were made out of white leather—sturdy, with leather straps crisscrossing her legs from ankle to knee.

She didn't bother with a headdress. She would never carry the Egyptian red sun disc, ever again. Not after Ra had betrayed her.

A long, skinny altar, made of granite with beautiful rosettes of gold filigree scattered across the top stretched across the center of the room. It wasn't as fine as the altar she'd had when she'd been in her prime and worshiped by millions, but it would do.

Sweet incense burned on the ends of the altar, the thick smoke hiding the ceiling of the temple. Sekhmet had enchanted the smoke to help hide her from the gaze of Ra. Finely-made clay lamps full of refined oil cast light from the corners of the small, square room.

Yellow rock walls echoed back Sekhmet's song, making it seem as if she was part of a large chorus of voices. Hieroglyphics covered the walls and told of her many feats, warned of her seven arrows, as well as showed how she once wreaked vengeance on all of humanity, killing scores before the god Ra had stopped her.

The center of the altar still held the many implements of worship that Sekhmet had laid out earlier: an icepick, a chisel, even an ankh with a sharpened end. However, the human had chosen a screwdriver this time as the appropriate tool with which to worship Sekhmet.

It was growing easier each time to convince the humans who traveled the planes that by worshipping Sekhmet they would gain foresight as well as immortality.

Silly humans.

The latest supplicant's blood spilled prettily over the sand. Sekhmet had already lapped up quite a bit of it, gaining power from the rich life force.

However, Sekhmet had to be careful about the blood she drank. Ra had tricked her once by dying beer red to fool her into think that it was blood. Then the bastard had kept her drunk for millennia so she would stay calm and pliant instead of roaring and killing like the war goddess she was.

Behind the altar, tucked away in a hidden crevice, sat a tall jar. It was similar to the canopic jars that the pharaohs had used to store their internal organs after death. However, Sekhmet had spent decades crafting this jar herself. Instead of plain pottery, she'd learned how to spin sand into glass. The head on the jar was Horus himself, not one of his sons. She'd baked him out of clay, then painted his face ash white. She'd only given him a single eye, and he grimaced instead of looking stern or godly.

Human eyeballs filled about half of the jar, floating in golden beer.

Ah, what power that jar held! Sekhmet had already added her latest acquisition to it. She only allowed herself a few drops of the golden brew daily.

But with each human sacrifice, the brew grew more potent.

Sekhmet wasn't trapped in her temple, cocooned here by the myths of the Greeks and the Romans and all those who came after them. She could leave the sacred space and travel to the plane of the Egyptian gods anytime she liked.

However, she rarely visited with her fellow gods anymore.

Instead, she focused on the human plane. That obnoxious bastard Loki had been right about that. Humanity was the future. The gods were as dried up as the mummies of the old pharaohs.

What Loki hadn't realized when he'd suggested that Sekhmet start killing her followers was the *power* that each sacrifice brought her. How much strength she now had. He'd probably been thinking that with fewer followers, Sekhmet would be weaker. That on the human planes, Loki would manifest as the strongest of the gods.

Such a fool.

Sekhmet would manifest as a great goddess once she had the power to travel, and stay, in the human planes.

Then, she'd rebuild her diminishing supply of followers. The people would worship her. They'd have no choice. If they didn't, they'd suffer her vengeance again, only this time with no Ra to stop her.

A loud *caw* split the air.

Sekhmet wailed out loud. *No! Too soon!*

But what had to be, had to be.

An Egyptian black hawk circled her head. Its feathers were the color of dried blood instead of the more familiar rust-brown. Black tipped the ends of its feathers and its beak. Its eyes were golden and full of unnatural power. Its black talons curved dangerously and were oversized compared to the rest of the bird, who was still larger than most, with a three-foot wide wingspan.

It cawed again, a deep, unearthly sound, warning her away from the body.

Sekhmet reluctantly stepped back. That, too, had been part of her deal with Loki for teaching her how to influence humans well enough for them to gouge out an eye and kill themselves while worshipping her.

The creature circled again, then dropped the ice it carried in one giant claw onto the center of the body. With one last ringing call, it disappeared.

Sekhmet didn't know where the bodies went, nor did she care. Loki had some use for them once she was done. The bodies still carried Power. They had, after all, been blessed by a goddess.

A brilliant light that held all the colors of the rainbow filled the temple. Sekhmet resumed her dance, though she'd stopped singing. She bid the body farewell as it disappeared, the light consuming it.

The darkness afterward made her blink once, twice, as her eyes adjusted. The burning lamps in the corners dimmed. The brightest source of light remained her canopic jar.

Maybe she could have just one more sip of that divine liquor before she concentrated on calling her next victim…

Sekhmet stopped herself just in time, her hands like claws as she reached for the jar.

No.

That was the trouble with holy beer. She couldn't deny its hold on her.

She could only push away her cravings for so long before she gave in and drank her gut full. Then her war-like features would dissolve and her healing aspect would rise.

However, this time she wouldn't be under that bastard Ra's

thumb. No one would keep slipping beer into her morning meal or would spike her tea with palm wine.

This time, she'd only have to be a goddess of healing for a short while. She would be able to sober up quickly, then wreak havoc once again.

7

WHILE HUNTER and I waited for Ferguson in the parking lot at the top of the Minnehaha Falls, I figured I'd try to see if I could follow the body back in time.

I closed my eyes and went back to my *area of knowing*, finding the tagged timeline that had the latest body that had shown up in.

The smell of incense flowed over me as soon as I opened up the timeline. I nearly gagged. That smell came from something that was ancient and evil—a god who was up to no good.

However, I couldn't follow the poor guy back into his past. Was it because he'd been traveling through planes? Going from a plane where the gods existed and back to the human plane?

Phil Chao was never going to believe that theory.

When I opened my eyes, everything seemed brighter. I glanced up, but the sky still held clouds.

I looked over at Hunter. God*damn*. He was glowing like a fucking candle. The trees beyond him as well. Not so much the cars in the parking lot.

I blinked and tried to clear my eyes, wiping a cold gloved hand over them.

When I looked again, I saw ghostly figures in the periphery. Tall figures made out of mist. They disappeared when I looked at them directly.

"Fuck," I said, though I hadn't meant to say anything out loud.

"What's wrong, boss?" Hunter asked. His voice sounded incredibly gentle, as if he was trying to calm a wild animal.

Maybe he was.

"Starting to see things," I told him truthfully. I didn't know how else to explain it. "Lights and ghosts."

"How large has your *area of knowing* gotten?" Hunter asked, still using that quiet voice.

I didn't want to close my eyes again. What the hell would change when I opened them again?

I found I wanted to do what Hunter suggested, though. Not quite a compulsion. Just for some reason I wanted to please him, which, believe me, weirded me out enough that I nearly didn't.

However, I closed my eyes and reached for the blue light, the wavy lines of the timelines.

"Holy fuck!" I said, my eyes shooting open. The lights of the trees surrounding the parking lot flared again, before steadying out to a warm glow.

"My *area of knowing* is fucking huge," I told Hunter. "It's at least a mile square." On a good day, I could generally know everything that had happened in a couple of blocks around me.

Hunter nodded. He looked sadly determined. "Drug's gotten ahold of you."

I blinked, surprised. "How is that possible?" I asked. "I took the *poisoned pearls* on the first of January, as always. It's been six weeks. It's almost Valentine's day. The drug should be wearing off, not getting stronger."

Hunter shrugged. "That's just how it happens, boss."

"I don't believe you," I told him flat out.

"When did you take the second dose?" Hunter asked.

"I didn't," I told him. "I wouldn't. I wouldn't take it without telling you about it. I'm not addicted to it."

Hunter kept a straight face, though I could tell how much he wanted to roll his eyes at me.

I knew I sounded like every junkie who'd ever lived. But I honestly wasn't addicted to the *poisoned pearls*, not like Hunter had been. I only took the drug once a quarter, and I always took the exact same amount. I didn't crave it, not like I craved cigarettes and sex.

"It's something else," I told him stubbornly. "It's the case and the fucking rainbows. Or something."

Hunter pressed his lips together and looked away, as if he was afraid to say anything more to me, afraid that he might drive me further into lies.

I *wasn't* addicted. I hadn't taken more of the drug, not unless Loki had slipped it into my coffee some morning when I wasn't looking.

This grand expanse of my powers had to be something else.

But what?

Phil Chao looked as pissed as I felt by the time he arrived with Ferguson in tow. I was fucking freezing and could barely feel my toes anymore.

Seemed the dynamic duo were riding in Phil's fancy BMW today instead of the standard police sedan.

Maybe they'd been out having a blowjob together. I knew whores who gave a discount if two guys came in at the same time. I wasn't about to ask, though. There were some things you just could never unsee.

"Another body," Ferguson commented dourly as he walked up to us.

Funny, he didn't glow as brightly as Phil Chao. Was that because he was mundane? And Hunter was, well, Hunter?

However, Ferguson still had quite a light about him. I could barely see the features of his face through the glow. Oh, sure, he narrowed his beetle-like eyes at me and he frowned. But that was the extent of what I could make out. And he still needed to take some fashion advice from Phil instead of wearing those round parkas all the time.

Phil looked as pissed as Ferguson. Or I figured he did. His anger radiated from him in a red cloud.

I suddenly knew that they'd both been out to a late lunch before the call had come in. Ferguson had stiffed Phil again, making him pay for lunch. While Phil was happy to do it, he wanted to be asked, not tricked or forced.

I shook my head and pulled back. I did *not* want to learn more about their relationship. Like most of the cops I'd met, they needed marriage counseling.

"Hey, you there?" I heard Ferguson ask, snapping his fingers in front of my face.

"Yeah, yeah," I said. I faked a yawn, then winked broadly at him and gave him a leering smile. "Late night, you know?"

I had to throw him off the scent. He couldn't suspect that there was anything wrong with me, that I was seeing and smelling things that couldn't be there. I didn't know if I'd pass Dennis' next test, not when I was like this.

Damn it! Was this an aftereffect of talking with Odin? I was going to string that bastard up if it was.

Even through the light pouring off Ferguson I still managed to catch a glimpse of his disgust. What a hypocrite. He'd been visiting a girl-on-girl pegging site just the night before.

Ugh. WHY couldn't I get out of his brain? I really didn't want to know any of this shit.

"Look," I said before Ferguson could start pestering us with more questions. "I'm freezing here. Why—"

"Then you should have thought about that before dumping a body here," Ferguson interrupted.

"How the hell am I here, watching a body fall out of the sky through a goddamned rainbow portal, yet at the same time on the other side of the portal tossing said body through?" I demanded. I was getting angry at his stupidity.

Phil took a step back. Ferguson didn't. He did reach down to his belt and flip open the holster for his gun.

Hunter put a gentle hand on my arm and said, "Cassie. Cassandra."

That seemed to break the spell of whatever the hell had gotten hold of me. The world suddenly shrank down to normal proportions. The extra glowy lights disappeared and everything looked normal again.

Ferguson glanced over his shoulder at Phil. "Did you see what I saw?"

Phil was watching me carefully as if I might suddenly bite. "She appeared to grow taller and larger, yes," he said. "And she glowed like a spotlight had hit her. Then she became normal again."

"That's not possible," I said, flatly denying it. "Think about it. How the hell could I do that without some grand special effects department?"

Ferguson and Phil exchanged a look. I was right. For once, Jacobsen Consortium's lies worked in my favor. No one had that power of illusion. Particularly since I was a known, and registered, post-cog. I didn't have telepathic abilities, and no telepath could influence the thoughts of others, at least according to the lying Jacobsen lawyers. Fuckers.

The cops weren't thrilled with letting us go. But they had

nothing to hold us there. Ferguson still insisted that I freeze my toes and my tush a while longer while he filled out a report.

Then Hunter and I escaped, practically running up to the street where Hakeem's warm car should be awaiting us.

But getting out of the cold wouldn't really help with the big questions: What the hell had just happened? And why?

HOWEVER, because that was the way this lousy day had been, Hakeem's car was *not* where it should have been.

Fuming, I pulled out my phone and told it to dial Hakeem. Hunter frowned at me, but I wasn't about to risk further frostbite by pulling off my glove in order to punch in Hakeem's number. It was bad enough that Hunter rarely remembered the phone I'd gotten him, let alone to charge it.

Cars cautiously drove along the snow-covered street. It had just been too cold and snowy to plow down to the concrete. White stretched out as far as the eye could normally see, making islands of the dark trunks of trees. I knew that houses lay north of us, but I didn't try to look and see what the residents had been up to that morning.

I knew I could. My senses stretched out far more broadly now.

"Hello, friend! Hello!" came Hakeem's friendly voice over the line.

"Where the hell are you?" I said, not bothering to hide just how pissed off I was.

"I'm sorry, I'm truly sorry," Hakeem said. "But I *had* to take this ride."

It didn't take extra senses to know who he was picking up. "Josh? You've abandoned us to go and pick up Josh?" I felt betrayed. I knew Hakeem was working as a double agent. He'd never hidden that. However, this was far beyond merely tattling on us.

"I couldn't tell him no," Hakeem said. He even sounded sorry.

"That's too bad," I said as I felt my rage change from red hot to icy cold. "Guess you've made your choice now, haven't you?"

"Cassie, I—"

"Don't even bother," I told him. "Don't call us. We'll call you. Maybe."

I hung up with an angry jab of my gloved finger. For once, a device actually followed my wishes and the phone shut off.

Hunter didn't look scared, not exactly. He did look extra on-guard, as if he'd just spotted an idiot carrying a concealed weapon in a crowded mall.

"What?" I asked.

"You're, ah, glowing," Hunter said.

I looked down at my hands. Fuck if he wasn't right. I shook myself, trying to shake it off, but that didn't work.

I remembered that the last time I'd started glowing Hunter had called my name.

I said it out loud. "Cassandra."

With a great *whoosh* all the glowy bits left, as did the extra power. I swayed and would have fallen over but for Hunter's solid hand wrapped around my bicep.

"Whatever the hell is happening, it isn't being caused by the drug," I told Hunter firmly. "This is…something else."

Hunter pressed his lips together as if preventing himself from arguing with me. Finally, he gave a curt nod. "You may be right."

Of course, I was right. How dare he not realize I was right? Wasn't I always right?

I forced myself to take a deep breath. I needed to keep hold of myself, as well as my too-ready rage. Getting angry seemed to be a surefire way that I'd "hulk out" as it were.

"Now what?" Hunter asked.

No taxis were about to be running up and down this stretch of road, not during the winter, at any rate. "I'll get us a ride," I told him, calling up the GirlFriend's Car app.

I refused to use one of those testosterone-riddled, frat-boy car services. Instead, I used a local crew who provided the same service. The company had originally been formed by a pair of lesbians. They still ran the service, but it was no longer just women drivers.

"Kris" promised to be there in three minutes.

Hunter looked at me expectantly. "What next?" he finally asked when I didn't say anything.

"It's just after one o'clock," I told him. "I'm going back to the office to do paperwork and research. Figure you should go do some research as well."

Hunter nodded. He knew me well enough to know that I needed some time alone and was getting rid of him.

I was *not* about to summon another god, particularly not a trickster like Loki. If that boy wanted to talk to me, he could just mosey on into my office like the other clients. However, I also knew that it was much more likely that Loki would come and visit, or gloat—if I was alone.

So I planned on giving him that opportunity. Asshole had better take it, too.

I PUSHED OPEN the door to my office, still located on the second floor above *Chinaman Joe's Good Luck Parlor*, a sex and toy shop. I rarely did shifts in the store anymore as I had enough business coming in. Still, I would work the occasional weekend in a pinch, like the time that Thomas had come down with the flu. Someone who smells like vomit is a turnoff for most people.

Not all, mind you. Just most.

I waited in the hallway just outside the office for a moment, looking through the open door, making sure that nothing appeared *off* or out of place.

I had the corner office just above the store. Tall rectangular windows took up most of the two walls looking out on the street. Despite the cloudy day, the wavy glass that filled the tiny, lead-lined panes cast a lot of light. My broad desk, battered and scarred and full of character, still took up most of the space. Papers and folders lined the edge of it, and I could tell from where I stood that no one had disturbed them.

Two guest chairs, my own incredibly well-architected chair, and a couple file cabinets were all I could see from the door. The coffee maker just behind the desk was empty—seemed someone was desperate enough to drink the sludge I'd left behind. Or they they'd grown tired of the smell and had thrown it away.

My "out" board was still prominently perched on the top of the file cabinet to the right. I had a generic "out tracking leads" note pinned to the center of it, the words written in large block letters on a neon-orange piece of paper.

Sane people would come into my office, find I wasn't there, and —oh, I don't know—would call me on the phone to try and find me. But too many (like my mom, Chinaman Joe, hell, even Hakeem, once) freaked out when I wasn't where they expected me to be. I'd come up with the solution of the "out" board and would change the message regularly so that people wouldn't assume a robot had replaced me.

I took down the note, since I was obviously "in." It didn't take long for me to make a fresh pot of black coffee, swipe on my phone, and start to do some more pantheon searching.

However, I felt as though I was spinning my wheels. There were just too many gods. So I said into the empty office, "You know, Loki, a clue sure would be helpful right about now."

A gust of nasty smelling air whipped past me. I coughed, gagging. It smelled like corpses that had been rotting in the sun for a couple days. Gore had its own distinct stench, like fat spilled and spoiled.

Don't ask me how I knew that smell, I just did. I could hear the buzzing flies and the cawing of ravens feeding off the flesh of the dead.

When I looked up, Loki sat in one of my guest chairs. He wore a brown leather vest with large iron rings sewn into it, over a white shirt that had seen better days. He'd placed his war helmet on my desk. It was made out of a shiny metal, rounded over the top like a dome. The front of it opened up in a T shape, exposing his eyes and nose. Long white feathers stuck up along the sides of it, as if to suggest wings.

"Sorry about the smell," Loki said, though he didn't sound sorry at all.

"What the hell was that?" I asked, narrowing my eyes at him. Shit. Now *he* was all sparkly and stuff.

"Just cleaning up," Loki said. "You know. Planes of useless gods. All gone bye-bye now."

"Any reason in particular why you're killing gods?" I asked, not that I expected him to answer me.

"Of course!" Loki said, beaming at me.

I waited, but that seemed all that Loki had to say about it.

"Want to tell me about it?" I asked after at least a minute had passed by. I was comfortable in the silence, a trick I'd learned to use with clients. However, I wasn't about to try to out-stubborn Loki. He was too much like a cat.

"No, not really," Loki said. "You'll find out soon enough. As you're already starting to realize, I have *plans* for you."

I couldn't help but roll my eyes at him. "Really? That's all you've got? Some vague threat of *plans*? Honey, I hate to tell you, but the preacher down the block is more threatening than you at times." The street preacher was just nuts and went on and on about how this city was becoming Sodom and how the LORD would cleanse it.

It wasn't that the street preacher had ever physically threatened me. However, there were days when he was a lot less coherent. I assumed those were the times when the meds had completely stopped working, or he'd stopped taking them. I'd learned long ago when I'd been living on the streets that unmedicated assholes tended to be unpredictable, which sometimes made them deadly.

"Tell me, Cassandra," Loki said, purring and sounding, well, sexy for once. "How are you feeling? How far are your senses stretching? How powerful have you become? Does it feel good?"

I shivered. Loki hadn't ever really tried to seduce me. Sure, he'd teased me about it, transforming into one of the most mouth-watering women I'd ever met.

The tone of his voice, though, had its hooks in my sex drive and was tugging on it, hard.

What The Hell?

I was *not* attracted to men.

"Are you getting aroused? Feeling more sexually confident?" Loki continued.

"You sound like an E.D. commercial on late night TV," I growled at him. Good. I was starting to feel more like myself. Sarcasm to the rescue!

"I'm much better than some pill," Loki said. He wiggled his eyebrows at me.

I couldn't help it. I laughed at him. "Really? It must be the end of the world. You're trying to *flirt* with me? Seriously?"

Loki, however, wasn't offended. He appeared to be "in" on the joke. "I *am* flirting with you. And soon, you'll see why."

"You wouldn't happen to want to give me a clue first, eh?" I asked, trying to wheedle at least some useful information out of the asshole before he disappeared, going back to the battlefield and his buddies.

"Just keep using your powers," Loki assured me. "You'll grow into them in no time!"

That powerful stench filled my office again. My eyes stung and I couldn't help but hack and cough some more. When I looked up, my office was empty again.

And despite it being fucking cold outside, I was going to have to open a window.

LOKI HADN'T BEEN any help. He and some friends of his were killing gods. But why? He had *plans* for me. But what? And I couldn't get angry, or rather more angry, or I was going to start glowing like a fucking lava lamp. Somehow, that increase in my powers was related to whatever the hell Loki was up to.

Stupid bastard.

Hopefully, Hunter was finding more leads than I was.

I couldn't keep a window open to my office for long, though it still stank of the battlefield. It was just too damned cold.

That was another thing. Sure, I often bitched about the cold weather. Everyone did.

This was the first time in a long while that I remembered really *feeling* it, as if every cold wind blew straight through me, icing my bones and freezing my blood.

If Loki thought that keeping me cold all the time would make me warm up to him, he had another thing coming.

Normally, my office was my safe spot, the hidey-hole I could pull in over me to just drink coffee and think for a while. However, instead of a sanctuary, it felt too small, dim, and closed in. Even my magnificent office chair didn't feel comfortable. I had to get out of here.

I texted Tess. For once, I had some luck. She was working in the funky tarot and such store that afternoon. If it had been a nice day,

I may have taken the time to walk to the Uptown neighborhood. If I'd been Hunter, I might have just *flowed* there, probably in less time than it would have taken riding the bus.

However, I was merely human. The bus, it was.

I timed it perfectly and reached the corner stop with the bus just a block away. Fortunately, the bus wasn't too smelly, despite the homeless guy sleeping in the back. The defroster was working overtime, blowing loud, blessedly warm air up against the windows. I leaned against the glass and let the bus carry me away, not really thinking or planning too much.

I remembered being newly homeless and loving the bus. Other homeless kids disdained it, but I still rode it, despite them. I could almost pretend to be "normal" again when I did, as though I was riding the bus on my way home or even to some made up job, instead of just using the bus as a safe place to get warm.

Buses were a necessity as far as I was concerned. Particularly living downtown with no access to parking. Sure, I had the expense of renting a car now and again, but in the long run, it was so much cheaper to do that than to deal with insurance, gas, and parking.

The bus hummed along and everything felt lighter. Though I was good with the weird shit my job threw at me, the bus's normality grounded me and helped me, well, feel more human again.

I felt so much better by the time I reached the Uptown neighborhood. Tess's store was just south of Lake Street, where the bus had dropped me off. The sidewalks here were all clear, the concrete bleached from the constant salt used to melt the ice. The day remained overcast and stupidly cold.

I walked past the yuppies texting on their phones, trying to persuade their compatriots to join them for an early happy hour. The textile store beside the bar had never interested me—I wasn't crafty—but I had always loved the colorful yarns and the rich smell of lanolin.

The incense from Tess's store floated down the sidewalk to greet me. I was getting pretty fed up with all the bad incense I'd been exposed to recently. A prayer wheel stuck out from the brick wall, a long cylinder about two feet tall. It was made of green-patina brass, with wooden handles on the top and bottom. The center of the wheel held prayers punched out of the metal, written in Sanskrit. When you spun the wheel, the prayers would go out into the world.

I always spun the wheel every time I passed it.

This time, I found myself hesitating before I reached for a handle.

What exactly would I be praying for if I spun the wheel? Did I really want to be praying to some foreign god? Or were the prayers just for peace, not for intervention?

Fuck it. I spun the wheel anyway.

Then I stood stock still and watched a sliver of pale white fog separate from the wheel and float away, up into the air.

Shit. Was that part of the power flares I kept having?

"Cassandra," I said out loud, feeling like a fool.

Nothing changed. The day didn't grow lighter or darker. I felt the same.

But I wasn't about to take a chance and spin that wheel again.

THE BELL over the door tinkled as I pushed it open. The smell of sweet incense washed over me. I couldn't decide if it made me want to gag or break into a writhing dance.

Maybe both, which was one of the stranger things that had happened that day. Honestly, that was saying something, as I'd summoned Odin that morning, seen another dead body fall through a portal, as well as chatted with Loki.

The store itself was wonderfully warm and humid. As well as tiny. Hell, my shithole apartment was bigger. If two people stood with their arms outstretched, they could reach the walls on either side. It would take three, maybe four, to reach from the front to the back.

Shelves holding merchandise covered every inch of wall space: tiny statues dedicated to every god imaginable; plastic self-service bins filled with rock crystals, agates, and other mysterious stones; three coffee cups with dancing Ganesh on the side; tall brass vases filled with rolled up small posters of gods, while underneath was a barrel with bigger posters; ceremonial daggers and blades of cold black iron; as well as pyramids of power in wood, crystal, and obsidian.

I didn't roll my eyes at all the doodahs. Much.

On the left side of the small space, at the back, stood a short counter with even more statues inside the glass case along with stacks of tarot cards. Opposite the counter was what looked suspiciously like an old CD rack holding boxes of incense.

A doorway in the center of the back wall led to the back room where the supposed psychics did tarot and palm readings. A purple velvet curtain covered the opening, the curtain bedazzled with silver and gold crystals in a pattern of ocean waves and a bright half-moon.

Tess pushed aside the cloth and came out into the store. She had frizzy hair that was colored like a peacock's tail today, bright blue-green on top and dark blue "eyes" around her shoulders. She was tall for a Hispanic girl, not quite my height but close. She was also skinny with no boobs or butt to speak of.

"Cassie!" she said happily as she walked toward me, her hands out.

Tess didn't hug. I didn't know her full story, but I knew that gang rape was part of it. Instead, she always squeezed hands with people. And air kissed.

She wore a beautifully soft black alpaca turtleneck over her jeans, looking more chic than anyone should at her day job. Then again, she was probably meeting her girlfriend later on that evening, after work.

"Tess," I told her after I'd gotten not just one cheek air kissed, but both. "Looking good, girl," I told her with a smile, squeezing her hands one last time before letting go.

Tess beamed at me. "Thank you. So are you," she said. "Very colorful."

"Thanks," I said. At least going too deeply into this case wasn't making me change my style. Colorful had always been my thing. Or at least as long as I'd had a choice and could rebel against the multitudes of beiges, creams, and browns that my mom wore.

"So what are you looking for?" Tess asked. I hadn't gone into any details in the text I'd sent her earlier.

Tess walked further into the store, then stopped midway when she realized I wasn't following her.

I didn't know why I was hanging out just inside the door, why I felt reluctant to go further inside. There wasn't anything there that could hurt me. Right?

Fuck being scared. I deliberately marched up to Tess.

"Not sure if you can help me," I told her. "It's for this case. Weird incense keeps getting burned near the dead bodies. I'm trying to see if I can identify the incense."

"Is it very sweet? Or more of a musty smell?" she said, walking back to the case full of boxes of incense.

I thought about it. The smell had definitely started off sickly sweet, but it had mellowed by the time the third body hit. (Had there been a scent with the first body that I just hadn't noticed? I regretted not tagging the area.)

"Musty," I said after a moment's recall.

Instead of reaching for the boxes of incense, Tess opened up one of the large glass mason jars standing on the shelves beside the rack. The bottom of it was filled with what looked like brown rocks that had had white sugar drizzled on them. A white and black label taped to the front of it said, "Copal."

I stuck my nose in and sniffed. That was a mistake.

I reared up, coughing. Damn. Pieces of that scent had accompanied Loki this most recent visit. I gagged, trying to get the odor out of my nose.

"Obviously that's not it," Tess said dryly after I recovered and wiped my running eyes.

"Nope," I croaked, my voice still hoarse. "But what type of gods would you burn that incense for?" Might as well see if I could figure out who Loki was killing.

"South American gods," Tess told me as she closed the jar. "The Mayan and Incan. A few of the East African tribes used it as incense as well."

For the first time, I regretting have trained my hunches and instincts so well. Either that, or it was another one of those damned spikes of power.

I suddenly knew that Loki had been visiting the Mayan gods. And killing them. I shuddered and turned my sight away, not wanting to look further and catch a glimpse of the battlefield.

Why was he doing this? What did he hope to gain by killing the other gods?

Tess opened a second jar and handed it to me. This time, the rocks inside looked golden, like hardened sand. The scent that flowed out even before I stuck my nose in the jar was sweet and fresh. It didn't smell like newly-cut grass, but it had that same essence.

Yet, at the same time, that mustiness that Tess had asked about coated the back of my throat. The label said it was Frankincense.

"That's it," I said. It was like the second body had been bathed in a fake version of frankincense, while the most recent one had been smoked in the original stuff. "What sort of gods would use this?"

Tess sighed. "Frankincense is ancient. But it's middle-Eastern, not Asian. So if you're looking for old gods, you've got a range between Mesopotamia through the Egyptians, to the Greeks and Romans, then onto the Jews and Christians and beyond."

Egyptian? My hair-trigger sense of "wrongness" locked onto that one.

I bought an ounce. Figured it was a business expense. However, I couldn't justify a cute brazier to hold it. An ashtray would do well enough when I decided to burn it.

Tess rang me up, giving me her employee discount. It was good to have friends. I stuffed the small brown paper sack into an inner pocket of my black leather jacket, feeling odd all of a sudden, like a wino who'd just hidden away a bottle of booze.

"So what can you tell me about Horus?" I asked, shaking my head and trying to dispel the sensation.

Tess talked about how Horus had been a good guy, inheriting the throne from his father Osiris after a huge fight, his mother Isis helping him along.

"Who was he fighting against?" I asked. Sounded like Horus wouldn't be the one killing all these people, even if he was a one-eyed god.

"Set," Tess told me. "Don't have a statue of him. He's frequently represented as the Set Animal, a dog-like, pig-like amalgamation of creatures."

"Great," I said. Would Loki pair up with a monster like that?

What was I thinking? Of course Loki would, thinking that he was smart enough to control such a beast.

Stupid god.

Tess led me over to a section where all the small statues of the Egyptian gods stood. Isis, Osiris, Ra, Anubis, Horus, even Sekhmet, a lioness-headed statue who was both a goddess of healing as well as a goddess of war.

I couldn't help but joke after Tess had told me a little history of each, "So where's my statue?"

"Huh?" Tess asked, looking adorably confused.

"The statue dedicated to me," I said, standing up straighter.

Shit. I was starting to glow. I could tell by how Tess's eyes grew huge that I was probably starting to change size as well, grow larger, looming over her.

"Where is my statue?" I boomed. I couldn't stop myself. My *area of knowing* blossomed and I knew everything that had happened to everyone during the past three days, along with tantalizing hints of what was to come. I found myself craving that knowledge, pressing against it. I felt like I could fly.

"We don't have a statue for you, Cassie," Tess said quietly. She wasn't about to back down, though, despite how scared she looked. "I'm not sure we have anything for you."

I shook my head and shrank back down.

What the hell? Why had I thought there needed to be a statue for me?

Oh.

A spike of fear ran through me. I turned wide, horrified eyes to Tess, who still looked scared.

"It's okay," I told her, though I knew she didn't believe me. "I have to go now." I rushed out the door, the cold wind nearly knocking me on my ass when I reached the sidewalk.

I stopped just past the window of the shop and leaned against the solid brick wall where Tess couldn't see me.

I suddenly knew what Loki's *plans* were for me.

He wanted me to become a goddess. Hell, for all I knew, he wanted me to reign by his side.

That wasn't the nastiest part of it. No.

The worst thing was that Hunter was right.

That level of power was addictive. Sooner or later, I would give in to it. Or do anything to keep it.

8

———————

I DON'T KNOW how long I stood outside Tess's shop, shaking in the cold. Normally, the weird shit didn't even phase me. It was kind of my super power, to surf the tsunami of strangeness. Usually only mundane things tripped me up.

This felt bigger, somehow. I'd been targeted by a god before, like that asshole who wanted to use me as a *receptacle* since I was technically a virgin. But that had been a single god.

Loki had friends this time. Other gods he'd conned into going along with his plans. What did those sorry bastards want? What did they expect to get out of the deal? Didn't they realize that Loki would double-cross them in the end? Or did they think they'd outsmart Loki?

I don't know how long I stood there, trying to get a handle on this new turn of events. I could see the connections clearly, though.

Every time I used my psychic ability, I was going to get stronger, as well as more addicted. Shit, every time I let my temper rise as well.

I didn't have any training, not like most PAs, not like Sam. I'd never had to tamp down on my powers, despite going too far into every case.

I needed help. Not some stupid AA program, but something practical to do with training powers.

The only person I could think of turning to was Theresa. She might be able to guide me in this. Heh. She'd certainly helped "ground" me the night before.

Yes. I needed to go home. Meditate. Wait for my lovely consort.

No. Girlfriend. I needed to keep thinking in terms of human, as well as here and now.

"Cassie? Cassandra? My friend, are you all right?"

Hakeem's voice penetrated the serious funk I'd wound around myself. I blinked. The sounds, sights, and smells of the city came rushing back: cold wind whistling up the street, the hoppy beer from the yuppie bar in front of me, that musty taste of incense still coating the back of my throat, my tiny Ethiopian driver standing in front of me.

"Hi," I told Hakeem. My voice cracked and sounded out of place. I cleared my throat and tried it again. "Hi," I said, finally sounding normal. "What are you doing here?" I asked.

I remembered being really angry at him for ditching us to go pick up Josh. Suddenly, it didn't seem important anymore.

I needed a friend. Hakeem was there. It was meant to be.

"I promised to take you to my cousin's shop," Hakeem said, beaming up at me. He was only wearing his green, gold, and black argyle vest over a white shirt, no jacket. He didn't shiver despite the cold, though I suspected he'd been there for a while, trying to call me back. "To buy an amulet, to ground you," he added.

"Right," I said. "Good." I still wasn't thinking straight, but despite everything, I trusted Hakeem. Kind of. Mostly. When it came to being my royal chariot and carrying me to where I needed to go. "Lead on."

Hakeem grinned and turned, walking three steps up the

sidewalk to where his black town car was parked. He opened the backdoor, bowed his head, and said, "My lady."

I shook my head and said, "No. Riding in the back will be a mistake." My voice almost sounded normal, though I could tell I wasn't completely there yet.

"Right," Hakeem said, nodding, though he looked puzzled. He closed the backdoor and opened the front for me.

I slid into the blissful heat of the car. However, despite the warmth of the interior, I could still tell that the cream-colored leather seat hadn't been warmed.

Hakeem hadn't expected me to sit in the front. That hadn't been part of the design.

I was breaking Hakeem's patterns. Maybe I could break Loki's as well.

Feeling better, I strapped myself in as Hakeem pulled smoothly out into traffic. I just breathed for a bit, deeply and evenly, counting as I did so.

Theresa would be proud of me for meditating. I hadn't told her that part of the problem with meditation was that I'd never been able to achieve some sort of Zen state. However, she was also right —just trying made me feel better most of the time.

I watched Hakeem drive. Normally, I didn't get to see him do his pattern thing, since I generally rode in the back. He seemed perfectly calm, like a pool of still water. He didn't make a single move in haste. His eyes didn't dart from side to side, looking in the rearview mirror, the side mirror, then to the front again. Instead, his awareness *flowed* from one area to the next as he marked all the cars around him, drawing their patterns from them, then plotting his own.

It was like watching a master chef at work. I knew he could talk while he drove, despite how focused he appeared to be. However, he also seemed to be waiting for me to speak. I wasn't sure what I could say to him, though, that he wouldn't report to his other master, that wouldn't get me a "surprise" visit from Dennis and possibly a determination that I was no longer sane.

I was perfectly sane. It was the rest of the world that had gone nuts.

"So what happened this morning?" I asked Hakeem as I continued with my deep, calming breaths.

"Ah, Cassie my friend. I am so sorry," Hakeem said. He kept his eyes forward, watching the traffic and flowing into yet another hole in the stream of cars. "Josh can be an asshole, no?"

That cracked me up. "Yes, Josh can be quite an asshole." I suddenly felt sorry for Hakeem who was caught between a granite wall and a towering mountain cliff, with no way out. "How do we get you out of this?"

Hakeem shrugged. "The time will come. Soon."

I didn't like the sounds of that. "You're not leaving or being deported, are you?" I asked. Then I took another deep breath, trying to delay the anger that threatened. Given the current political climate, the threat of deportation had a lot more teeth than it used to.

"No," Hakeem said. "That isn't my way."

"Good," I told him. "If Josh gets to be too much, let me know. I'll deal with it."

I wasn't sure exactly how I was going to do that. Maybe a little bit of goddess power thrown his way would do the trick.

Hakeem actually glanced at me before returning his attention to traffic. "I will do that," he promised, nodding.

I could tell he meant it. I could also tell that it hadn't really occurred to him before. Or possibly, before now there wasn't a lot that I could have done.

We rode a short while longer, reaching Richfield, the first suburb south of Minneapolis. The neighborhood had seen better days. Shops had been built along the main avenue back in the '60s, then had been reconfigured many times since then. They were an eclectic collection of yuppie goods stores, pot shops, and ethnic restaurants, with a few chains thrown in.

Hakeem pulled into a strip mall that was just past the first business district. The shops all had bars on the windows and signs in English, Mexican, Korean, and Ethiopian. However, the cars in the parking lot were all upper-middle-class SUVs. No BMWs, but no junkers either.

I got out of the car before Hakeem could come around and open the door for me. I knew having him wait on me would be a bad idea. I had to do everything myself for a while to keep me grounded and human and not giving in to the feeling of being a goddess.

It seemed a little warmer here, though I still walked quickly to the door Hakeem held open for me.

The shop looked like the others, though instead of bars it had metal gates that could be pulled up across the windows and door. A string of red paper hearts was taped to the front window under the words "Find the perfect Valentine's Day gift here! Act now!"

As if I could possibly forget the day was coming. This Friday, actually.

Then I saw the name of the shop. "All American Pawn."

A pawn shop? Not a jewelry store?

I nearly turned and walked right back to the car. How could I find *my* amulet here? I sure as hell wasn't going to see it among secondhand, used goods.

I stopped myself though, taking a deep breath and batting away at the anger. Hakeem had a good reason for coming here. There was sure to be something.

The store smelled like machine oil and rust. Summertime equipment like leaf blowers, lawnmowers, and edgers hung from the wall immediately to my left. Past them and piled onto the shelves on the next wall were amps, equalizers, and other musical equipment. To my right hung winter-type gear, shovels, overalls, along with new cheap gloves and hats.

The rest of the store was filled with shelves carrying the same eclectic mix of goods: collections of matching plates and bowls held together with aging masking tape; fancy stemware that was merely old, not yet vintage or collectable, and so only gathered dust; cookie jars of cartoon figures that I recognized from the unfortunate times I'd babysat as a teenager.

"Come in! Come in!" came a cheery voice from the far corner. A small black man stood there, looking like he might actually be related to Hakeem. He wore a navy-blue vest over a black hoodie. He had very white teeth and a huge smile, with his black hair cut short.

I raised an eyebrow in Hakeem's direction, but he was already walking briskly toward the counter and speaking rapidly in a language that I assumed was Amharic, Hakeem's native language.

I trailed after Hakeem, still fascinated by what looked like junk to me but hopefully were treasures to other people.

"Cassandra, this is my cousin Bassam," Hakeem said, making the introduction.

I nodded at the man, my attention caught by all the sparklies in the glass counter. The shelves rotated on their own, like a slowly turning Ferris Wheel, bringing tray after tray into view. Rings. Broaches. Necklaces. Tie clips. Belt buckles. Diamonds galore, but also rubies, emeralds, and sapphires.

Though Theresa had teased me about Hakeem's "cousin" making me an amulet out of burlap and chicken bones, I hadn't considered that he might, instead, take me someplace with proper jewelry.

Sadness washed over me as I watched the wheel turn. So many of these pieces represented broken promises, lost dreams. Particularly the wedding rings, which sparked with hate and anger.

It also freaked me out a little. I shouldn't have been getting such readings, not without touching the items. My powers were still too strong. I was going to have to figure out how to either tone them down or ignore them. And soon.

Still I watched, fascinated by the half-heard stories each piece had.

"What are you looking for?" Bassam asked after the wheel had turned for the third time.

"Something other than these," I said, gesturing at the merchandise I could see. I turned to look at Hakeem, who held up his hands, silently asking me to wait.

"Ah, someone with a discerning eye!" Bassam said. He sounded like the slickest merchant I'd ever met, and that was saying something since I'd been introduced to more than one of Hakeem's "cousins."

"Let me show you the special case," Bassam said with a wink.

He knelt down below the counter, unlocked a sliding door, and brought out a large jewelry box. It was an antique made out of a nubbly black leather, like alligator skin. It looked like an old-fashioned hat box, tall and round in the front, with a flat back. The brass latch holding it closed had a pattern of interlocking diamonds etched into the metal.

With a flourish, Bassam opened the box. Faded blue silk lined the top and sides. It actually opened up like a tackle box, expanding upward with many trays.

The piece I was supposed to pick up rested in the center of the top row. It sang to me of power and responsibility. It was teardrop shaped, about two inches long, with a brilliant blue sapphire in the center, edged with three rows of diamonds. The color flashed even nestled in the case.

It called to me. *Pick me! Pick me!*

Fuck that.

Fuck Loki and his patterns and expectations. Taking the blue amulet would be playing into his *plans*.

The future tugged at me. I could be a queen—no, a true goddess, worshipped by all. I only had to pick up the piece. Pin it to my chest. Let all see the goddess I truly was.

My fingertips tingled and my palm ached, empty of the amulet. I clenched my hands into fists, though I felt my body leaning forward.

One of the things that saved me was that I was a post-cog, not a pre-cog. Peering into the future had never been my thing. It unsettled me, seeing the path before me.

I turned away from that future, physically turning myself away from the counter, determined to make my own.

I closed my eyes and returned to my deep breathing. There had to be something else in that box. Something that would be *mine*, not something prescribed by some asshole god to force me into a particular future.

When I opened my eyes again, I saw it. Or rather felt it, as it was sitting on the third shelf of the jewelry box, tucked away in the back, out of sight. I risked reaching for it, pulling my hand back from the blue teardrop and sliding it toward the right shelf.

The warmth of the piece surprised me when I first touched it. I was expecting it to be as cold as the other stones in the box. Instead, the heat melted right into my fingers, making my bones feel warm for the first time that day. Hell, maybe that week.

I pulled it out, delighted to find that it was a double-headed axe —a labrys—a symbol of lesbian power and gay pride. My powers told me that the piece I held was a museum replica of an ancient Minoan design. The gold felt heavier than it should—it was probably merely gold plated. The axe took up most of my palm. The front of the blades had been decorated with braided wire, while the edges remained sharp enough to cut thread—or slice skin if I wasn't careful. A smooth brass handle trailed down from the head, flaring out around the bottom to balance the axe and make it easier to swing.

It was perfect. Just the thing to thwart Loki as well as stay true to myself.

I turned the piece over and saw that there was a pin on the back so it could be worn on a jacket. That may have worked if I only wanted decoration, but I needed something more. Though I considered my leather jacket a part of me, I did take it off too often for pinning something to it to be effective.

"Maybe this will help?" Bassam asked.

I looked up. He held out a long thin piece of black leather.

It took me just a moment to loop the leather firmly around the axe blade itself, ignoring the pin in the back.

When I tied the necklace around my neck, I knew I was not going to be taking it off again, not for a long, *long* while. It felt too good there, making me feel as though I stood on healthy green grass in the summertime, the solid earth lending me her power. I was *warm* finally, all the way through.

The blue teardrop still called to me. It held a cold, lonely future, though. It was more powerful than the piece I'd chosen. But sapphires and diamonds just weren't me.

I'd been thinking recently about changing and what that meant. While I still would have been me if I'd chosen the teardrop, the axe meant I was *more* me.

I knew I hadn't voided all of Loki's plans. This axe gave me power as well. I was going to have to be very careful with it. In fact, if I transformed into a goddess, I knew the axe would suddenly grow to be full size and appear in my hand. I could already hear it singing as I swung it from side to side, like a demented baton twirler. The sharpness of both edges would cut through bone as easily as paper.

I wasn't looking forward to killing anyone.

Okay, maybe that was a lie.

I didn't want to kill any *humans*.

Gods, on the other hand…

"How much?" I asked.

I didn't like the gleam in Bassam's eye. He knew he had a sucker on his hands and that I'd pay pretty much any price he'd quote me.

However, the price surprised me. Only low three digits, not four. Maybe that was because Hakeem was there and he'd vouched for me, so Bassam was treating me like family.

I still bargained him down by half. I wasn't comfortable doing that sort of dealing; however, I knew it was expected of me and Hakeem had been coaching me.

Soon, Hakeem and I were headed back into the cold, though it wasn't as cold anymore. Winds blew and the sky remained overcast, but I felt better. Stronger. More able to cope with whatever the hell Loki threw at me.

Now, I just had to learn how to control my urge to lash out or to use my powers.

Piece of cake, right?

<hr>

HAKEEM DROPPED me off at Theresa's house. Though I probably should have gone back to the office as I had paperwork to fill out, I couldn't face that closed-in room again.

Besides, I had work to do here as well.

The brown paper bag with the frankincense made a crunching sound as I took off my coat, reminding me that it was there. I could smell the sweet and musty resin without opening the bag. My fingers felt the chunks through the paper.

I realized it was another temptation. I could see myself setting the incense alight, then dancing naked around the living room, cavorting in the smoke.

While that might not be such a bad thing at some other time, right now it wouldn't be wise.

I suddenly felt like a junkie who had to avoid the whole goddamned world or be *triggered.*

I was going to have to learn some self-control, something I'd never been that good at. I was much more of a go-with-the-flow kind of gal.

However, it was more important that that fucker Loki didn't *win.*

I did strip down to just my bra and panties. I nearly changed when I realized they didn't match—my bra was smooth and black, made out of a fake satin, while my panties were cotton and had pink and white stripes.

Then I said fuck it. They didn't have to match, not if it was just me.

So how was I going to learn control? I'd never been good at denying myself, well, anything.

Except…I didn't drink alcohol. Not really. Not much beyond the occasional glass of wine or mug of beer. I could drink alcohol. I wasn't addicted to it physically.

Emotionally, however, I liked it too much.

Could I use that?

I thought about how powerful and strong I felt when I was transforming. I instantly started to beef up, growing taller and larger. Bra grew with me, so I wasn't going to have to worry about suddenly being naked, not that I cared about that. Cops had a different view, though.

So, I could make myself loom large.

Could I reverse the process? Deny myself this power?

The easiest way was just to say my name out loud. "Cassandra."

I felt myself start to shrink, but the process was slow.

I said my name again, only this time I put my mother's intonation into my voice, making it cut like a knife.

Yup. That did the trick. Shrank right back down like a guilty schoolgirl.

However, I could tell that just saying my name wasn't always going to work. The more I used that trick, the more blunted it would become.

Thinking about my mom helped make me human, though. She'd always been the one in charge, the one with all the power. As long as I thought about her and didn't let myself grow too angry about it, that would bring me back down to human.

What else could I use?

Memories of Theresa didn't work. Nor Hunter being disappointed with me. Chinaman Joe being upset with me did bring me back to earth.

I concentrated next on my amulet. As part of my research for a case once, I'd learned about total physical response, or TPR, for teaching kids, particularly for older students learning English as a second language.

Researchers had found that if teachers taught the sign language version of each letter of the alphabet along with showing a picture of the letter, as well as saying it out loud, kids learned it better and faster. The integration of physical movement with sight learning and speaking made stronger connections in the brain.

So, I reached up and tapped my amulet once with my middle finger. "Grow," I told myself.

Whump. That worked.

Then I tapped it twice, using the same finger. "Human sized," I said out loud.

The shrink down was a bit slower. However, I achieved it.

I played around with various gestures and commands for the next hour. It felt like magic to me. Except that I wasn't generating this power for myself. I was tapping into energies that already existed. It was, but wasn't, like my psychic abilities.

I didn't allow myself to explore the expanded *area of knowing* when I went goddess-like. That way lay madness. I was going to need help taming that aspect of myself. My psychic powers were just too addicting, and I wasn't sure where the balance would fall.

I couldn't just stop using my abilities, either. I'd learned that early on. With the advent of those powers came the unfightable urge to use them.

Either that, or go crazy and kill myself. The inability to turn psychic abilities off was part of the reason why the *blessed* had such a high suicide rate.

Maybe I needed to do some research on people with food issues, because you couldn't just stop eating. A very different type of addiction than to alcohol or gambling.

By the time I finished, I was sweating like a pig, delightfully fragrant, and starving for both food and sex.

Fortunately, I'd texted Theresa earlier and she'd agreed to come home from work as soon as she could.

I felt her approach the house from the rear. I'd missed her driving up and parking in the garage back there. I frowned, then shook my head.

No, I was pulling back from my powers. Not pushing them out further. I was safe here. This was my home, my sanctuary.

I stayed where I was while Theresa entered the kitchen, putting down her purse on the kitchen table. Her keys rattled as she tossed them there as well. "Cassie?" Theresa called out.

I smiled beatifically.

Soon.

Theresa walked into the living room next and stopped stock still just inside the door.

"Cassie?" she asked softly.

The glow from my nearly naked body filled the darkened room. "It is I," I told her solemnly.

"What happened?" Theresa asked, using her "Dr. T." voice. "Are you all right? How do you feel?"

She still wore her white lab coat and marched straight over to me, unafraid. Or at least able to ignore her fear. Science was her thing, and I was presenting as a definite puzzle, something for her to measure and solve.

"I'm more than fine," I assured her, taking her hands in mine. Okay, so maybe I was going slightly overboard as my hands dwarfed hers. I released one and tapped on my amulet twice, shrinking back down immediately.

"Shit, how'd you do that?" Dr. T asked, that analytical edge still tinting her voice despite her profane words. "That wasn't an illusion. You weren't clouding my mind. You physically grew. How?"

Interesting. Jacobsen Consortium knew about telepaths who influenced other people, despite their claims to the contrary.

Of course, they did. She'd always believed me when I'd told her about Dennis.

I led Theresa to the loveseat just under the window and explained my very weird day. She liked my amulet, though I wouldn't take it off to show her, just let her examine it (and me) up close.

"It makes sense that Loki would try to make you a goddess," Theresa said. She'd kind of climbed into my lap and her womanly scent was making it hard (harder) to think straight.

"What—what did you say?" I asked, forcing my head up instead of worshiping her neck.

Theresa pulled back so she could look me in the eye. "Remember what you told me once? How Hunter said his powers worked better around you? As did Hakeem's? They called you a catalyst."

My anger spiked but I pushed down on it. I did *not* want to lose this moment with my love. "Loki wants to make me stronger so I'll make *him* stronger?"

"That would be my guess," Theresa said.

Boy, was I going to have some choice words for that asshole the next time he showed up.

Speaking of which…

At least this time Loki didn't carry the stench of the battlefield with him as he walked into the living room. He still wore a brown leather chainmail vest, though this time over a black poet's shirt with ties around the cuffs and a floofy collar. He also had on black leather pants that looked good on him, as opposed to all the bad-boy wannabes. The patch over his one eye was made of beaten silver filigree. Scars filled his face, tracks of pain and humiliation.

"Please, don't let me stop you," he said as he sank into one of the chairs. "I enjoy a good show."

I looked down at Theresa. She was kind of frozen on my lap, her jaw slack, her eyes wide open but unseeing. I carefully picked her up and put her on the loveseat, her dead weight not straining my muscles in the least.

"What are you doing here?" I growled at Loki as I stood up.

"You called. I came," he said, staying in his seat.

"This is *my* sanctuary," I told him. "My house. Neither you nor anyone else is allowed to come in here without my explicit invitation. If you *ever* come back, you stop outside the door, knock, then wait until I let you in. If I do."

Loki waved an indulgent hand in my direction. "Yeah, whatever."

I taped my amulet with my middle finger, suddenly *looming* over the trickster. I fisted the front of his chainmail and physically hauled him up out of the chair, then shook him. Hard.

Loki looked surprised. "My, we *have* grown into our powers," he purred after a moment's recovery. He suddenly changed aspect as well, growing as tall as I was. (Much taller and we'd both have to either break the ceiling or bow our heads, something neither of us was likely to do willingly.)

"You do *not* belong here," I told Loki firmly. "You want to see me, you come to my office like a regular client. You hear me?" I said as I let go of his ringed vest.

"I think it's so adorable that you think you can order me around like that," Loki said, his eyes glittering with amusement. "Go on. Just what do you think you can do to me?"

I bit my lip. I was *not* about to call my axe to my hand. Theresa would kill me if I spilled blood all over the carpet. Particularly a god's blood, which I suddenly knew would be impossible to clean up.

A part of me was tempted to call on that training that Hunter had tried giving me so long ago. I finally understood how I could use it, could *flow* and strike.

But Loki was spoiling for a fight. And I wasn't sure I could win. He had a lot more training than I did. Which was something I was going to have to fix, I realized. And soon.

I could have just left. I didn't know about transporting myself to another plane, but I did think I could reach my office before this jerk.

However, that would leave Theresa sitting alone. I didn't trust Loki to be around her. Especially not with how he'd treated Hunter when he'd had him alone.

Instead, I shrank back down to human sized. I deliberately turned my back on the asshole as I walked back to the loveseat. I sat down and took my time draping Theresa's legs over mine, pulling her close.

Finally, I spoke. "Oh, you're still here?" I said casually.

I nearly laughed at the look of surprise on Loki's face.

"I don't need anything from you, little man. I don't need to do anything *to* you, either," I said. I was proud of how nonchalant I managed to sound. "Go away. You bore me."

Something I'd learned ages and ages ago: The best way to deal with bullies, as well as asshole gods, was to treat them like they were nothing, or to laugh at them. Never take them seriously.

Loki wasn't quite sure what to do. He hadn't expected that response.

He glowered at me, the natural glow of his Presence growing brighter.

I yawned. "Go take your special effects and show them to someone who might be impressed."

Loki narrowed his eyes and glared at me. "You will regret this," he said.

"Promises, promises," I told him, maintaining a strong edge of *and I don't really give a fuck* in my voice.

"You don't want to make me your enemy," Loki said, sounding more than a little hurt.

I snorted. "You're not worth my time or energy to be made into an enemy. Don't you get it? I don't care about you."

Love and hate were two sides of the same coin.

Apathy was the opposite of both, and my only way out.

"We'll see about that," Loki declared. He disappeared with a resounding clap of thunder that shook the walls and rattled the windows, leaving behind the stench of sulfur.

Theresa stirred in my lap. "What happened?" she asked. "Did I fall asleep?"

I didn't want to tell her about Loki's visit. However, I owed her the truth.

I'd just made an enemy of a god.

How could I fight him, when push came to shove?

No, that wasn't right. In a physical altercation, Loki would always come out on top.

How could I beat him at his own game?

9

Theresa lay on her side in her bed, breathing in the musky scent of sex, watching Cassie sleep. Normally, Cassie was insistent on making Theresa come, then either taking care of herself afterward or foregoing her own orgasm.

Tonight, Theresa had been the aggressor. She knew that Cassie had needed the attention, the adoration of her girlfriend. Consort. Whatever.

Soft light from the streetlight outside came through the slatted metal shades. They'd been too involved in each other when they'd first come in and had forgotten to close the curtains over the windows to block out the light.

Theresa decided to wait until Cassie dropped into a deeper sleep, then she'd get up and close the curtains to make the room completely black so that her girlfriend would sleep better and longer. It was important that Cassie got sleep right now.

The bedroom itself held touches from both of them. Two dressers instead of one were pushed together and took up most of the wall opposite the foot of the bed. They didn't match, of course.

Cassie didn't believe in coordinated sets of anything. Theresa sometimes teased her about wearing socks that actually did match.

The alarm clock had a distinct orange glow to it, as Cassie had been too freaked out by the previous one that had red numbers. ("Looks too much like demon eyes," she'd claimed. Theresa had been happy to buy a new one if it meant Cassie slept here more nights.)

Theresa's glass of water beside her thyroid pills stood on the small table next to her side of the bed. Cassie's water bottle stood on her side, locked and closed so she wouldn't spill water over everything. Again. (Theresa had to admit that Cassie was *not* a morning person, as that was when accidents were most likely to occur.)

A pile of Cassie's books also sat on the table on her side of the bed. (Cassie would never admit it, but she was something of a nerd when it came to reading. It was part of why her job suited her so well—she bitched about the research, but she was good at it and secretly enjoyed it.)

Theresa sighed, contented. She didn't want to change a thing. She was happy. And she loved Cassie, more than she'd ever loved anyone before.

Though Theresa had hinted about it, she'd never flat out told Cassie that it had been a case of love at first sight. There was something about Cassie that had immediately attracted Theresa, despite everything: the fact that she considered herself mostly straight, that Cassie was a client and therefore off limits, and that Cassie had abilities while Theresa was boringly normal.

Cassie had never asked Theresa to give up her job at Jacobsen Consortium, though Theresa knew she'd give notice in a heartbeat if (or when) Cassie did ask.

It was simple. Cassie mattered more than Theresa's job.

Yes, there would be consequences if Theresa just quit. Money and insurance were the first two that came to mind.

However, Theresa felt certain they'd be able to work through them.

That was something else Theresa hadn't told Cassie yet: That even without Cassie asking, Theresa's days at Jacobsen Consortium were going to reach an end sooner rather than later.

Julie, the evil H.R. minion, had been pestering Theresa again. There had been a "voluntary" survey that Julie had been pushing Theresa to fill out.

Theresa had opened up the document, glanced at the questions, then closed it again in a hurry.

After going out to lunch with two of the other researchers, Theresa had had her suspicions confirmed. She was the only one being asked about her home life and a possible conflict of interest living with a PA.

The survey was illegal as hell.

Julie had tried to tie Theresa's most recent job review to her filling out the survey until Theresa had pointed out that filling out the survey constituted a breach of privacy, and that she'd sue the company for discrimination if they insisted on it. Publically.

Other researchers had partners who were PAs. Jacobsen Consortium hadn't bothered any of them. No, this special survey had been created just for *her*, to find out more about her and Cassie.

On the one hand, Theresa supposed it was a good sign that the company wasn't getting enough information about Cassie from Hakeem, and so they were searching for other areas.

It was a bad sign, however, that they were desperate enough to consider breaking the law to find out more.

Theresa couldn't help but smile as Cassie turned over flat on her back, her breasts rolling and making interesting patterns as she moved. Even her slight snoring—more like a purr—was cute.

Jeez, Theresa had it bad. She was in so far over her head. She never wanted this relationship to end, not ever. If Cassie left,

Theresa would diminish to half a person, a shell of her former self. There would never be another love of her life, not like Cassie.

Cassie was rightfully concerned about taking the next step. It wasn't that she didn't love Theresa. Stepping closer to each other meant changes. A new stability for Theresa, but Cassie thrived in some level of chaos.

How could Theresa keep Cassie beside her for the rest of her days? Or were those days numbered as well? Of course, Loki trying to turn her girlfriend into a goddess threw more wrinkles into their future. It didn't surprise her. Cassie was already a goddess in her eyes.

Theresa didn't reach out to touch Cassie, though she really wanted to. Her girlfriend was a light sleeper and would wake when anyone touched her. It was a skill she'd developed when she'd been out in the streets. She slept better now with someone else in the bed than she had when they'd first gotten together. Theresa liked to assume that was because Cassie felt safe here with her, as opposed to Cassie just getting used to it.

So Theresa kept watch over Cassie, letting her love sleep and recover, so tomorrow she could go save the world. Again.

ODIN KNOCKED YET another damned bird out of the air with a lightning bolt.

The sky was dark with the flocks who'd come to invade the land of the Norse gods, picking off claw-fulls of ice from the Bifrost bridge. Cold winds blew up from the gorge, carrying the scent of stale ice and the promise of death. Storm clouds massed above them, thick and unforgiving.

Heimdall stood beside Odin, rooted to his rightful place at the end of the bridge. He shot down the birds who dared come near, the supply of arrows at his feet never ending.

Other gods had joined Odin and Heimdall that morning, trying to defend their single access point from the birds: Thor wielding his mighty hammer, Tyr throwing spear after spear, even Freyja in her falcon-guise, tearing birds out of the air.

The rest of the Norse gods stood arranged behind those fighting. They bore great implements of destruction and would die defending their homes. Beyond the gods ranged the heroes and the Valkyrie.

At the far end of the bridge, a massive black cloud gathered, full of ill-formed shadows. Occasionally, hot winds carried the stench of the desert across the ice bridge.

Odin's precious foresight, so dearly bought with his one eye, was finicky at best. It often showed him merely possible timelines, as thin as the threads of fate spun by Norns standing at the foot of Yggdrasil.

Today, the outcome of this battle seemed more certain than most events that Odin had ever witnessed.

The future held only death and defeat. The damned birds would drain the Bifrost bridge of most of its magical protection. Anyone would be able to cross it without harm.

Though Odin's foresight didn't clearly show what would happen after the bridge had been conquered, he already knew. It was the only possible outcome.

Before Odin and his brethren could refortify the bridge, other gods would attack. Foreign, alien gods who worshipped sand and the sun instead of snow and ice.

Odin knocked another bird out of the air. He'd tried electrifying an entire flock, but the birds were too spread out. Plus, his magic didn't work that way. Humans were the ones who'd perfected mass slaughter. The gods generally fought one on one. No god had even invented something like a machine gun. Even though Odin might wish for one, it was against his nature to use an implement like that. Despite staring at the face of sure annihilation.

He hummed a mighty battle verse and continued waging war.

The war today, with the other gods, would be epic and worthy of songs and poems to echo through the ages.

Would there be anyone left to write them?

SAM DIDN'T LIKE the cold winds blowing down the concrete canyons of the buildings in downtown Minneapolis. They carried strange smells, scents that didn't belong, like baked sand and overly sweet incense. She tugged her long coat tighter around her, glad that she'd worn wool slacks and a mustard-colored, thick-knit turtleneck, as well as warm black boots.

Sam had been taught to never accredit her "feelings" to anything significant. Jacobsen Consortium had trained all their psychics to use only what the company had defined as their individual psychic abilities, as well as to ignore anything that couldn't be tested and quantified.

However, Sam now questioned everything Jacobsen Consortium had indoctrinated her with.

Cassie had ridiculed Sam's training, saying that it was like trying to fry an egg with one hand tied behind her back. While it was possible and master chefs could do it, it was also limiting.

Sam didn't know how to track her feelings, how to follow the ill winds she smelled. If she closed her eyes, she didn't feel drawn to one place or another. There wasn't anywhere she could go in order to escape.

Doom whirled around her. No place was safe.

So Sam ignored her impending feelings of destruction. She could go cower in her apartment, or she could continue to hunt for that chink in Mrs. Lewis's armor that would send her house of cards tumbling down.

Sam felt a little like Loki hunting for mistletoe, that most inoffensive of plants that would take down a mighty god. Everyone Sam had talked to had either signed non-disclosure agreements (even the cooks and maids) or had been paid off well enough that they wouldn't share any dirt they had. And Sam didn't have the leverage (or deep enough pockets) to make them tell her anything.

She had to admit she felt dirty, worse than a grubby boy in a garden turning over rocks and looking for worms.

It had to be done.

Sam didn't trust Mrs. Lewis. The more power the woman gained, the more uneasy Sam felt. And while Jacobsen Consortium wasn't all puppies and rainbows, at least the control was spread out across the board, so there was some wiggle room.

As opposed to everything being controlled by a single pair of hands.

It had taken some digging on Sam's part to find Emanuel. Cassie had mentioned him in passing, how her mother had started dating again, a Cuban immigrant. Cassie had never met the man and so hadn't passed on much more information. Plus, though Cassie's father had died years before, it had still pissed her off that her mom was seeing someone else.

Sam had been surprised when Emanuel had agreed to an interview with her right away.

Maybe he, too, had decided that Mrs. Lewis needed to be stopped?

Emanuel lived in an expensive condominium complex just north of downtown, with great views of the city as well as the river. White marble shot through with gold covered the floor in the lobby. Dark, reddish wood wainscoting came midway up the walls, topped with a rounded, polished brass bar. All the fixtures matched, the lights with creamy glass and red-and-brass accents. The chairs in the lobby were made of dark-red leather with brass thumbtacks around the edges for decorations. Everything was picture perfect, like a spread in a style magazine.

No one sat behind the reception desk just opposite the doors when Sam was buzzed in. Maybe it was only manned on weekends.

Sam stepped into the waiting elevator. The doors closed and the elevator lifted off right away.

The only button on the front wall of the elevator was clearly labeled, "Lobby." Beside the starkly empty panel, an electronic key-fob reader jutted out.

When Emanuel had buzzed Sam into the building, had the elevator been alerted as well? Was it automatically programed to go to a particular floor? While for residents, would their fob tell the elevator which floor to stop at?

Based on how long it took for the elevator to reach the mystery floor, Sam assumed that Emanuel lived close to the top of the building. A sign listing the numbers of the various condos pointed her in the right direction. Inoffensive beige carpet muffled her steps. The walls were painted a sage green, with a white chair rail splitting the high expanse. No pictures hung there, no mass-produced art. The people who lived here were too rich to be bothered by such banalities.

The doors to the three condos Sam passed were all plain with nothing to distinguish one from the next except the stark, black apartment numbers.

Emanuel lived at the end of the hallway. A merry, "Come in!" greeted her knock.

Sam hadn't known what to expect, but it hadn't been a wide open room with a hospital bed pushed up against the far end. What had at one point been a luxurious, open-floor-plan condo had been turned into a hospice. Windows filled the walls, showing spectacular views of downtown Minneapolis and the river. Shabby rugs covered the beautiful hardwood floors. The smell of urine and chemicals overwhelmed the air systems.

"Emanuel López?" Sam asked as she approached the shrunken man lying on the very white sheets.

He nodded and gestured for her to come closer. "I apologize for not getting up," he said, still smiling. "But as you can see, I'm a little preoccupied."

An oxygen breathing tube nestled under his nose. Two clear bags of fluid hung on a stand beside the bed, the tubes connected to Emanuel's left arm. He was emaciated, the bones of his skull showing starkly. His dark skin looked jaundiced. Despite his cheery grin, Sam still saw pain in his rheumy brown eyes.

"Thank you for agreeing to see me," Sam said. She'd had no idea of his condition—nothing she'd read about the man had even hinted that he'd been sick.

Emanuel shrugged. "I don't have much to amuse myself with these days. Your request for an interview regarding Debra intrigued me. Pull up a chair."

Sam sat down primly on the European desk chair that she found next to the bed and drew her notebook out of her purse.

"I can call a nurse if you'd like something—coffee, tea, water," Emanuel offered.

"I'm fine, thank you," Sam said, though she would have liked more coffee. However, she didn't know how much time she had before Emanuel would ask her to leave, particularly given the state of his health. "Let's get started, shall we?"

Emanuel nodded. Sam could tell that his sharp, alert state was mostly for show—a bone-deep tired resided in the man. He was likely to sleep for hours after she left.

"How long did you date Debra Lewis?" Sam asked. She had approximate dates, but she didn't know for certain.

"About three years," Emanuel said. "And we were doing more than just dating. I had mostly convinced her to leave this place and come with me back to Florida."

"Really?" Sam said, surprised. She knew that Debra had been born in Minnesota. Cassie called her mom a Scandihoovian Ice Queen for good reason. Sam couldn't imagine Debra agreeing to leave her hometown and live anywhere else, particularly someplace that didn't have four seasons.

"Debra wanted to run for the senate again. We would have started with a Congressional district in Florida. She would have won. The people would have loved her," Emanuel said.

That made much more sense to Sam. Mrs. Lewis would leave Minnesota in search of power. However, Sam doubted that the people of Florida would have cared for her that much. Maybe Emanuel had enough money and influence to buy their love, though.

"What happened?" Sam asked. "Why didn't she leave with you?"

"Cassandra happened," Emanuel said. His cheery smile turned melancholy. "I hadn't even known that Debra had a daughter. They didn't talk for years."

Sam nodded. She knew that. She also knew that Cassie and her mom now had monthly lunches, like clockwork. They'd never have what Sam would consider a normal mother-daughter relationship— Cassie was too much of a smartass, and Mrs. Lewis was…well, an ice queen always in search of more power.

"When it turned out that Cassandra had psychic abilities, Debra's focus shifted." Emanuel sighed.

Sam could tell that even the memory was tiring to him.

"Debra's always been very good at finding the appropriate lever, or the right pressure, in order to get her way," Emanuel said. "She knows what promises to make, as well as what promises to keep. However, she is not good at sharing."

Those simple words held a wealth of information about Debra Lewis and her former partner. "Why are you telling me this?" Sam had to ask.

The hacking cough from Emanuel startled her.

A fleck of yellow spittle remained on Emanuel's chin when he finished. "I'm dying," he croaked. "Doctors gave me six months to live over eighteen months ago. I've fought as long as I could. This week? It's a race whether the cancer or the pneumonia will get me first." He shrugged.

"What do you expect me to do?" Sam said, her curiosity unassuaged.

With great effort, Emanuel pushed himself up on the bed until he was halfway to sitting up, leaning close to Sam. He smelled of stale sheets and cold death. His watery eyes stared directly into Sam's soul. "Debra dreams of control of you and your kind," he stated flatly.

"I know that," Sam said. Or she'd assumed that was in part why Mrs. Lewis was pursuing Jacobsen Consortium as diligently as she had been.

"Cassandra is the key," Emanuel said intently, as if he was sharing state's secrets with her. "She's the chink in Debra's armor. Pressure on her girl will get Debra to bend. If you want to stop Debra, you must use the daughter."

With another great coughing fit, Emanuel fell back against the hospital bed. Even amidst the racket, Sam heard a door click open. A tall African-American woman in bright pink-and-green scrubs came into the room, hurrying across the floor in white sneakers.

"You need to go now, Miss," the nurse said firmly.

"Thank you," Sam said, standing. She felt dizzy, as though the world had just shifted under her feet and she hadn't found a solid place to stand on yet.

Emanuel waved at her and continued to cough. Sam saw herself out, the door to the condo blocking off all sounds and smells, isolating Emanuel's death room from the rest of the living.

Sam did *not* want to use Cassie in her upcoming battle with Mrs. Lewis. Cassie had once been her lover. She wasn't a pawn for Sam to move around.

What if Cassie knew what her mother was up to? How Debra

planned on controlling all of the *blessed*, particularly her daughter? Would Cassie stand up to her?

Sam knew the battle would be epic. However, she didn't think that Cassie's disapproval would do any good. Mrs. Lewis had determined her course and nothing short of an act of god was about to dissuade her.

Sam didn't want to become like Mrs. Lewis in order to fight her. She didn't want to know about the leverage points she could use against people, the proper ways to blackmail someone into getting her way, the appropriate bribes one could or should pay.

She'd learned those things, true, but she'd always imagined that she'd be able to walk away in the end.

Now, contemplating how to use Cassie against her mother, Sam wondered if she'd ever feel clean again.

HUNTER HAD a bad feeling about meeting Mac for dinner. The other vet wanted something. What exactly, Hunter didn't know.

The dive Mac had suggested they meet at served breakfast all day long. He swore that the hash was a religious experience—instead of corned beef, they used pastrami. It sounded like sacrilege to Hunter, but he'd been willing to meet Mac there for dinner anyway.

Hunter had expected a dark, dim room, not a brightly lit place with sunflower-yellow booths lining the two walls to the right. The front counter stood on the left, with round metal stools topped with red padded cushions. A huge machine took up the far side of the counter. A clear tube, about six inches in diameter, rose up from the machine, going along the ceiling toward the door, then back down to the floor, where it curved and returned to the machine.

It took Hunter a few minutes to figure out that it was for roasting coffee. The beans would travel through the air pipe, tumbling while they heated. Though the scent of bacon grease filled the restaurant, Hunter could now detect the burned popcorn scent of the roasting coffee beans as well.

Mac wasn't there yet, so Hunter took a booth in the back with a good view of the room. The kitchen was directly behind him, but Hunter didn't feel any threat coming from that direction.

No, the threat would come walking in the front door.

Hunter shifted in his seat, uneasy. He made himself smile at the waiter and ordered both water and coffee while waiting for Mac.

Mac had hinted more than once that he'd really wanted to learn more of Hunter's story. Why was it so important that Hunter tell his tale of addiction? Was it just because Mac thought Hunter needed to tell his story in order to make further progress in the program? Or was there some other, darker reason?

Hunter had done what he could to check Mac out, including some vaguely illegal searches on the web, ferreting out all of Mac's background.

As far as Hunter could tell, Mac was a regular vet with more than one tour to the Big Playground. He'd received an Honorable Medical Discharge after he'd seen his squad blown up all around him and the nightmares wouldn't end. Mac still struggled with his addiction to pain meds and alcohol, the self-medication he'd started on after he'd gotten back to civilian life. It was part of why he lived in the shared housing with guys who understood that Mac's brain had been rewired wrong by the PTSD.

While some of the guys in the house were pretty religious and went to church faithfully, Mac had never struck Hunter as someone who prayed regularly. Sure, there was the whole "believing in a higher power" thing that came with AA, but Mac had never emphasized that part of the program with Hunter.

Hopefully, Mac didn't have a secret altar set up in his room dedicated to a god who wanted Mac to *influence* Hunter in some way. While Mac might seem like an upstanding guy, you could never tell about gods.

A few minutes later, Mac finally came in. He spotted Hunter right away, sliding into the booth. "Waiting long?" Mac asked as he picked up a menu with one hand, unzipping his khaki colored parka with the other.

"Naw," Hunter said, sipping his coffee. "They haven't been that busy."

The waiter came up right away. Mac ordered the pastrami hash. Hunter did as well.

When the waiter left, Hunter stirred uncomfortably under Mac's stare. "What is it?" he finally asked.

"You seem different. More relaxed," Mac said.

Hunter kept his shit-eating grin to himself. *Relaxed* might be one way of looking at it. Audrey had certainly been helping in that regard. Instead, Hunter merely nodded. When Mac didn't say anything more, Hunter said, "Go on."

"You ever going to tell me your full story?" Mac asked.

Hunter blinked, but he didn't stiffen up. He'd been expecting this confrontation. He shrugged. "Why is it so important to you?"

"It isn't for me," Mac said. "It's for the others."

"What others?" Hunter asked. "Who do you want me to tell my story to?" He should have known that there was something else at stake here.

Mac sighed. "Look. I know that Jacobsen Consortium gave you a raw deal. As did the government."

Hunter merely nodded. He figured Mac had been able to piece together that information, same as anyone else who'd paid attention.

The *details* though, were more difficult to figure out. The devil always danced in the details.

"Some of the other vets I've talked with, they've had similar stories. Being deliberately strung out by the government, then kept that way by Jacobsen Consortium," Mac said after a few moments of silence.

"So why do you need my story?" Hunter asked. "Since you already know what happened?" There *had* to be something else at stake.

Mac sighed. "You know that there are people who are working to take Jacobsen Consortium down, right?"

Hunter shrugged. He hadn't, not really. And he didn't think it would make any difference. They'd just replace one set of privileged bastards for another set. "Why would you care about Jacobsen Consortium?" Hunter said pointedly. "You're not one of the *blessed*."

"I was a soldier," Mac said stubbornly. "They taught me to protect those who couldn't protect themselves. To defend the honor of this nation. To give my life for my fellow soldier."

Hunter had been taught all those things as well. However, he felt as though those lessons hadn't stuck as well with him. Maybe it was because he'd been so addicted that the addiction had come first, replacing everything else.

"And there's another war coming," Mac said firmly.

Hunter blinked. What was Mac going on about? Was this about the coming apocalypse? What did he know about bodies falling out of portals and what that portended?

"And?" Hunter said when Mac didn't continue.

They both paused as large plates were carried over to their table. It looked like a mess, a scramble of potatoes, meat, and red and green peppers, with pumpernickel toast on the side. However, the smell set Hunter's mouth to watering, though he wasn't certain he actually wanted to eat anything. Not until they'd finished this conversation and he knew if he'd have to run. Or possibly kill someone.

"What war is coming?" Hunter asked after Mac had taken his first bite.

"You know. With the gods," Mac replied, his mouth full.

"With who?" Hunter said, not sure he heard right.

"Look, I've seen some weird shit in my life," Mac said finally. "Heard voices. Been visited."

Shit. Did Mac have an altar to some strange god? A god who'd decided to come calling on Mac some night?

"I've also seen you spar. The way you move. That's not human," Mac continued.

"What are you saying?" Hunter asked when Mac stopped again to shovel more food into his mouth.

It occurred to Hunter that Mac was eating very quickly, as if afraid that he was about to be called back into action. Hunter had known a lot of guys who ate that way, particularly when on duty, too aware that any break was temporary.

"I know you were kept addicted for a long time," Mac said as he paused from inhaling his food. "I also know you have one of the strongest minds I've ever met. There aren't many who can handle their addiction as well as you can."

Hunter snorted at him. He'd been a *mess* when he'd been addicted. Strong mind or not, Hunter hadn't been capable of fitting in, of passing. He'd never been a *functional alcoholic*, not like some addicts he'd heard talk at meetings. The only reason he hadn't ended up dead in a gutter was because of his paranoia. And maybe a touch of luck as well.

"So what do you want?" Hunter asked after Mac had put away half his plate. Mac had to want something pretty badly if he thought buttering up Hunter was the way to get him to agree.

Mac stopped shoveling his food into his mouth long enough to give Hunter a grin. "Always know when the brass is shitting you, right?"

Hunter nodded, still waiting. Tension coiled around his belly, making it impossible to eat the meal sitting in front of him. However, he still felt loose as well, aware of the *flow* of conversations in the half-empty diner, anticipating the waiter coming up with more coffee, the rhythm of the line cooks in the back.

Was this how Hakeem saw things? As an always shifting pattern of inconsequential events sliding into each other as they marched toward an inevitable outcome?

"I've already put in for a transfer from the house," Mac said as he reached slowly into his jacket pocket.

Hunter stiffened. Mac was telegraphing his movements, making sure that Hunter saw what he was doing and had a chance to react.

Sadness coursed through Hunter. He realized he no longer trusted Mac. Not in the least. Mac had been compromised, probably by an asshole god.

"I'll be moving out of the shared space tonight," Mac continued as he pulled out a crumpled brown paper bag. "I know you won't understand this betrayal. Not for a while."

Hunter still wasn't sure what the hell Mac was talking about until he put the paper bag on the table and pushed it carefully toward Hunter.

The realization of what the bag held sent a jolt of electricity through Hunter.

"What the hell?" Hunter said, his voice a harsh whisper. His palm itched to reach for the bag holding the *poisoned pearls*. The rush of his *area of knowing* expanding shot through him. That certainty of safety made his mouth water. He craved the drug more than food, sex, anything else.

"You're going to need this," Mac explained. He wouldn't meet Hunter's eye. "You got to trust me, though you have no reason to. But believe me, I wouldn't do this to you unless there was no choice. No other option. I would never order another soldier in civilian space to certain death unless I knew it would not merely win the battle, but end the war."

"What are you talking about?" Hunter said. He couldn't take

his eyes off the innocuous-seeming bag. Where had Mac gotten the pills? How pure were they? Or were they cut with crap that would keep Hunter addicted forever?

It hadn't been that difficult to get clean—he'd been in prison and hadn't had any access to the drugs.

Staying clean had always been his issue.

"Ask your taxi driver if he's seen what's coming," Mac said in a harsh whisper. "Or ask one of the gods. There's a war coming. Here, to where civilians live. And we need to win it."

Mac rose up from his seat. He dropped two twenties onto the table. "You can hate me all you want for the rest of your days," Mac said. "I've betrayed you worse than Loki did."

Hunter's eyes shot up to meet Mac's at *that* reference. He'd only ever talked to his therapist about how Loki had *used* him.

Mac's eyes looked as haunted as Hunter felt. "I won't apologize for this betrayal," Mac continued. "That would imply that I'd done something I wouldn't do again. But I would. In a heartbeat. Have a good night, soldier. I expect you to join the battle, fight, and win."

Mac gave Hunter a proper salute. The gesture felt final, as formal as a kiss of death. Then Mac turned and marched out of the diner.

Hunter knew he'd never see Mac again.

Of its own volition, Hunter's hand reached out and touched the bag.

He shuddered. No. He did *not* want this. He wasn't going to break his sobriety.

He still had the bag tucked deep inside his jacket pocket before he left the restaurant.

10

———

I'D BEEN as surprised as hell when Hunter had actually *called* me using the cell phone I'd given him, making sure that I'd be in the office at the usual time in the morning.

Then again, the apocalypse was coming. I didn't know exactly what form it was taking, except that it involved the death of a lot of gods and myself transforming into a goddess. Hunter using a cell phone might be at that scale.

I made it to the office a little early so I could get started on the paperwork I'd been putting off. Though I had no idea in hell how I was going to report some of the shit that was going on.

The office still felt cramped to me, though nowhere near as claustrophobic as it had. I figured my amulet had something to do with that. When I thought about it, I found I still loved my desk, that battered huge expanse of oak that I'd found second hand. My chair was still a marvel of modern ergonomics that made sitting comfortable. Even the bitter, black coffee was a just right.

However, I did find myself constantly looking out the window, as if to reassure myself that there *was* an outside that I could escape into. Soon.

About five minutes after eleven, Hunter showed up.

Now, Hunter is one of the whitest white guys I know. That morning he looked like a kabuki actor, or as if his face was covered with baby powder. His eyes darted this way and that as soon as he stepped across the threshold. Who was he looking for? Or was it just his general paranoia amped up to eleven?

"Hey there," I told Hunter softly as he drew closer to the desk. "What's up?"

Hunter tried to smile at me. It came across more like the rictus grin of a skeleton, stiff and scary. "Not here," he said, shaking his head. "I'll tell you outside."

"Fuck," I said. He was trying to avoid saying anything illegal in the office. Not that Dennis was any kind of post-cog, but still, it had been one of my hard boundaries for Hunter.

I grabbed my coat, glad that I was wearing my thickest leggings. They had broad zebra stripes that curved around my legs and ran into my docs. I also wore layers on top, starting with the brightest blue winter-silk camisole I owned, then a thick, darker blue short sleeved shirt, with yet a third, long-sleeved shirt in another shade of blue over top.

At least I had my longer leather jacket today, more of a duster than a coat. It wasn't as heavy as my regular jacket, but it was warmer because it covered more of me.

Though I wasn't feeling the cold as badly today as I had been earlier that week. The amulet was doing its job keeping me grounded, more in this plane than in the colder habitats of the gods.

I put a general note about hunting clues on my out board so that no one would freak too badly when they found I wasn't in my office, then led the way out of the building. I stopped on the sidewalk and looked at Hunter to find out where to next.

He seemed a little more at ease outside. Or maybe that was just me. "This way," he said, walking down the block.

I had a bad feeling about this, doubly so when Hunter turned up the alley. For a moment, I flashed back to when I'd found Kyle here, lying next to the door leading to *Chinaman Joe's Good Luck Parlor.*

The dumpster for the restaurant next door to Chinaman Joe's stank of fish guts and burned rice. I scanned the graffiti scrawled across it out of habit, making sure that it was just obnoxious, bored kids trying to leave their mark in the world instead of gang tags. The wind blew colder back here, making me shove my hands deep into my pockets.

The thought of lighting up crossed my mind, but I'd already had my first cigarette of the day walking from the bus stop to the office. I wasn't due another one until after lunch, unless I was too busy saving the world.

Once Hunter had made sure that we were the only ones back here, he started pacing back and forth in front of me. "I went out to dinner with Mac last night," he started with.

"Okay," I said, playing along. "How's Mac?"

"Bastard's a traitor," Hunter said, his jaw tightening so much I was surprised he got the words out.

"Really? Why?" I said, surprised. I'd always figured Mac was one of the good guys. However, if he'd seriously betrayed Hunter, well, I wasn't sure what I'd do. Except stay out of the way and then figure out how to get Hunter out of jail after he killed the guy.

I took a deep breath, followed by a second. I didn't want to get too angry all of a sudden. I still didn't have complete control on the whole goddess thing.

"Mac says there's a war coming. With the gods," Hunter continued. "And that we need to win it. He probably was told that by a god."

I nodded, though I wasn't sure where this was going. "And?"

Hunter gave a bitter, biting laugh, as cold as one of those Alberta clippers that blew through the city in the dead of winter. "He wanted to make sure 'our side' was well equipped." Hunter pulled a crinkled paper bag out of his pocket and shoved it at me.

I knew what it contained the moment I touched it. "What the hell?" I asked. I couldn't help the anger that washed over me. "Are you fucking serious? Isn't he, like, your sponsor? How could he just hand you this?"

Hunter took a step back. "Whoa," he said, his rant derailed.

Shit. I was glowing. I reached up and tapped my amulet twice with my middle finger, trying to bring myself back to human size and color. "Sorry," I told him.

Hunter blinked, impressed. "No, I think you need to tell me what's going on first." He sounded hurt and more wary than usual, as if by not interrupting him with my news, I'd also betrayed him.

I explained about Loki's visit, how I'd come to realize what the asshole's plans for me were, how he wanted me to become a goddess so that I would enhance his own powers, as well as acquiring my amulet.

"Show me," Hunter said when I'd finished.

"You sure?" I said. I didn't have anything to hide from him. I still wasn't certain that this was the right time and place. He was already shaken by what had happened with Mac.

Would my transforming throw him off his stride even more?

Hunter still said, "I'm sure." Then he pressed his lips tightly together, as if he was afraid of what else he might say.

I tapped my amulet again and let myself *become*. There was no other word for it. My senses expanded to the point where I could smell which dogs had visited the dumpster that morning on their walks. I could feel the pressure shifting in the clouds above us as a storm boiled and rushed toward us. I could see speckles of blood still on the brick wall from when Kyle had been killed.

My *area of knowing* grew as well, though I tried to reign it in. I didn't want to be distracted by who Tommy had slept with this week or by the cheerful murder that one of the neighbors was contemplating.

Hunter was nodding when I turned my attention back to him. "Yes?" I asked him, curious what he saw.

"The bastard may have been right," Hunter said slowly.

"Handing us these?" I asked, holding out the paper bag filled with pearls that would delight me. Despite how strong I'd suddenly grown, the drug would make me exponentially stronger still.

Hunter smiled and shook his head. He gently lifted the bag from my hand.

I allowed it. He was merely human, after all. If I truly desired the pills, I could easily retrieve them, even from the fastest man I knew.

And that was both terrifying and electrifying.

"Mac handed these to *me*," Hunter clarified. "You're becoming a goddess," he added as he quickly reached into the bag and grabbed one of the pearls. "Or already are one."

I could feel it in his fingers, that smooth, almost plastic exterior that was always slightly warm. The pearlescence of the drug looked the same as I'd remembered. However, now I saw how similar it looked to the rainbow portals, how it shone with a light all its own. It pulsed with energy from the multiple doorways that it had access to.

Somehow, this drug crossed the planes of existence, a side effect its makers probably hadn't intended.

"You need help training, in learning how to become *more*," Hunter said as he peered down at the drug in his hand, mesmerized.

Before I could stop him, he popped the pill into his mouth.

"You know that Dennis is going to have both our hides if you fail your quarterly pee-in-a-cup test," I warned him.

Hunter gave me an amused look. "Surely a goddess can spoof a blood test," he teased.

"True," I said. I hadn't thought of that. I wondered what else I might be able to do to our dear Dennis the next time he came for a visit…

"There," Hunter said after another moment.

He suddenly had his own glow.

I wasn't surprised that the drug had hit him harder and faster than it used to. When he'd been addicted, he'd grown accustomed to it and so had always needed more to achieve the same results. Since he'd been clean for eighteen months, his needs had changed.

Hunter pointed past my shoulder.

When I turned, I saw a misty white fog filling the end of the alley. Shapes started to coalesce out of the cloud.

Shapes of beings. Some human.

Most not.

"Who are they?" I asked Hunter. It amused me to realize that I'd taken a step back and let him come forward to protect me. When at this point, I was possibly the stronger of the two of us.

"The ghosts who trained me," Hunter said. "Now, they'll train you."

"Huh," was about all the comment I had to that. I recalled Hunter talking about his ghosts often, the ones who'd trained him to move and *flow* like he did. I'd thought they were partly figments of his imagination, that he'd called up beings in his mind to fight and train with.

Seemed they were real. Or real enough. They weren't of this plane, that much I could tell. But that didn't make them figments of Hunter's over-active, strungout imagination.

Hunter looked at me, waiting.

"Okay. Let's go meet the ghosts," I said.

I had no idea how I was going to write any of this up for my case report, or even if I would at all. Maybe in my special file where

I recorded what *really* went on, all the weird shit that no one would believe.

Least of all Jacobsen Consortium.

A DOG-HEADED guy stepped forward first. From the neck up he bore the head of a black dog with a long, skinny nose and tall ears. From the neck down, he was a human who had golden skin. He wore a white robe. It wasn't exactly a toga, but it looked kind of like that. A necklace made out of chunks of amber, each about the size of a baby's fist, hung down to the middle of his chest, with a shiny copper disc painted bright red in the center of it.

It took me a moment to realize that this was the Egyptian god Anubis.

What the actual fuck?

A tall Asian woman in flowing black robes stepped forward next. She wore her long white hair loose around her shoulders. I could tell that the curved sword she carried in one hand wasn't for show. She moved with a precision that I had seen in Hunter. She had that same god-glow as Anubis. My own power let me know that she was not just a white-haired witch, but *the* white-haired witch.

An older man joined them. He looked more human than the other two and of African descent. He wore a grass skirt, the better to show off all the muscles in his torso, I guess. White, red, and black paint striped his chest, making it seem even broader. He carried a staff that had a hook on one end and a blade on the other. He was merely a hero, not a full god, based on the light he emitted.

Other beings massed behind the three up front. I knew if I concentrated on any single individual, I could discern their origin.

I had no time for that shit. Instead, I took a step in front of Hunter, then turned to confront the bastard.

"Who are these beings?" I asked. I realized I'd already grown another head taller and so was glowering down on the man.

Didn't care. Asshole should have prepared me better.

"The ghosts who taught me how to fight," Hunter said. He looked surprised, as if he didn't understand why I was so pissed off.

"You never bothered to mention that they were gods," I said, fixing him with a stare that was strong enough to burn.

Hunter shrugged. "Didn't really understand myself, at the time," he said. "Not until you and I started doing research and I found pictures of them in books and on the internet."

"You could have told me then," I said. "That you'd met some of these beings, instead of making me write fucking poetry to invoke one of these assholes."

"You needed to talk to someone in particular, not just a god in general," Hunter said. "Plus, I never know who's going to show up. Often it's all heroes, no gods at all."

I sighed. He still wasn't getting the point.

"None of the Norse gods ever showed up," Hunter continued. "And I would have told you if you'd decided you needed to contact an Egyptian god."

"Have you met Horus?" I asked, my curiosity warring with my anger.

Hunter shook his head. "Just Anubis. And he only rarely appears."

"Why did you call them ghosts?" I asked as I turned and looked back at the massed beings.

"They're all kind of white and insubstantial," Hunter explained. "Plus, once I found out they were gods, it felt even more fitting. They're more like ghosts than gods now—forgotten, ignored—when once, they had millions of believers."

It kind of made sense. He and I were still going to have a *long* chat about what was appropriate for him to keep to himself and what he really needed to tell his boss about.

"Let's go do this thing," I said, squaring my shoulders. I knew already that I was going to hate every minute of what was about to come.

But being an adult meant sometimes doing the hard thing. And I'd learned how to adult some time ago, despite how it sucked.

"Fuck!" I said as my ass hit the hard cold concrete of the alley. Again.

Goddamned white-haired witch was wickedly fast. She gave me an amused smile with her scarlet red lips. Her skin had also been tinted white, making her eyes appeared like black holes.

At least we weren't trying to fight with swords, or my shirt, leggings—hell, even my hair—would have been sliced off. But she was awfully hard to fight using hand-to-hand combat. Especially in the close quarters of the alley.

We weren't actually in my physical plane anymore. We squared off in one of the alternate timelines for the same alley, a human plane that had recently been decimated. It wasn't easy to ignore the bodies piled up at the end of the alley, particularly when the winds blew the wrong way.

I sure as fuck hoped we didn't end up killing ourselves with some idiotic plague like these poor bastards.

Hunter was up a ways, fighting the African hero. It always freaked me out how *fast* Hunter could move. Now I finally understood why.

Still wasn't sure about the *how*, though. Hunter wasn't a god. Maybe he was a hero, and that was good enough for these beings to teach him. Plus, at the time he'd been completely strung out on the *poisoned pearls*—a drug that was also called *ghost tripper*.

I turned my attention back to the witch who was waiting

impatiently for me to get off my ass just so she could trip me up again.

I wasn't learning anything. I knew that. They kept trying to teach me as they'd taught Hunter, by showing me moves and then sparing.

I was never going to be able to fight Loki physically, not and win. It would take years of training, and even then I doubted I could learn enough. Loki had been around for *centuries*. I didn't have the time to pick up what he already knew.

I'd tried explaining that to the witch, but she insisted that I learn some moves anyway.

I figured in part it was to put me in my place. These were *old* gods. I was just some young upstart.

Finally, Anubis stepped forward. "Enough," he declared as I wearily rose to my feet. I shot him a smile, only to receive a blood-thirsty glare and a deliberate lick of his chops in return.

Ewww. I didn't know if he wanted to hump my leg or eat my face off.

Possibly both. At the same time. You never knew.

"While moving like the winds is a nice skill, I think you were right in your initial assessment," he said. He sounded like a scholar, with a surprisingly deep voice. "The physical fight will not be yours."

Thank fuck someone was listening to me.

"Hunter brought me here so that I could, uhm, *become* more," I said. I'd told that to the white witch earlier, but she hadn't wanted to listen.

Anubis nodded. "With Hunter, to become meant physically training him," he said slowly. "What do you think you need?"

"How the hell should I know?" I asked, trying to keep hold of my temper. "I've been human all my life. What does a fledgling goddess need to know?"

"Goddess of what?" Anubis asked.

I gave him a blank stare until he continued.

"I herd the dead to the Hall of Justice, where they can plead their case and explain their earthly deeds to Osiris," Anubis said. "Then I weigh that soul against a feather from the headdress of Maat, the goddess of truth."

"So?" I said when he looked at me expectantly. Sounded like a way to make sure the humans prayed to three gods instead of just one, getting the idiots to tithe more.

"I am a god of the dead," Anubis said slowly, as if explaining to an imbecile. "People would worship me so they might be judged less harshly after they died. Why should your followers worship you?"

I opened my mouth, then closed it again. Fuck if I knew.

Then I blinked. Nodded. "Loki wants to make me a goddess because I'm a catalyst," I said. "I make everyone around me stronger. Better at what they do naturally."

"A goddess of luck?" Anubis suggested.

"No," I said. People wouldn't suddenly win the lottery by hanging out with me, though that would be a cool trick. "Not luck. Skill." I paused, trying to find the words. "Those who have abilities, like the psychics, are stronger around me. So their telepathy works better, their cognition is stronger, they can match patterns better. That sort of thing." Or at least that was what others had told me—it wasn't something that worked on myself, so I had no idea.

Anubis gave me a doggy grin. "A specialized class of people would worship you if you could aid them that way. Yes. But that's just a single aspect. What else?"

I debated for a brief moment before I decided what the fuck. May as well show him what I already had.

I reached up and tapped my amulet with my middle finger. I felt myself *flow* out, my presence expanding. I didn't grow taller in this plane, like I did the human one. Instead, I felt as though I grew deeper, more solidly there. I also felt echoes of my presence ripple out across the nearby planes.

My axe found its way to my hand. I noticed that I'd physically changed as well. I'd always had an awesome rack. It became exaggerated, as did my hips. My shirt stayed modest though, despite suddenly changing to a triple E cup.

I twirled the axe easily in my hand. I knew what I hunted. "I am a protector of women," I said. My voice, too, had grown deeper. "I protect their virtue, and extract vengeance on rapists." Particularly those assholes who preyed on lesbians.

"Most excellent," Anubis said, as though he was praising a star student. He glanced at me, then deliberately looked over his shoulder at Hunter. "Rapists who only attack women? Or men as well?"

That shook me to my core. I almost lost my presence, shrank back down to my usual self.

I only suspected what had happened to Hunter, how Loki had treated him. I didn't know for certain.

The look of pity that Anubis gave Hunter told me much more.

Strength flowed to my hands from my axe, rooting me on this plane. It *thirsted* for the blood of those who'd taken advantage of another in that manner, violating them, making them feel helpless.

"All rapists," I intoned. "All must be wary of me."

I suddenly had a clue how I was going to fight Loki. Even if I made him stronger just by being there.

IT WAS WELL after lunchtime by the time we reappeared in our physical plane.

I felt powerful and *alive* in ways I'd never felt before. I was fully human again, with a normal *area of knowing*, yet at the same time, I felt bigger. I had a purpose, I guess maybe even a higher calling.

The cynical side of me rolled her eyes hard enough to strain something. Did I really want followers, worshippers? Women who would burn incense and dance naked in adoration?

Well, of course I wanted those things. I just wasn't sure about the whole "worship me and I'll help you for it" equation.

The world was tit-for-tat. I knew that. You scratch my back, I'll scratch yours. That worked to some degree, unless you didn't have anything to start with. Like the street kids. Like the broken down preacher reeking of piss and ranting on the corner. Like the women unable to escape an abusive relationship.

I didn't know how to reach out and fix all the problems in the world. Shouldn't that be what the gods did instead of greedily absorbing all the prayers they could?

I looked at Hunter. He appeared less solid than normal. Maybe it was because he still had a tinge of that glow the drug produced. He seemed more *other* now than he usually did.

Given enough time and training, could he become a god?

"You hungry?" I asked him as we both turned and headed down the alley.

"Starved," he said.

"How about we splurge and go to that steakhouse—"

I stopped at the same time Hunter did, feeling that tremor in the air. I *knew* what I'd see when I turned around.

"Goddamn it!" I said as I whirled around. "NO. Not now."

I peevishly put my hands up in the air, as if holding back a great weight. "I GET LUNCH FIRST," I roared.

The sparkling rainbow portal hung above the alley, surrounded by gray storm clouds. A body was about to fall through. I just knew it. And I knew that Ferguson wasn't going to be polite about it this time. We would be held for questioning all afternoon and through half the night. I'd be ready to chew off my own arm by the time we were released.

"Impressive," Hunter said. He looked drugged, his pupils so wide that he practically had no iris left.

Fuck. I had to get him out of here as well. The cops would take one look at him and realize that he was no longer clean. And while I could probably spoof a blood test, I couldn't change how Hunter reacted to their questions.

The weight against my palms increased. I knew a body lay there, caught between the worlds. Poor woman was already dead, so I wasn't torturing her by making her wait.

I wasn't sure how I was keeping the body there. As soon as I turned away, it would come slamming down.

Or would it?

Did I actually need to be here? Or did I just need to keep my focus here, holding the body in place?

"Body," I whispered to Hunter. "Move my body."

He nodded, though I could tell he didn't understand.

"Get me to the restaurant," I told Hunter. "I'll buy us some time."

Hunter grinned. "You ready?"

I nodded. I understood a lot better why Hunter moved as fast as he did. Didn't mean it still didn't freak me out.

Hunter grabbed me and we *flowed* out of the alley. I kept my hands up despite the fireman's hold that Hunter had on me. I closed my eyes and ignored how fast we were going, keeping my focus on that damned portal.

Moments later, we blew through the entrance of the steakhouse. I whispered, "Body" again to myself to keep my awareness there. Just another few minutes.

Hunter asked for a table in the back. The restaurant's theme could best be described as "Mafia Diner," with really tall, leather wing-back chairs instead of plain stools lining the bar, as well as secluded booths that also had tall backs and deep seats.

I let Hunter take my arm and guide me to a booth as if I was blind. I kind of was. I kept up my silent mantra of, "Body. Hold the body," the entire time.

If any nearby telepath could read my mind, they'd think I was insane. Fortunately, I automatically registered the abilities of everyone in the vicinity and knew I was safe.

Only after Hunter had ordered for us did I finally let my concentration slide. It had been more than ten minutes since we'd first appeared in the alley. Even a paranoid shit like Phil Chao wouldn't look much beyond that. There was a good chance we'd made a clean getaway.

The appetizers arrived first—wonderful calamari with a tangy fish sauce. I dove in, Hunter right behind me.

Only after I'd finished licking the grease and breadcrumbs from my fingers did I realize that Hunter was staring at me. "What?" I asked. Did I have a dollop of sauce on my cheek or something?

He shook his head at me. "I think...I think I understand now why you sometimes call me a freak."

I didn't know whether to bristle or laugh at him. "Really?" I asked, the sarcastic tone in my voice sharp enough to cut metal.

Bastard still laughed at me. "Yup. I kind of know how you did what you just did. I see the potential in myself. But I don't think I'll ever get there."

I paused, not sure what he was driving at. "Do you want to get there?" I asked. I hadn't chosen to become a goddess. I still wasn't sure I even liked the concept.

Hunter shook his head. "Don't think so. I have a different path, one that I'm supposed to follow. My speed...that flow...that's my calling, I guess."

"You missed being able to train with your ghosts," I said.

"I did," Hunter admitted. Then he shook his head. "The price of seeing them though...it's too high."

I didn't know if there was anything I could do to fix that. Was it possible for me to reduce Hunter's cravings for the drug? I'd only kept mine under control because I refused to become addicted. Plus, while the expanded *area of knowing* was kind of awesome, it still scared me.

Or it had, until I'd started *becoming*.

"Let me know if I can help," I told him.

The wary look he gave me informed me that I needed to say something more.

"Hunter," I said, making sure that he focused on me and not the demons already dancing in his head and clamoring for *more*. "I trust you," I said. "You will make the right call."

Hunter gave a visible shiver at that. "Really?" he whispered, as if he couldn't let the word escape into the world.

"Cross my heart," I told him. "Pinkie swear," I added, holding out my hand to him, little finger extended.

"I will live up to your trust," Hunter said solemnly as we joined pinkies.

What more could you ask for?

11

─────────

I MADE Hunter call Audrey after we'd finished eating. "You don't have to tell her everything that went on," I said. "But you can't be alone tonight. Particularly after what happened with Mac."

Hunter turned wide eyes to me. The food had definitely helped take the wild edge off his appearance. He almost looked normal. I hadn't realized before that the training with the ghosts was part of the reason why he seemed ethereal sometimes, as if he wasn't fully of this world.

While I was certain his training had saved his life more than once—hell, had even saved the world—that didn't mean I believed it was good for him. Hunter needed to be more in the world, not less.

I didn't understand why my training, the whole goddess thing and manifesting my powers, put me *more* in this world, not less. May have had something to do with the coming apocalypse, I don't know.

Hunter dialed Audrey's number from memory, then gratefully

handed his phone to me. (So he couldn't keep it charged when I asked him to, but he would for his girlfriend? Huh. But I didn't tease him about how low I rated. Not yet.)

"Hey Audrey, this is Cassie," I told her before she said anything beyond hello. I did *not* want her to assume that this was Hunter and for her to break into sex talk or something. There were certain things I never wanted to know.

"Is Hunter okay?" Audrey asked immediately.

"Yes and no," I told her. "Mac betrayed him. Forced drugs on him."

Audrey's gasp told me that she understood just what the consequences of that action entailed. "I'm going to string that bastard up by his balls if I ever see him again," she told me.

I really did like this woman. "Hunter can't be alone right now," I said. "Can you help?"

"Give me twenty minutes and I'll be on my way," Audrey assured me. I told her where we were and that we'd wait for her at the restaurant.

We ordered coffee and sat in silence, Hunter growing more antsy by the minute. "Out with it," I finally said.

"She's not going to like it," Hunter said.

I read between the lines easily enough. *She's going to break up with me for falling off the wagon.*

"A—while Audrey is a really nice woman, there are plenty of other fish in the sea," I told him. "Even for you. This is not your last chance at a relationship."

I could tell he didn't believe me, but I pressed on. "B—Audrey works with people who are on the street and probably addicted to who knows what. She understands that you're going to screw up now and again. You make a habit of it, that's one thing. If it's just *shit happens*, that's something else. And this choice you made, this time, falls firmly under the latter, not the former."

Hunter was still twitchy, but at least he was listening to me. "C." I paused. I really wanted to ask him, *why the hell are you asking me for relationship advice?* I certainly didn't have a sterling track record.

But then I realized it was as much about how to be human and fit in with the world as it was about relationships. "C," I said again. "What you have with Audrey is brand new. That makes it stronger in some ways because it's all about the potential of what you could have. It's also weaker because it's so new. You have no habits to fall back into, no coping mechanisms for dealing with being disappointed in someone else."

Hunter finally gave me a ghost of a smile. "You should write a book or something," he said.

I snorted at him. "Yeah, right. They'd have to edit all the swear words out of it."

"Not all," Hunter said. "Maybe half."

I grinned. He was finally looking better. Mostly human. And I knew he must be feeling better if he was able to tease me.

We made a good team. However, the morning had made me wonder if perhaps we wouldn't always be together, if maybe Hunter would be better off on his own and not dealing with the weird shit all the time.

***

After Audrey fetched Hunter, I went back to my office. I mean, where else was I supposed to go? I could have called off early, but I didn't want to go back to my apartment or to Theresa's place.

No, I needed to return to that dank space I called my own and think things through.

No one had visited while I'd been gone—or at least if they had, they hadn't left me a message. The place didn't have the stench of a battleground either, so Loki hadn't been there. The day was still overcast outside; the light coming in was dim. I cracked open one of the windows just a hair to get a fresh breeze blowing through. Then I grabbed a bottle of water from the tiny fridge (refilled from the jugs downstairs that Chinaman Joe kept for employees), sat my ass down in my comfortable office chair, put my feet up on the desk, and settled in.

I knew Loki wanted me to become a goddess and reign by his side, in part, so he'd get stronger. Loki was killing other gods for some reason that I was sure I wasn't going to like once I figured it out. Anubis had told me that Loki was using Set, as well as war/lioness goddess Sekhmet, to achieve his plans.

I still felt as if I was missing something, though I wasn't sure what.

It didn't surprise me that I felt the presence of someone in the hallway before they knocked on the door.

I kind of figured Loki would show up again. Hell, even my mom or Chinaman Joe would have been vaguely normal.

I never expected my ex-girlfriend, Sam, to come walking in.

She looked good. Hell, Sam always looked good, her soft brown hair professionally done, her makeup fresh and clean, a red wool long coat over a nice-fitting black turtleneck and grey wool slacks.

Except that her makeup couldn't cover how exhausted she was. Or disguise how haunted her eyes looked.

"Hey, Sam," I said, staying where I was in my chair, my feet up. I took a long drink from my water bottle. I wasn't sure what she'd see, but her being here made me uncomfortable, despite this being my turf and everything.

It was just another sign of the apocalypse, her showing up. I was certain of it.

"Quite an office," Sam said, looking around.

It wouldn't meet with her standards, that was for damned sure. The pre-owned wooden desk, the scratched-to-hell metal filing cabinets—hell, even the scent of burned, cheap coffee was not her thing.

Sam sat in one of the visitor chairs and peered at me. "You look good," Sam said.

I didn't bother telling her that the whole goddess thing really did it for my appearance. "Thanks," I said. I took a deep breath and waited for her to talk, for her to tell me what she wanted, why she was slumming it with me.

She nodded after a few moments. "I never thought you'd grow quiet like this," she admitted.

"Like what?" I asked, playing dumb. I knew exactly what she meant, though. I hadn't settled down, or grown up, or any of those stupid things that people said. I'd learned to deal with people better. Letting them talk about themselves was the best way to get information that they'd never intended to share.

"I've been working with your mother," Sam finally said.

"Still?" I said. "I thought you'd realized what a conniving bitch she is." The last time we'd talked, Sam had called to complain about my mom.

Sam gave me a quick grin. "Oh, I have no illusions about Debra Lewis. She's used me but good. I'd like to think that I've been successfully using her in return to get what I want."

I couldn't help but snort at her. Sam was, and always would be, junior varsity to dear old Mom. Sam was merely selfish, spoiled, and privileged. She wasn't a sociopath, at least not while I'd been dating her.

After the next long silence, I finally asked, "What do you want?" What was big enough that Sam would let herself be used by my mom? That she'd be willing to come here and seek my help?

"I'm trying to take down Jacobsen Consortium," Sam said.

That surprised me. I hadn't expected a teenaged rebellion from Sam against her pseudo-parent.

While I railed against Jacobsen Consortium, it wasn't worth my time to actively work at destroying them. Since I wasn't recognized as part of the club by the *blessed*, I only needed to take care of myself and Hunter. I didn't need to bother with the rest of them, unlike Sam. She defined herself as being one of the *blessed* first and foremost.

"Good luck with destroying the machine," I said. I actually meant it, though my tone may have been slightly sarcastic.

Then I waited. I wasn't about to ask how I could help her with that. Her cause was *not* mine.

Besides, I had to go save the world. Again.

"Your mom is determined to break the board of Jacobsen Consortium," Sam said. "She's been gathering dirt on the various board members, finding the right pressure points, so that at the critical time, they'll vote for her and put her as a full member on the board."

I nodded. Sounded about right. Though I also knew that Mom had found more joy being the power behind the throne as opposed to actually becoming Queen herself.

"She's also gathering political power," Sam said.

I shrugged. That was like saying, "Flowers like sunshine." Of course Mom was jockeying for a better political position. That was like breathing to her.

"She plans on taking over Jacobsen Consortium," Sam continued. "There might still be a board, but they'd rubber-stamp all her proposals. And no one in the government will stop her, either."

I had to admit that made me a little uncomfortable. Mom with a built-in constituency of powerful psychics at her command to further her own plans of power…

Then I put two-and-two together and I came up with a lot more than four.

"Shit," I said. "She'd be in charge of all the PAs. Including me."

"Does the phrase *mother knows best* ring any bells?" Sam said with a chilling smile, one that she'd probably copied from my mom.

I actually shivered at that. Goddamn it. Of course my mother would take over an international, multi-billion dollar company just to have more control over me.

Some would think that assumption would be egotistical.

They'd never met my mom.

"The funny part is," Sam said, her voice sounding bitter and harsh, her smile brittle enough to shatter. "The funny part is that she's the one who's ultimately behind the more stringent registrations of the *blessed*. She wants more, tighter controls. It wasn't easy to sift through her shell companies, but she's the one sponsoring a bill to make it *illegal* to be a PA and not be registered."

I shook my head. I'd heard of the bill, but I hadn't paid that much attention to it. I was already registered. It was no skin off my nose if the rest of the *blessed* were now going to be more controlled.

"She's trying to number us. Round us up into our own special district of the city. Boxcars will be coming next," Sam said.

I couldn't help but snort at her. "Really? You believe that hyperbole?" I'd heard some of the same arguments. They didn't make sense to me. The PAs were useful to the government, to the cops, to chemical corporations. We made them money. Why would they round us up and gas us?

Sam wagged her head from side to side. "I don't think they'll kill us. I do think that they'll try to control us more and more. Dictate where we can go, where we can't go. Try to restrict our lives." She paused, then added, "There's an old saying about how mankind doesn't want artificial intelligence. They want artificial slaves. And that's what they'll try to make of the *blessed*."

I chewed my lip, considering. Sure, the PAs were completely outnumbered. The latest statistic I'd heard was that there were over one hundred of them for every one of us.

We had unique skills. Skills that were valued. Of course, the government and corporations would like to get away with not paying us. However, because there were so few PAs, they could pick and choose their jobs.

Unless Mom's bills went through and the PAs *stopped* being able to pick and choose what work they did. Would the government really create an entire class of second-class citizens? Who were actually slaves?

Not if I had anything to say about it. This goddess wasn't about to be the object of worship for a downtrodden people. They'd be as powerful and feared as I could make them.

However, I had no intention of *manifesting* for Sam. It wasn't because I cared what she thought—I honestly didn't give a crap about that. I didn't trust Sam, however. She'd spread the news of my Coming and it wasn't the right time for that yet.

"I'm not saying you're wrong," I finally told her. "The government would love to control us completely and make us slaves. However, I'm not sure what you think *I* can do about it. You don't expect me to talk with my mom and that she'd suddenly have a change of heart, do you? Because that's fucking insane." My approval or disapproval had never once changed my mom's plans.

Sam shook her head. "No, I don't think you'd be able to talk your mom out of anything. She's too…determined."

"Focused," I said. That was one thing I both admired and hated about her—she had a laser focus on what she deemed important that nothing could shake.

"But we still have to stop her," Sam said.

I bristled at this *we* shit; however, I maintained my silence.

"Have you ever thought about having a kid?" Sam continued.

"Hell, no," I said. Sam knew how I felt about kids: sociopathic monsters who were only allowed to live because they ensured the continuation of the race.

Sam merely nodded, that brittle smile turning triumphant around the edges.

I suddenly saw her plan.

I had to hand it to Sam. A grandchild was one of the very few things that would shift my mother's focus away from Jacobsen Consortium. It was possibly the only thing in the world that would make Mom blink.

"You could adopt someone older," Sam suggested. "Not an infant."

I couldn't help but snort at her. "You do realize that if I had a kid, adopted or not, the first thing my mom would do would be to have me declared incompetent so that she could raise the child on her own, right? Away from me and my corrupt, gay lifestyle?"

Sam opened her mouth then closed it again. "You're right," she said with a sigh, looking disappointed. "What if it was your girlfriend's kid?"

"Would have to be related to me," I said. Which would mean for something this crazy to work, I'd have to marry Theresa first. So the kid would be mine as well.

Damn it. Now I was back to that other intractable problem. How much of my life did I want to change? And did I really want to help Sam that much? I didn't owe her a goddamned thing.

"If you could distract your mom for a short while, I can get our defenses in place," Sam said as if I'd already agreed to her insanity. "I still need for your mom to take down the current board at Jacobsen. But while she's distracted, I'll be able to replace it with members of the community. The *blessed* need to direct themselves and stop relying on Jacobsen Consortium, or the government, or anyone else."

"What, you think it's time for the *blessed* to grow the fuck up?" I asked, biting sarcasm firmly in place.

"I wouldn't put it exactly that way, but yes," Sam said, standing.

"Think about it. Your mom's grand plan will enslave us. You, me, everyone. Even your girlfriend, Theresa."

"You can see yourself out," I told Sam, stubbornly not getting up, or even removing my feet from where they rested on my desk. I was *not* going to be part of this insanity.

"It was good to see you," Sam said softly. "Goodbye."

A thread of her perfume, sweet and expensive, tickled my nose after she left.

God, we'd had some good times.

I also knew, down in the depths of my soul, that I never wanted to be with her again. What we'd had, while intense, hadn't been *real*, not like what I had with Theresa.

I didn't want to help Sam. I knew that supposedly innocent request of hers was as calculated as any of my mom's, designed to get me to jump in the direction she'd pointed me in.

On the other hand, it would be fucking awesome to pull something over on my mom and to ruin her plans.

How difficult would it be to fake Mom out? To get her to believe that Theresa was pregnant? Particularly if I could get Theresa to agree to play the part, then drag her with me to my next mother-daughter lunch in a couple days?

Who would be the father? While sperm-banks were supposed to be confidential, I would bet it wouldn't take too long before my mom found out if we'd actually been to one or not. No, it would have to be a mutual friend of Theresa's and mine, who Mom didn't know and couldn't reach.

Hunter? I couldn't help but snort out loud at the thought.

Then I sighed. Was I actually considering doing this? Was it that important to stop Mom from her plans of world domination?

She'd be angry as fuck when it turned out to be a con job. However, Sam was right. The *blessed* needed to be able to direct themselves. They should be running the corporation that trained them, not the lawyers and bankers.

They'd end up with an adversarial relationship with the government. They'd have to learn how to fight in a political arena, not just dump money on lobbyists but to actually get their own damned hands dirty.

I sighed. I couldn't believe I was actually thinking about going along with this crazy scheme.

But the appeal of pulling one over on my mom was irresistible. Of thwarting her plans.

And Sam knew that. She knew that would be the only string she could pull to get me to do this.

I sighed and finally stood up, stretching.

While the pregnancy could be fake, the marriage proposal would have to be real.

Luckily, I knew a guy who could find me the perfect ring.

HAKEEM SHOWED up less than a minute after I called, as if he'd been circling the block or something, waiting for my text. Maybe he had.

I nearly didn't get into the car. But the temperature had dropped again, and icy winds nipped at any exposed skin. Plus, though I believed in following my hunches, I was still officially a post-cog. Knowing something was going to happen before the deed disturbed me.

The car smelled the same, of pine and clean leather. The warmth was blissful, and it always felt decadent to be able to slide into the backseat of such a luxurious vehicle. Particularly with someone else driving.

"Welcome, my friend," Hakeem said, his smile as bright as it ever was when he caught my eye in the rearview mirror. His cheeriness didn't hide the worry lurked there as well.

"What's up?" I asked. I figured cutting through the bullshit would make this less painful.

Hakeem sighed, but threw me another smile. "I should know that you see the truth. Always." He slid into traffic gracefully, like a professional diver slicing through the water. "I need a promise from you. That you talk with me later."

"Later? As in, after what?" I asked, alarmed. I made myself take a deep breath. I sure as fuck wasn't about to go all goddess on Hakeem, though the rage pumping through my blood made it oh-so-easy to consider, oh-so-hard to fight. "What have you set me up for?"

"Your word," Hakeem insisted.

Well, if he wanted my word to talk with him after *something,* that at least meant that whatever he had planned wasn't deadly. Or he figured I'd survive it.

"Talk?" I asked, fuming, glancing out the window at the traffic sliding by. "Or just listen?"

"Both," Hakeem said firmly.

"Why should I listen to a traitor?" I asked him. I knew I shouldn't have gotten into the car. I knew that once he started reporting on me and Hunter to Jacobsen Consortium that I should have cut him off.

How dare he betray Me?

"Because I see truth that even you cannot, Cassandra," Hakeem said gently.

Strange, how Hakeem saying my name both elevated my awareness as well as grounded me, brought me back to human.

"I will talk with you once, afterward," I told Hakeem. "I make no promises for future conversation."

"Thank you, my friend," Hakeem said. "I expect no less."

It didn't surprise me when I finally realized that we were heading toward the University of Minnesota. I knew we weren't heading further east, though, going to a funky shop for me to buy a ring, like I'd requested.

We were on our way to Jacobsen Consortium.

However, Hakeem didn't pull into the parking lot. Instead, he glided into a spot that had just opened up out front.

I looked at him, catching his eye in the mirror, wondering if he really expected me to get out of the car and walk into the building like a lamb to the slaughter.

He shook his head, responding to my unasked question.

For the first time, I saw his true age in his expression. I rarely remembered that Hakeem was older than me, older than Hunter. In his fifties, I believe. Never married, but acting the uncle to dozens of relatives.

Too fucking bad if this pained him. I knew it would end up hurting me more, in the end.

Both of the back doors of the car opened simultaneously, cold wind instantly seeking me out, sending chills down my spine.

It didn't surprise me when I realized that Josh was one of the new passengers.

The other fucker, though, was Dennis, the asshole telepath who worked for the government and ran my evaluations every quarter.

Dennis, who had abilities that Jacobsen Consortium continued to deny. A telepath who didn't just receive thoughts but who could influence people, too.

Well, most people. I'd always appeared to be immune to his "charms."

I started reciting addition tables immediately to keep Dennis the fuck out of my head.

One plus one equals two. Two plus one equals three.

I shot Hakeem a look that should have cut his soul. How dare he trap me in here with the enemy this way?

I knew I'd survive the encounter. Hakeem's demand of talking afterward guaranteed that.

This was a much worse betrayal, however, than I think Hakeem realized. He'd just taken a safe place and made it no longer safe.

I could never ride with him again.

"Hello, Cassie," Josh said, sounding smug.

"You've gained weight," I told him honestly. His face was flushed from the cold, making his cheeks seem fatter than the last time I'd seen him. He wore a cheap, gray wool jacket that was already coming apart at the shoulder seam. He stank of sweat and the greasy tacos he'd had for lunch. He still wore his brown hair in a bad comb-over, his skull shining ghostly white through the strands. His brown eyes had paled with age. Seemed like he was aging pretty badly.

Dennis gave me a grin when I glanced over at him. What, did this asshole think that I was suddenly on *his* side? Fuck him and his stupid skinny tie that I wished would suddenly come alive and choke him to death. I visualized his dying face as strongly as I could, his pale blue eyes bulging out of their sockets, his fat tongue hanging out of his mouth, the way his breath would rasp, the stench of the shit draining out of him as he gasped his last.

The way Dennis paled told me *that* had been effective. Might have to do it more often. Though I suspected that anything I did to Dennis would come back to bite me later.

Josh didn't have the power to affect me or my work.

"What the hell do you two fuckers want?" I asked. I went back to my tables. *Four plus one equals five. Five plus one equals six.*

"I just wanted to talk with you for a few minutes," Josh said, trying to sound reasonable. "Since you never return any of my phone calls."

I shrugged. "Can't help it. I'm a busy girl. Dance card is usually full." I paused, then turned to Dennis. "And why are *you* here?"

He seemed to have recovered his equilibrium. "I'm here to ensure that you speak honestly with Josh."

"Does he know all that you can do?" I asked, giving Dennis a sharp smile.

He blinked his eyes and looked confused. Could have won a statue for that act. "I'm not sure what you mean," he said.

So no, Josh had no idea that Dennis was a fuck-ton stronger than a normal telepath. It made me wonder who the real target was. Was Jacobsen Consortium really wanting to question me? Or did they expect me to help set Josh up for some kind of fall, given our history? Had this meeting even been Josh's idea?

"Never mind," I said, turning back to Josh. "Talk away," I instructed him. Fuck if I was going to let them direct the conversation. "Since you've trapped me here."

"Cassandra, stop being so melodramatic," Josh said, scolding me. "Now, we know that your mother has been working to influence Jacobsen Consortium."

I snorted at him. "Dude, she wants your head on a pike." I wasn't about to tell them or even think about Sam's plot. *Six plus one equals seven.*

"What do you mean?" Josh asked, sounding hurt.

"After your treatment of me and Hunter? You're fairly high on her personal hit list," I brazenly lied. I deliberately thought back to the most recent brunch that I'd had with mommy dearest, how hot the restaurant had been, how cool the glass of ice water had felt when I'd wrapped my hand around it, how good the decadent blueberry crumble had tasted.

I didn't think about the conversation. That was, in many ways, a false detail. Remembering the physical sensations around the time was a much better way to lie to a telepath. And I'd had some practice by now.

How else are you going to be able to defeat your enemy if you don't engage them on a regular basis?

I didn't bother looking at Dennis to see whether he verified my lie or not.

I heard Dennis's coat shift across the seat. Shit, I was super wired if I could distinguish that from the sounds of the outside traffic. I figure he shrugged, neither confirming or denying my claim.

"Your mother's opinion of me is of no bearing here," Josh said stiffly after a moment.

I didn't laugh at him or his hurt tone, though I really wanted to. I figured that my mom's opinion didn't affect him or his position, but Josh was such a kiss-up that he always wanted to be thought of well by those higher on the food chain.

"What does she want with Jacobsen Consortium?" Josh asked after another moment.

"How the fuck should I know?" I asked, maintaining my outrage. I answered completely honestly. "She's never talked with *me* about her plans." I threw a glance at Dennis. "Not once."

Grudgingly, Dennis had to nod at that. It was the truth, after all.

"Can you at least speculate?" Josh asked, using a wheedling tone.

"That's easy. Mom wants what she always wants," I told him. "Power. Control. World domination. Why the hell do you need *me* to tell you that? It's obvious."

"But she's also trying to control the *blessed*," Josh pointed out. "Restrict them. Cut them off from the rest of the world."

"Why the fuck should I care?" I said. "I'm not part of their little club. Remember? You ensured that by how I came to my powers."

"I'm not going to apologize for that," Josh said sharply.

"Have you been enhancing your powers recently, Cassie?" Dennis said, sliding the question in, trying unsuccessfully to be subtle.

"Hell, no," I told Dennis. Again, truthfully. "There isn't a thing that I've been doing. Haven't taken any drugs."

Again, technically that was the truth. I hadn't done anything to increase my powers. It was that damned Loki tossing bodies at me, like a determined suitor would throw roses in my path.

"But you're stronger," Dennis said quietly. "You've changed."

I turned and blinked at him, trying to earn my own award for my performance. "I have no idea what you're talking about," I said. "I'm still the same girl trying to make a living in the big, bad world." I blinked my eyes at him, like an ingenue.

"There's something else," Dennis said, peering at me. "Something different."

Seven plus one equals eight. Eight plus one equals nine. Nothing else.

Damn that ability of mine to make the other PAs around me stronger. Dennis obviously didn't believe me. I couldn't feel him rooting around in my head, though I know he was trying.

Nine plus one equals ten.

I knew I had to give them something, or Hakeem would drive us around the city for hours.

"I didn't want to tell you this," I said slowly. "But there is something new in my life. As I said, it isn't me who's changing. Or not the only one, rather."

Dennis raised a single eyebrow. Josh gave a greedy smile, as if he'd finally found the ice cream center of the cake in front of him.

"It's my girlfriend," I said. I looked from one to the other, then, as if I couldn't hold it in anymore, I said, "We're pregnant!"

The pair of them looked distinctly uncomfortable at that. It sure as hell hadn't been what they were expecting. "My pal Hakeem here was taking me to a jewelry store so we can get officially engaged," I said all in a rush.

Again, telling them just enough of the truth to throw off Dennis.

Neither of the men seemed to know what to say at that. I know they both were curious who the father was. Their mothers had beaten enough manners into them so they didn't ask.

"Congratulations," Josh said belatedly.

"Yes, yes, congrats," Dennis said.

Seemed as though Sam had found the perfect distraction for just about anyone. No one expected that news, and there evidently was something gauche about continuing an interrogation after being told that someone's expecting.

"Drop us off at the next corner," Josh directed Hakeem before he turned back to me. "And you have my number. I expect you to call me after your brunch with your mother on Saturday."

I bit my lips together rather than telling him to fuck off. Maybe I would give him a call after brunch, just to gush about the coming baby. It seemed to make him uncomfortable as hell. Even Dennis appeared off his game thinking about that.

Shit, that might make it worth talking to these bastards.

Unfortunately, the cold wind that whistled through the car didn't clear out their stench after they exited the vehicle. The smell of the pine that was usually so sweet felt overpowering. And Hakeem's didn't pull easily into traffic. He swerved, as if he was blind. Or distracted. Or maybe not looking, as he appeared to be trying to stare at me in his rearview mirror instead of watching traffic.

"What?" I asked him belligerently. "What did you want to *talk* about now?"

"A baby?" he asked softly.

"Nothing I'm telling you about," I said. It was none of his business. Though I knew now that he was going to get hell from Josh for not knowing this before now.

Hakeem shook his head. "No, there is no child," he said softly. His eyes took on that distant look, as if he stared into a chilling future. "I will never tell them," he added.

"Good for you," I said. "Is that all?" I had had it with Hakeem, with never being sure of his loyalties, with not being able to speak freely around him. That just wasn't me. And he'd destroyed my sanctuary.

"I didn't have a choice," Hakeem finally said. He looked as guilty as a dog who'd just been caught chewing up his owner's favorite slipper. "They—Jacobsen Consortium—have my youngest brother. Yonas."

"What do you mean?" I asked. I couldn't help but snarl. I didn't like the thought of Jacobsen Consortium having their claws in anyone. Even a traitor's brother.

Hakeem gulped, then nodded. Again that swerve instead of sliding easily from one lane to the next.

"We cannot find Yonas," Hakeem admitted. "According to the reports we found, he passed through customs. He came to this country legally, I swear. He had visitor's visa. He was leaving the airport. Then…he disappeared."

I couldn't help my shiver. Had Hakeem's brother really been taken by Jacobsen Consortium? Was he being held in that mythical prison that Hunter swore existed under consortium headquarters?

"Why didn't you see this?" I asked. Hakeem saw patterns, and in some ways was one of the strongest pre-cogs I knew. Except his ability wasn't the same as pre-cognition. He worked best with solid, immediate objects rather than timelines and possibilities.

Hakeem sighed. "You see something. Cannot swerve around it. Some fates are real. Others just shadows."

I opened my mouth then closed it again. I knew that from Hunter. It was part of the training all PAs got—sometimes fate was just that. Fate. Knowing what was about to happen didn't mean you could always avoid it. That was why no pre-cog tried to see into their own future. The ones who did went crazy. Fast.

"And so I'm supposed to feel sorry for you? Forgive you for setting me up? Become a *victim* or sacrifice for you? So you can exchange one body for another?" I asked. It frosted my ass that Hakeem would treat me—or honestly, anyone—this way.

"No, Cassie, my friend, no," Hakeem said. "I know you not forgive. Or forget. Just know. *I had no choice.*"

That gave me pause. It didn't seem to me like an excuse so much as an explanation.

"Not enough," I said after a moment.

Hakeem sighed. "I know," he said softly. He pulled to a stop at the next corner. "Thank you for being my friend," he said.

I slid out of the car. I didn't have anything more to say to him. He'd crossed a line too far. I'd stopped trusting him when he'd turned into a double agent, though I'd been willing to do business with him. He was convenient. Made my life easier.

However, I didn't trust him at all now. In particular, I didn't trust him not to turn Hunter and I in on a trumped-up charge if it meant getting his brother out of Jacobsen Consortium.

I stood on the cold street corner and watched Hakeem's black town car slide into traffic like a shark among guppies. My heart lurched.

I'd never been one for impracticalities. I tried to always be a realist. The world was as it was.

I still wished with all my heart that Hakeem and I could have ended differently, or not at all.

I was never going to call Hakeem again. And neither would Hunter, or Theresa, or Audrey, either, if I had anything to say about it.

However, that didn't mean that I was about to turn my back on Hakeem's brother. Hunter had always claimed that Jacobsen Consortium had a dungeon where it kept some of the more dangerous PAs, the ones who went through the training successfully but turned out less than human afterward.

Maybe it was time to perform a jailbreak.

Because that, too, would put more pressure and more distraction on the board. Particularly if there was some publicity about it…

Humming, I turned and walked to the bus stop just a few feet away. The bus I needed arrived within a minute. Hakeem always did have good timing.

I didn't know if I was still working within the patterns he'd seen. I didn't care.

Because unless the fates conspired against me, I was never going to see my tiny Ethiopian driver again.

12

ODIN FELT HIMSELF TIRING. He roared his disapproval. He thrust with his spear more fiercely, fighting the *creature* in front of him. She had the head of a lion and the body of a luscious woman. Her muzzle was stained red from the blood of Tyr, who'd lost his other arm fighting her. The robe she wore appeared soaked in blood, or maybe it had just been dyed that color.

She swung out with her own weapon, a long pike with a wickedly sharp hook on either end. She seemed crazed, a true berserker. She didn't gnaw on the edge of a shield though to achieve her fighting state. Instead, she licked at her clawed hand, seeking the blood there whenever she appeared to be fading.

She snarled at him with his next thrust, but she didn't back away as far. Even on that foreign face Odin could read the smug satisfaction there.

So many others had already fallen. Odin couldn't allow himself to think of that. He had to fight to the end, through this Ragnarok and beyond. He could survive this twilight of the gods and live to fight another day. He had to.

That damned traitor Loki had been the one who'd weakened the bridge. Where was he? He wasn't fighting with this foreign army. Odin feared that the traitor might be causing further trouble in Asgard, behind the line where Odin and the gods fought to keep the strangers from invading.

Heimdall was the only one who didn't engage with another god directly. He continued to defend the Bifrost bridge from the huge flocks of birds attacking it.

Why were the birds still attacking the bridge? What did they hope to gain from it? Surely there weren't that many bodies that Loki wanted to send through the portal?

Odin didn't know how long they'd been fighting already. The bodies of the birds lay heaped like a black snow bank, up to his waist. He shivered when he heard a wounded cry, the light in his own chest suddenly lessening.

Another of the Aesir had fallen. He didn't know which one.

Would any of them survive?

He pushed forward, trying to drive the creature he fought back. He slashed with his spear, trying to catch the damned woman unaware.

She took one hesitant step backward, then another.

Ah ha! Maybe Odin could drive her off the edge of the cliff behind her, make her fall between the end of the bridge and the crevice, fall deep into the endless pit there.

He didn't realize his mistake until it was too late. She wasn't backing up. She was making him step forward.

He was in the path of her weird scythe before he knew it.

Odin found himself on his back. The woman had caught his legs with her hook and dragged them out from under him.

Except there were no more legs just past his knees. She'd cut them off. Bright blood pumped onto the brilliant ice. Rainbows sprang up around Odin, as if where he lay held a stupid pot of gold.

The woman immediately dropped to her knees. Odin failed to bat her hands away where they clenched at his chest.

With a single, strong scoop of her claws, this creature reached into his chest and pulled out his heart.

The world paled around Odin. He was fading. He couldn't help his revulsion. Was this creature about to eat his heart?

No, she held it up, high in the air.

Odin gasped as a great vulture flew up and gripped his heart in its claws. He could feel the damned bird squeezing the still beating organ.

As his sight faded, Odin watched the bird fly up into the darkened sky with its prize. Where was it going? What was it going to do with Odin's heart?

He groaned as the lioness leaned over and lapped at the blood still pouring out of his chest. He hadn't died yet.

They were going to do something with his heart. Something terrible.

Something he couldn't prevent, not as the twilight reached up and claimed him.

SAM KNEW that a hot shower wouldn't be able to wash away how slimy she felt. She took one anyway, turning the water to near scalding and scrubbing at her skin with a fresh bath scrunchy.

When she finished rubbing her skin red, Sam stood with her head bent under the pounding water, letting it beat away at her senses. She breathed in the humid air and swayed under the heat.

She only shut the water off when she realized how dizzy she felt. Sam dried herself off with her fluffiest towel, then put on her fuzzy robe and slippers and padded out to the kitchen.

She'd just poured herself a small glass of wine (no, really! Just a couple fingers worth!) when someone knocked at the door.

Sam put the glass down, worried. She lived in a secured building. No one should be able to just come and knock on her door. Unless it was an emergency with one of the neighbors?

Sam walked slowly through the open space of her living room/kitchen/dining room. There was place to hide if this turned into a robbery or a home invasion. "Yes?" Sam asked loudly as she approached the door. "Who is it?"

"Debra Lewis, dear. I just have a minute," came the voice from the other side.

Sam stopped dead in her tracks. Debra? Cassie's mom? Had she already discovered their plans? Sam's heart beat hard and her mouth was suddenly dry. She wished she'd poured herself an even larger glass of wine and had already finished it.

"I'm not really dressed for company," Sam said even as she drew the chain back.

"I'll just be a minute," Debra said, though with a hint of impatience, as if Sam was delaying her.

"Fine," Sam said, unlocking the deadbolt and sliding the door open. "What is it?" She stayed where she was, not inviting Debra in. Really, it was a bit rude for her to just show up this way.

Debra wore a slick blue coat that had silver woven into the material, so the color shifted every time she moved. She'd worn her blonde hair up that day, a more formal style. Maybe she was going to the opera later that night and wouldn't have time to change it. Pearls ran around her neck, showing off the beautiful red-and-off-white cashmere sweater set. A small black purse hung from her arm, the one that Sam swore was actually a bag of holding, given the things she'd seen Debra pull from it.

Sam could tell that Debra debated just brushing past Sam and walking into her apartment as if the space belonged to her. She seemed uncertain when Sam stood there, blocking the way.

"May I come in?" Debra asked, frost edging her tone.

Sam shrugged. "Sure," she said, deliberately turning her back to

Debra so the other woman could follow her. Sam walked directly back to the kitchen counter where her wine waited her and took a large gulp. Thus fortified, she turned to face her mentor.

"Can I get you any?" Sam asked, indicating the wine.

"No, as I said, I just have a minute," Debra said, her eyes narrowing. "It's a bit early to start drinking, isn't it?"

Sam just smiled at her. "The police called to let me know they'd solved the latest case I was involved with. This is to celebrate."

While Debra had her fingers in many, many pies, she didn't know all the details regarding the other parts of Sam's life. The case had been solved the night before, though the police wouldn't make the announcement of having caught the killer until after the arraignment.

"Ah," Debra said, nodding as if she understood. "Congratulations," she added.

Sam took another sip of her wine and waited, her one arm wrapped across her stomach, holding in the warmth of her shower.

"So I take it you weren't consulting with Cassandra when you went to see her this morning?" Debra asked.

Sam let her confusion show. "Why would I consult with Cassie?" she asked. "And why were you checking up on me?"

"I know about your visit to Emanuel," Debra said lightly. "He's dead now."

Sam shivered at the frigidness of Debra's tone. As well as the implication that somehow Debra was responsible for the man's death.

"I'm not sure why you're going to visit these people, trying to get them to talk about me," Debra continued. "I'm not about to ask you to stop, though. I just wanted you to realize I knew what you were doing."

Sam nodded. "Warning received," she said, taking another sip of wine. "Is there anything else?" Sam could tell that Debra really wanted to ask about Sam's visit with Cassie. Debra couldn't just come out and say that, though, not without losing some of her perceived power.

Debra's eyes narrowed and she drew herself up to her full height. While Sam had been aware that Debra was tall, she'd always believed that Cassie was taller. Now she wasn't sure, particularly given the way the woman loomed over Sam.

"I honestly don't care what you're doing," Debra announced in frosty tones. "Go and talk with whomever you like. However. If you hurt my daughter, I will *break* you. Do you understand that?"

"I do," Sam said, not adding, *probably better than you realize.* Emanuel had been right. Cassie *was* her mother's soft spot.

"I approve of this girlfriend of hers. Theresa," Debra said, taking a step back. "I believe they are a successful couple."

Sam blinked, unsure how to respond. Did Debra think that Sam had gone to see Cassie in order to try to talk her into getting back together? "I'm glad you like Theresa," Sam said quietly. "I think she's good for Cassie. Stabilizing, you know?"

Debra gave Sam a smile that had warmed to at least a few degrees above freezing. "Stabilizing. Yes. It is good for Cassandra to have a stabilized relationship."

"I'm glad we agree about that," Sam said. She had a feeling that Debra would have said something more at that point, but instead, she turned and walked toward the door.

"Lovely place you have," Debra said. "We should get together here for cocktails some night."

"It would be my pleasure," Sam said as she followed Debra out. She was uncertain if Debra actually meant it or if she just expected to be invited and would turn the request down. Somehow, Sam didn't believe that Debra really wanted to spend time "slumming" with Sam.

Debra paused at the door. "I'm glad we had this little chat," she said, sounding like a politician's wife. "I'm glad that you're creating your own schemes and plots as well. I find them amusing to unravel. See you at the fundraiser tomorrow night?"

"Of course!" Sam said, trying her best to sound delighted by the prospect.

Debra gave Sam one last long look before adding, "Alcohol is never a good, long-term friend, you know." Then she swept out of the door.

Sam shook her head as she closed and bolted the door. She understood better what Debra had wanted. Not only had she been trying to determine exactly what Sam was up to, Debra had also tried to throw sand in Sam's eyes, to indicate that there wasn't anything she could do that Debra wouldn't eventually find out about or figure out.

Sam nodded and went back to her wine, walking to the window to look out over the garden area in the back of the condo building. It wasn't snowing, but the temperature had dropped and it looked foreboding outside, gray and cold.

It didn't matter that Debra had now turned a portion of her attention on Sam, trying to figure out her angle. It would only be a few days longer before the board of Jacobsen Consortium would call a vote of "non-competence" and oust the chairman.

Sam's people were almost in place.

Now, all Sam had to do was to ensure that Debra missed the one, all important meeting.

***

Theresa made soothing noises as Cassie wound herself up, pacing back and forth in their cozy kitchen while Theresa stirred the pasta. The spaghetti sauce was already finished and simmering on a back burner, smelling of garlic and oregano. The table was set with bowls and silverware, a glass of red wine for Theresa, and a bottle of sparkling water for Cassie. A small salad waited them as well.

Once Cassie had finished her rant, an icy silence had descended on them.

Not the comfortable quiet that Theresa was familiar with, where Cassie hummed to herself and thought things through.

No, this was different.

Theresa wasn't certain, but she was afraid that it was yet another sign of the upcoming apocalypse.

Cassie was nervous.

Cassie was *never* nervous. Sure, she'd been scared before. She'd readily admit to that. Pissed off about this, that, or the other? Frequently.

But not nervous. Not like the cute geeky boy down in I.T. who'd finally gotten up the courage to talk to Theresa about maybe perhaps hanging out Friday night, if she wanted to, only to be shot down when he'd found out she had a girlfriend.

Theresa drained the pasta, shocking it with cold water (she loved knowing the proper terminology for such things, even if she had to learn it on TV shows) then set it in a bowl along with the sauce.

Finally, after everything was on the table, Theresa asked, "So what else happened today?"

Theresa wasn't sure about the look crossed Cassie's face.

Surely that wasn't guilt. Cassie was incapable of guilt. More so than nerves.

"Sam came to see me," Cassie said.

Theresa could tell Cassie was aiming for casual.

She missed it by a mile.

"Oh?" Theresa said. She was certain that she at least sounded vaguely casual. Maybe.

Theresa was never sure exactly how she felt about Sam. On the one hand, Theresa knew that Cassie would never cheat on her. If Cassie was going to break up with her, she'd tell Theresa to her face, probably after a magnificent argument.

On the other hand, Sam was a lot of things Theresa wasn't: rich, beautiful, and one of the *blessed*. Cassie said it didn't bother her that Theresa was mundane, and most of the time Theresa believed her.

Sometimes, though…Theresa knew her job came between them too often. There were too many times when Theresa couldn't talk with Cassie about what she'd done during her day.

"Yeah. Sam." Cassie heaved a big sigh. "I'm not sure where to start."

"The beginning is generally a good place," Theresa teased.

Cassie made a sour face at her. Then shook her head. "I don't think I should go into too many details. It involves Jacobsen Consortium."

"Okay," Theresa said slowly. Was Sam somehow involved with Jacobsen Consortium? Of course, she was. She was on important boards and attended charity dinners. The sorts of things rich people did.

"However, part of it involves my mom," Cassie continued after a short while.

That surprised Theresa. "How is Sam connected to your mom?" She would have thought that once Cassie and Sam were no longer involved, Cassie's mom wouldn't contact Sam.

Theresa knew that Sam's fiancé had been a member of the board of Jacobsen Consortium, something that Sam hadn't found out until very late. Evidently, he'd been some sort of spy. Cassie had felt sorry for Sam that her former girlfriend had been betrayed, yet on the other hand, Cassie felt that Sam deserved it, and excused the feeling on "having a small soul."

"Sam's been doing dirty work for my mom," Cassie explained. "Mom's trying to take over the world. As always."

Theresa merely nodded. She'd heard Cassie's claims about her mother being a complete egomaniac control-freak who would interfere with her daughter's every move if given a chance.

Yet, Cassie continued to have monthly mother-daughter lunches. Something about it being better to know her enemy.

"So why did Sam come to see you?" Theresa asked when Cassie didn't continue.

Cassie sighed and shook her head. "Sam had this lame-brain scheme that was supposed to distract my mom at a crucial point. A plan that involved you."

"Me?" Theresa said. She wasn't sure why she was so shocked. Was Sam trying to come between her and Cassie? Or did Cassie's mom not approve of Theresa? Debra had been nice the two—no, three times that Theresa had met her, if a little stand-offish.

Both Cassie and Theresa preferred Theresa's parents, who were casual and always inviting them over for dinner.

"Sam came up with the one thing that would completely distract my mom and take her focus away from Jacobsen Consortium." Cassie seemed to be girding herself for a fight. "She wants us to claim that we're pregnant."

"We're what!?" Theresa said. Okay, maybe shouted. She knew Cassie had the same opinion she did about kids—that most were sociopathic imbeciles who should have been shot when they turned into teenagers. She'd bet the world would be in much better shape if poor Johnny knew he only had until he was thirteen to prove that he could make the world a better place.

"Look, I told her it was a lame idea," Cassie said. "Neither of us want to have kids. Right?"

"Right," Theresa said, though now some of Cassie's prior nervousness had infected her. What was Cassie going on about then?

"So we'd have to pretend we were pregnant. Cause it ain't happening on my dime," Cassie said firmly.

"Wait. So you want me to pretend I'm pregnant? What the fuck?" Theresa said. She didn't swear very often, but she felt that the occasion merited such an extreme reaction right now.

"No," Cassie said. "Probably. I figure there has to be some other way to distract the Snow Queen."

Theresa knew that Cassie frequently called her mom that, though Theresa had never understood why.

"So what are you going to do?" Theresa asked. "To distract your mom?" And why the hell was Cassie going along with this harebrained scheme of Sam's?

There. That nervousness. It flooded the small kitchen, making the oregano scented air suddenly smell sour.

"If the pregnancy is fake, then the rest of it had better be real," Cassie said. She stood up suddenly and walked over to the other side of Theresa's chair.

Theresa found herself swallowing against a dry throat when Cassie got down on one knee.

A small green box was in Cassie's hand. Nestled inside was a beautiful emerald ring with tiny diamonds on either side of the green stone.

"Theresa. There's only you. Will you be mine?" Cassie said.

As wedding proposals went, Theresa had heard worse. Like her brother who'd merely put the ring for his fiancé on the breakfast table, said, "So. There's that," then left the room.

"I don't know, Cassie," Theresa said, though her heart was longing for her to say yes. "Is this really what you want?" They'd talked about the change this would bring to both of them, how their lives would be different.

"Yes. No. I don't know," Cassie said.

"Well, at least that's honest," Theresa said. She found tears in her eyes. Happy tears? Sad? She wasn't sure. "If you don't know if you want to marry me, then why are you asking?"

"I do want to marry you," Cassie said.

Theresa hated the hesitancy that followed.

"But?" Theresa finally said.

"Like you said, it means change," Cassie said. "Change for the better," she added.

"Who are you trying to convince? Me? Or you?" Theresa asked.

"Fuck if I know," Cassie admitted.

Normally, Theresa found Cassie's honesty refreshing.

Right now? It burned.

"If you aren't certain, then why the hell are you proposing? So that I'll go along with some fake-pregnancy scheme of yours to *distract* your mother?" Theresa asked, not bothering to hide her anger and hurt.

"I'm not proposing just because I need your help," Cassie said.

"Oh, really?" Theresa said, hiding how much *that* stung by getting to her feet. She wasn't going to be used like that. She had to get out of there. Now.

"That's not what I mean," Cassie said, getting off her knee and standing up.

"Until you know what you actually mean, why don't you just hold onto that ring?" Theresa said.

She fled the kitchen, racing for her—their—no, damn it, *her* bedroom and slamming the door behind her. The tears came bursting out. Theresa sank down on *her* side of the bed and let them flow.

"Theresa!" Cassie called after her.

At least Cassie had the sense to stay on the other side of the door and to not come storming in.

"Look, I'm screwing this all up," Cassie said.

"Ya think?" Theresa replied through her tears.

"I—just a second. That's the door," Cassie said.

One minute turned into two. Theresa heard Cassie arguing with someone.

She told herself she didn't care.

Finally, Cassie called out. "Uhm, T? The cops are here. I have to go with them."

Though Theresa didn't want anyone seeing the evidence of their most recent fight, she still walked out of the bedroom and went to the front door immediately.

At least Cassie wasn't handcuffed. Yet. Theresa wondered if it was just a matter of time, though, given the angry looks the cops were giving her girlfriend.

"They've found another body," Cassie said.

Theresa could tell the cops weren't pleased that Cassie was sharing any information about the case with anyone.

"They think I may know him. He has my business card in his front pocket, and no other ID," Cassie continued.

Theresa wasn't sure if Cassie was trying to piss off the cops or if she just didn't care. Probably some of both.

Or was it something else? Fear spiked through Theresa. "It isn't Hunter, is it?"

"Fuck," Cassie said. "I hadn't thought of that."

"Go," Theresa said. "We'll talk. Later."

"Promise?" Cassie said.

There it was again. That nervousness that had haunted them all evening.

"Yes. We'll talk. I promise," Theresa said. "Though I don't promise anything else."

Cassie nodded, her expression grim as she followed the police out of the house.

Theresa locked the door after they were gone, then collapsed on love seat under the window.

She'd been wrong before.

Seemed she wouldn't do anything for Cassie. Particularly when it involved her heart.

13

─────────

GOD*DAMN* IT. I hated this. Hated this case with a fucking passion that I generally only reserved for stupid people acting privileged. Here I was, riding in the back of a police car like some sort of common criminal. The car smelled of puke and fear, overlaid with those nasty pine "fresheners."

Made me want to puke, too.

I don't know what made me fuck up that marriage proposal so badly. Maybe I'd come to believe my own press. That goddess shit had really played with my head. Made me think on some level that I could do no wrong.

Obviously, I'd been *way* off the mark believing that Theresa would do anything for me. I could see how much I'd screwed up, believing that if I proposed to her she'd go along with pretending to be pregnant.

If I could have banished the stupid cops, I would have. Would have left them sitting in their car in the parking lot of some donut shop wondering what the hell had just happened.

Then Theresa had had to ask if it was Hunter. Of course, the asshole wasn't answering his phone. Now I *had* to go see the damned body.

Who could it be? The cops would have mentioned if it was a black guy, I was certain. Minnesota tried to be progressive, but I knew cops who'd pull Hakeem over just for driving while Ethiopian.

Evening rush hour was mostly over, so at least it didn't take hours to get to the downtown police station. I had Michael John's number on speed dial in case the cops decided to try to put me through the ringer. I was *not* up for their shit tonight.

I had too much of my own crap to deal with.

You know how on cop shows, the morgue is a clean, open place? That's just for the camera and crew. The morgue for the Minneapolis police department—situated in the basement, of course—was all closed in. The hallways were at least a foot narrower than upstairs. Bright lights shone down from the ceiling, but there were still nasty shadows in the corners. The amount of industrial disinfectant in the air made my eyes water.

The room the cops took me to was tiny—the gurney standing in the center of the it took up most of the space. Instruments of torture lay on the table beside the body, along with a tray that held bloodied swabs. Of course, they had a white sheet over the face of the damned corpse. Out of respect for the dead? Or just because they wanted the opportunity to shock me? I didn't know and I didn't care.

One of the cops walked around to the far side of the table while the other stood next to me. I knew it was so they could watch my face as they did the big reveal.

Damned if I was going to show them anything. I steeled myself, trying to hold my face as neutral as possible. Then I nodded to the cop, letting him know I was ready to view the body.

The old white guy under the sheet wasn't Hunter. I have to admit I was relieved.

Then I looked more closely.

One of the guy's eyes had been plucked out a long time ago. Scar tissue ran across the hole, making it look as though pale skin had grown over the eye. He had blond hair that had gone gray along the temples, along with a braided, white-streaked beard. He was a big guy—well over six feet tall. More scars ran across his shoulders and neck, remnants of old battles.

His heart hadn't been neatly cut out, though. No, it looked like something with huge claws had ripped it out.

I swallowed nervously. That hadn't been a human hand. I knew that instinctively.

But there was something about this guy. Something familiar.

"Do you know him?" the cop asked.

Shit. I did.

"Nope," I lied.

I could tell they didn't believe me.

They wouldn't have believed the truth either, though.

How the hell could I tell them that the guy on the gurney had at one point been the god Odin?

I TEXTED Theresa when the cops were finally done with me. However, as I expected, she told me to wait until tomorrow before I came back over.

Would she have invited me over if it had been Hunter? Of course, she would have. I wasn't about to tell her on a traceable device that the guy had been Odin.

I might have been crazy, but I sure as fuck wasn't stupid.

Most of the time.

So I made my way back to my shithole apartment. Like my office, this had been my safe hidey hole for quite a while. I could always come here and blow off steam, take some "me" time, smoke my cancer sticks and just be.

However, like my office, this tiny place no longer fit. I wasn't certain if it was because of the whole goddess thing or not. Or maybe I was changing regardless of choosing.

I sat on the loveseat with my feet up on the coffee table, staring at the TV silently playing some stupid sitcom. I toyed with the cigarette in my hand, but I wasn't actually smoking it.

Did I want to give up this place? Move in with Theresa?

If I reframed the question, such as *lose Theresa or keep this place*, my answer was immediate and obvious. I'd give up this place—and so much more—to be with her, to keep her in my life.

Not everything, though. And that, in part, had been my mistake. I had asked too much. Though the engagement had been real—I truly did want to be with her—I hadn't gone about it the right way.

All that shit about love being selfless was right in some ways.

Now, I just had to show Theresa how I really felt about her.

Woke up Friday morning, Valentine's day, alone.

Not how I wanted to start a day that was supposedly all about romance.

At least the storm had blown through the night before, only dumping a few inches of snow. The day was clear and cold as fuck, the blue skies lying about how nice it was outside.

I decided to forego my morning cigarette, though I still made myself coffee, still sat on my loveseat and thought about my upcoming plan of attack.

I agreed with Sam in principle. Mommy Dearest running the board of Jacobsen Consortium would turn into a fate worse than hell. No one believed me when I told them how grasping and power hungry my mom was.

Though I suspected Sam now did.

However, Sam's method of distracting my mom wasn't going to work. I should have realized that earlier before I blithely told Dennis and Josh that we were pregnant.

It had been fun to mess with them.

But I'd done it at the expense of my sweetie. And that wasn't right.

Speaking of which…my phone binged. A text message had just come through. Though it wasn't Theresa. She had her own ringtone.

Maybe it was that ass Hunter finally replying to my calls.

My hands started shaking as I read the words.

This is Dr. T. I have to cancel our appointment today. I'm tied up at the office for the next couple of days.

Fuck.

I knew, *knew*, what had just happened.

Josh had reported to his upper management that Theresa was pregnant.

And they'd grabbed her.

<hr />

"Fuck," I told Hunter as I paced in front of him. We were in my office but I was too agitated to sit. Hunter was having to be the calm one that morning.

Yup. Just another sign of the coming apocalypse.

"We have to go rescue her," I said.

"Are you sure they won't release her? Once they figure out she isn't pregnant?" Hunter asked reasonably.

"Sure. After someone like Dennis rapes her mind? I don't think I want to wait that long," I said. Though chances were that awful things were already happening to her. I couldn't let myself dwell on that, though.

"How long do you think they'll hold her?" Hunter asked.

"The message said she'd be tied up for the next couple of days," I said. "So maybe through the weekend? Though it probably was an automated program with a canned message."

I hadn't realized that my love had been tricky enough to sneak my number in as one of her regular clients. I had to admire her for that.

Why hadn't she told me? I knew the answer to that as soon as I wondered about it. She didn't trust her employers, not completely. A strong telepath—such as, oh, say, Dennis—would have been able to pluck that information from my mind without me knowing it.

"What are we going to do?" Hunter said.

I couldn't predict the future. I was a post-cog, not a pre-cog. But I knew what Hunter was proposing. I shouldn't even bother going after her on my own. He was attaching himself to my side. Blood-brothers.

"We're going after her. Together," I told him.

And woe be to those who stood in my way.

Being a goddess had to have its uses, right?

I swear that was the longest day of my entire fucking life.

Hunter insisted that we go in after nightfall. He'd already scoped out the place and knew the times when the guards would change. Had he foreseen the need to break in? Or was he just being his usual paranoid self? I couldn't say.

I stayed in my tiny apartment for most of the afternoon, pacing and experimenting with the whole goddess thing. I didn't think anyone would be coming to pick me up. Good luck to any police who tried.

Jacobsen Consortium knew better than to mess with me. Or they should.

Except that they'd grabbed my girl.

I regretted my fucked up proposal the night before more than ever. What the hell had I been thinking? My love for Theresa was real. That was all that mattered. We'd figure the rest of the shit out.

While being with her meant change, being without her meant change as well.

Bad change. Changes I didn't like.

So I paced. I practiced. I didn't smoke. I was actually kind of proud of myself, how I managed to avoid the cancer sticks.

Maybe transforming into a goddess had its bright points. Like purifying my blood of all cravings, making sure that my need for cigarettes was no longer physical.

I still required sex with Theresa. That was an addiction I wasn't about to give up.

Hunter and I met at the bus stop closest to the University about 8:30 that night. The consortium headquarters were located this side of the west campus.

All those luckless, cheap interns they could draw from.

I wore my longer black leather jacket, my black twenty ring docs, and black, fleece-lined leggings. I couldn't make myself wear all black, though I knew it would have been smart. Instead, I had on a maroon shirt over a bright white camisole.

It was Valentines' Day. Red was appropriate.

Hunter was in his long brown wool jacket, heavy jeans, and black military boots. He moved like a shadow, though I could see him. I'd been experimenting with just viewing the world though my *other* vision instead of fully transforming.

Hunter fucking glowed like an electrified ghost.

Hopefully, I was the only one who could see that.

"You ready, boss?" Hunter asked.

I could tell he was gathering himself up, getting ready. It was like the light inside of him concentrated in his torso, so his chest was slightly brighter than the rest of him.

Huh. I would have thought his legs would have grown brighter.

"Ready," I told him. I tapped my amulet once with my center finger. I felt myself *become.*

I didn't gain height or mass this time. Hopefully I'd managed to kill my own glow.

But I was now *more* than I had been.

Hunter *flowed* away, heading toward a door that had remained hidden until just now at the base of the consortium headquarters.

I knew that Hunter was moving faster than the mortal eye could follow.

I moved with him, just as fast.

However, not as easily. While I could do this, I felt unsettled. This wasn't how a human was supposed to move.

I was more than human at that point.

At my core, though, I knew the truth.

My mantle of godhood was merely borrowed. A cloak I'd thrown on in order to fit in. While I made it look good, it just wasn't me.

Something that nearly losing Theresa had finally made me figure out.

THE DOOR to the basement of Jacobsen Consortium had been cleverly hidden. Most people wouldn't have noticed it. Decorative evergreens had been planted in front of it, and it had been painted the same pale gray as the stone of the walls. Hell, they'd even gone so far as to texture the metal, making it look more like stone.

With my goddess sight firmly in place, I could see it. It had a dark quality to it, like the entrance to Hell.

It didn't stand a chance against Hunter's attack. He *flew* through the air, his foot landing solidly above where a handle would normally have been placed.

The metal dented with a solid *thump*.

Hunter whirled and kicked it again, this time just below where a handle should be.

The door bounced in its frame, shivering under the impact.

Hunter kicked it a third time, this time squarely between the other two marks.

The door clicked open.

I grabbed it before it could close again. A mechanical lever fought me, trying to pull the door shut. I wrenched it open, using all my strength.

Hunter's eyebrows reached the top of his forehead as he stared at me.

Huh. Might have used too much strength, as the door now appeared to be hanging off a single hinge.

Oops. My bad.

The back of my skull tingled, as if a cold oil had just been smeared there.

Silent alarms were going off. The kind that usually only dogs could hear. Maybe there was a reason that dog spelled backwards was god.

"Going to have company soon," I told Hunter.

A guard booth was set up directly in front of the door, with bulletproof glass up top, reinforced steel underneath. I paused for a moment, reaching into the empty space and smashing the control panel with one hand.

Yup. A little too much strength still, as the panel was now just a gaping hole.

Too bad. I wanted their system going into complete fucking overdrive at this point, with no one being able to figure out what the fuck had happened.

That was one of the nice things about *becoming*. None of the human's recording equipment actually was capable of revealing my greatness. It was one of the things we were counting on, something to work for us during this prison break.

Hunter *flowed* down the hall behind the guard booth. I followed him, marking the places that I could touch later on our way out, such as the open door to an office that held cabinets full of paper and the lab with very volatile chemicals. The sheetrock making up the walls would be more difficult. However, the studs they were nailed to were merely wood.

I sure as hell wasn't about to set fire to our only escape route. Not unless there appeared to be another way out.

Hunter fought (and won) two additional doors, then came to an absolute standstill. I nearly plowed into him.

I gulped as I looked around. My sense of *being* diminished slightly.

It turned out Hunter had been right all along. It hadn't just been his overactive paranoia.

Jacobsen Consortium did have a prison of sorts in their basement.

Well, fuck.

They weren't going to have it for much longer.

Though Hunter had broken down the door, I slammed it shut after us, restraining it with power. No one, at least no human, could come in after us until I allowed it.

The room had a regular office desk at one end. It looked like government issue, with plain gray metal sides and leg, the top made of brownish Formica. Biometric locks secured all the paperwork hidden inside it.

Next to the desk stood a chair with restraints. Not just arms and legs—no, it had a high back so someone could have their forehead strapped down as well.

Evil curled around the seat of the chair, like a dark miasma.

Did they have eye retainers? So the victim couldn't avoid whatever horror they were being shown?

I destroyed it with a single touch, splinters flying everywhere.

Just past the office was a half-circle made up of eight segments. Locked doors stood in each section. Red blinking lights on the control panels beside each door showed the system was in shutdown mode.

Had the guards figured out this was a prison break? Probably. I was certain they'd trained for that.

Though not for someone like Hunter and how he moved.

Hunter attacked the first door, but it appeared to be made of sterner stuff than its cousins. It shuddered under his kicks, but didn't open up.

"Let me try," I said. We didn't have much time. The guards would be here any moment now, though we'd timed our attack when they'd be at the far end of the building, in the middle of a change over. We didn't want them gathered outside the door in force before we left.

Instead of trying to punch my way through the several layers of steel that made up the door, I ripped the control beside the door out of the wall.

The way it sparked made me jump. *I should be afraid* said a very distant part of my being. I vaguely remembered fear. *I could get electrocuted.*

I felt myself grow into the challenge. I determinedly reached out and grabbed the sparking wires, then pulled, hard.

Seemed that if the system became completely disabled, the door would automatically unlock. That seemed like something of a flaw to me. Wouldn't they want the doors to stay locked if the system failed?

Maybe there was a heart somewhere in this place.

It didn't take long to free all the prisoners. Only six of the eight rooms were occupied.

Theresa was *not* there. Where were they keeping her? I couldn't sense her in the building at all.

Had the consortium already released her?

One of the former prisoners, a tiny black man who looked like a younger version of Hakeem, thanked me profusely.

Most of the others did as well, except for the older gentleman who still seemed shell shocked by the whole thing.

Of course, that was when our luck ran out.

"So, what do we have here?" came a sardonic voice from behind us.

A half dozen guards stood between us and the exit. How the fuck had they gotten there? The door was still closed.

I knew that Hunter and I could *flow* past them. We wouldn't be able to take all the prisoners, though.

"What do you think this is?" I replied, my sardonic tones heavy enough to smash bricks. "It's a jail break. You will let my people go."

I found myself *becoming* more, though I hadn't willed it. It was just the situation.

These were *my* people. They all had power. I could tell. Hakeem's brother Yonas was the strongest of them all.

"You're wrong," the main guard said.

I paused for a moment. That voice. It sounded familiar.

"It's time to choose a side, Cassie."

What the hell? How did this pipsqueak know my name?

At least by saying it, the asshole hadn't made me shrink back down to human. If anything, I suddenly became bigger. Stronger.

More of the goddess.

"Are you going to stay small and weak? Powerless while the ones who are worthy take their proper place? Or are you going to join us?"

Goddamn it.

The guard was changing, transforming, growing taller and more pale.

Loki.

I'd always known that it would come down to this, a battle between us.

I just hoped that somehow, I could win.

"Here I call on my brothers and sisters," Loki said in a weird chant-like voice. It echoed strangely, as if he was speaking not just in this world, but in many.

He was dressed as I'd seen him before, wearing a brown leather vest with large iron rings sewn into it over a brilliantly white peasant shirt that tied around the collar and cuffs. Only someone like Loki could pull that off and have it not look incredibly poofy. His war helmet was made out of a shiny metal, rounded over the top like a dome. The front of it opened up in a T shape, exposing his eyes and nose. Long white feathers stuck up along the sides of it, suggesting wings.

"Come to me now. Let us reform this place. Let us make a new home for the gods."

Oh, crap. Was that what the asshole was up to? Kill off the weaker gods, then bring the survivors here?

Mess up humanity even more than it already was?

Not just no, but *hell* no, was my response.

Loki held his hand up. Something appeared in the center of it.

Ugh. What was that thing? Was it dripping blood?

"I give you the power, now, to cross the worlds, come into this plane. Be at home, here."

I suddenly knew what Loki held.

Odin's heart.

Odin, the one who'd tied himself to Yggdrasil, the World Tree, so he could learn everything. He was connected to it in more ways than one.

And that damned tree had roots in all the worlds.

By using Odin's still beating heart, Loki could open up every plane of existence that Yggdrasil touched.

The "guards" standing beside Loki began to transform.

I recognized Sekhmet from the descriptions I'd read of her, with a lioness head and a human body. The mussel on the beast was already stained with blood, a quick appetizer of one of the human guards, I bet. The Set animal came next. It looked like something between a boar and a dog, with square, pig-like ears and a hound's sharp jaw, ready to tear his opponents to pieces. Nasty piece of work that needed to be put down.

Other gods showed up: a red-faced demon with four knife-wielding arms and a bad attitude; an old Chinese man with white hair falling from his bulbous skull, bulging eyes, and a gaping black hole of doom where his mouth should be; even a black woman who seemed to be part spider.

How the *fuck* was I supposed to fight all of them?

Even with Hunter, I knew I didn't stand a chance.

I was going to die before I'd made it right with my girl.

That was *not* going to happen.

I transformed as the other gods did, stepping sideways onto a glorious plane of battle. My curves became broader, more pronounced. I wore the same black leggings and twenty-ring Docs as always, but over my eye-searing pink shirt I had on a silver vest made up of tiny metal links. It was soft and warm to the touch, and I knew would protect me from the sharpest blade.

My amulet changed as well, becoming a huge double headed ax. It sang as I swung it through the air, thirsting for the blood of the wrong-doer.

And these gods were about as nasty as it got.

On the human plane, my body stood where I'd left it, rigidly frozen. My muscles strained with tension. Light streamed from every pore. The strong scent of burning Frankincense swirled around me, followed by the smell of burning pine.

I was going to be as sore as fuck in the morning, though I was aware that my physical body wouldn't be holding that position for that long. While battling the gods, hours would pass, but on the human plane it would be mere minutes.

Of course, Loki didn't need anything as trivial as a human body and had merely left the guard he'd been using behind.

Bastard.

Whereas I would have to split my focus, making sure that my physical body survived so I'd have something to go back to after this was all done.

Assuming I lived through the upcoming battle.

———

I swung my ax at the damned lioness again. And missed. Again. She was fucking fast.

I'd already dispatched that Set animal thing. Not that I believed that I'd killed him. Gods never really died, you know?

Hunter still fought that four-armed demon. He moved faster than that thing; however, he was tiring. It wouldn't be much longer before one of those knives took off Hunter's head.

And he wasn't a god. I didn't know if I'd be able to bring him back.

My left arm had been shredded by the asshole in front of me. Fortunately, being a goddess had some advantages—if I'd been a human with that amount of damage, I'd probably be in a coma due to blood loss. As it was, my arm was still usable, though it hurt like a son-of-a-bitch.

The battlefield we stood in had once been an actual field. Burned stumps of corn crumbled under our feet. Ashes made the ground slippery. I couldn't escape the stench of rotting gore. A purpled sky lingered above us, as if it couldn't make up its mind whether to bring back the sun or to kill all the light.

Maybe it, too, was waiting on the outcome of this final battle.

I felt the air changing as I sidestepped the latest nasty swipe of Sekhmet's claws.

A light suddenly shone on the horizon. Was that the sun? Had dawn finally come?

No. It was a fucking rainbow shooting across the sky.

What the hell?

Sekhmet stopped her attack, looking up as well.

I did a quick check on my body back on the physical plane. It seemed to be holding up well.

Odin's heart lay on the ground before me back there.

That messed up organ had also suddenly sprouted a rainbow. Light raced crazily around the room, touching the rescued prisoners who stood with shocked expressions on their faces.

I crowed with delight when I realized that Loki hadn't thought things through. Of course.

By opening up the planes between worlds, he'd invited *all* the gods to come to the party. Not just his buddies.

My tiny Ethiopian friend changed first, growing tall and even blacker, suddenly spouting the head of a dog.

Anubis, faithful defender, had arrived. As had the others, the ones who'd trained Hunter, taking over the bodies of the *blessed* that the Jacobsen Consortium had been holding. They joined me on the battlefield.

Suddenly, the sides were more evenly matched.

Maybe I could survive this after all.

14

I SIDESTEPPED Loki's sword while I swung with my own ax, missing by a mile, as usual.

"Surely you can do better than that?" Loki taunted.

I ground my teeth together and didn't bother replying. Stupid bastard. I was still trying to wipe that smug smile off his face.

As I'd always suspected, Loki had centuries of experience when it came to fighting. The smarmy asshole was just too damned slippery for a novice like me.

My double-handled ax thirsted for his blood. He was a rapist, not merely of bodies but of minds and souls as well. I knew all of his misdeeds, how he'd ruined entire worlds. I wouldn't introduce him to my mother, the Ice Queen. Hell, I wouldn't even leave that asshole telepath Dennis alone with Loki, and that was saying something.

A thick rainbow filled the sky above the battlefield, which gave me hope. The gods on both sides struggled on. All the charred remains of the former corn stalks had been smashed down by the feet of the gods. My boots and legs were covered in charcoal and ash. Ravens cawed at us from the sidelines, impatient as always, wanting us to finish up so they could feast on the flesh of the fallen. The smell of sweet incense mingled with the coppery tang of divine blood.

I had the strength of a goddess, and I wouldn't tire for a while yet.

But I couldn't seem to catch the slippery bastard in front of me. He'd already made a hash of one of my legs. I'd been lucky he hadn't taken it off at the knee. It still hurt, but I was too angry to let it stop me.

Hunter and his friend Anubis had finally finished off that damned four-armed demon and were now dancing with the spider woman. What was it with gods and multiple appendages?

I couldn't help them, though. I had to defeat Loki.

I just didn't know how.

A shadow suddenly crossed in front of me.

It took me a moment to realize that it existed on the physical plane.

Someone was approaching my human body.

I rushed at Loki, forcing him back, giving myself a moment of breathing room while he gathered himself for his next attack.

It gave me a second to glance down and see what was happening on the physical plane.

Hakeem stood beside me.

What the fuck?

The words came slowly, due to the stupid time difference between the planes.

"I give you my gift. Freely," Hakeem said as he slid his hand into mine. "It is yours for the taking."

His skin felt cool as glass, smooth and solid.

Power pushed through my physical body, then flowed up to my goddess aspect. Warmth suffused my blood. The morning became brighter. The pain of my knee and my arm vanished.

I wasn't suddenly twice as strong, though that would have been nice.

Instead, I could *see*.

It was similar to when Hunter and I shared our *area of knowing*, hunting together, the pre-cog and the post-cog working like a single well-oiled machine, sensing what was just about to occur and then confirming it had happened.

But Hakeem dealt with physical entities in the here and now, not with timelines and probabilities.

Suddenly, I *saw* the pattern of Loki's attacks. Before, his attacks and his blows had seemed random to me.

Loki had been trained by masters. It was a complicated dance, but a dance nonetheless, with steps I could now follow.

I tried to leave a remnant of Hakeem's power still in his hands. It didn't seem right that I should take all of his gift, even freely given from a traitor.

I knew this was his way of apologizing to me for working as a double-agent.

No matter what else he might have done, Hakeem had a good heart, a heart I now knew as intimately as my own.

I laughed in the cool morning air, my voice ringing out over the entire battlefield. "Though this has been fun, boys and girls, it's time to end this. One last push."

The look of surprise on Loki's face was priceless. Then his usual sneer returned. "So you think a little foreknowledge will save you?"

"No, I am as doomed as all of mankind," I told him honestly. "I have no desire to be a goddess and live forever."

"I should have known you were too simple to appreciate what I've done for you," Loki said. He actually sounded disappointed. Give that man an Oscar.

"That little bit of foreknowledge will, however, end you," I told Loki.

With ease, I stepped around his next attack, bashing him in the back with the flat of my ax as I passed.

Good. That got him angry.

Angry gods stopped thinking and relied on "instinct," which was just another name for deep conditioning.

Loki used both hands to swing his great sword at me, forcing me to take one step back, then another.

A black form appeared out of nowhere.

Loki's next step landed solidly on Anubis's tail.

Anubis gave a dog's yelp that would have done Lassie proud. It conveyed all the hurt and surprise one could hope for.

Loki, now off balance, awkwardly stepped sideways.

I followed right behind, swinging my ax after him, cutting his head cleanly from his body.

It sailed through the air, carried by the feathers flowing up on either side of his helmet, then landed with a soft *thunk*. Ash covered it instantly, the skin lined and cracked, like an ancient stone statue.

A loud hiss followed, like all the air being let out of a balloon. The sky sagged, the rainbow started to dissolve, and the true sun began to rise.

All the steam went out of the other players. Sure, they got in a few more blows, but it was like the still-writhing body of a snake after the head has been cut off.

As the gods fell back from one another, they began to dissipate, fading like ghosts at dawn. The spell that Loki had spun to open the portal dissolved.

Only Anubis remained behind, standing beside me.

"You must close all the gates," he said, his voice a surprisingly high tenor when I'd expected a low growl.

Odin's heart suddenly appeared at my feet.

Shit.

Well, at least the old guy was really going to owe me one after this.

Anubis took me to the top of an ice covered mountain. Freezing cold winds gusted around us, trying to steal the last remnants of my warmth. Clouds boiled across the sky and the air smelled of snow and iron. The snow crunched under my boots, sounding like breaking Styrofoam. More mountains surrounded us, rugged and desolate.

Around a sharp boulder we found Odin's body. He lay with his arms outstretched, as if he'd been stopped while trying to make a snow angel. A large red blotch spoiled his bright white shirt, opening around the wound in his chest. His single eye reflected the gray of the sky, and his mouth was open in surprise.

Or maybe he'd been screaming.

The heart in my hand felt warm. It still beat, albeit slowly. It wasn't as gross as it might sound. Though it felt slippery, it wasn't slimy. It smelled like burning pine logs.

I glanced over at Anubis. He merely nodded at me, as if encouraging me to get the job done. He wasn't shivering, but I bet he was cold as fuck, too.

I remembered from my research that Anubis was familiar with hearts. He weighed a human's heart against a feather of truth, judging whether or not the beast Ammit would eat the heart or if the human would go on to live forever in the golden fields.

Had Anubis already judged Odin's heart to be worthy?

I sank down, kneeling on the hard snow easily. I would have sworn that even fifty years of yoga every day wouldn't have made me that graceful. I held Odin's heart up above my head for a moment, gathering my thoughts.

I had no prayer for the old man. All I could think of was a warning.

"Be good," I told him.

Then I carefully lowered his heart, sliding it back into his chest.

Odin took a shuddering breath a moment later, then lay still, looking vulnerable in his sleep.

I knew it would be a while before he woke up.

I still had nothing to say to him. He could find his own way down the mountain to his hall.

I had more work to do.

THOUGH I'D SEEN and done some strange things, the next place Anubis took me to was the strangest of all.

I knew it instantly. This was Yggdrasil, the great tree. It existed in its own plane, the horizon bending around it, forming a slightly pink bubble that surrounded it. Night and day flowed above and below the great tree, one chasing the other like a crazy cat-and-mouse cartoon. Hundreds of branches forked above the huge trunk, while just as many roots spread beneath it. No leaves, flowers, or berries grew on it, but I had no doubt that the tree was alive.

We stood on one of the roots, looking up. I felt like an ant contemplating a sequoia. The world tree was vastly tall and broad, bigger than any skyscraper. The space was full of warm, humid air, which surprised me—I'd figured it would be cold here, like the snowy north. The trunk smelled like good cedar bark, fresh and warm. The silence was eerie, my ears straining for any noise, expecting but not finding any *shush* of wind.

While this was all new to me, I didn't hesitate. I knew what needed doing.

I placed the hand still coated in Odin's blood against the rough bark, then *pushed* with all my power.

The resistance I felt didn't surprise me. Yggdrasil wasn't merely alive, but *aware*.

It wasn't like we would ever be sitting down and having coffee and a chat together. The All World tree was too alien for that.

But it knew me, and it knew its place as an access point to every plane.

I pushed more power at it, willing the tree to grow into more than just a gate. Like Hakeem, I gave all my abilities to it freely.

Slowly, understanding grew. The bark beneath my fingers grew smoother, the cracks along the trunk disappearing, rounding it out, until it stood like a mighty spear. It was still wooden, a living thing. However, now the tree had grown wary of all trespassers.

I felt myself shrink down, my godhood leaving. I had a brief pang of regret, but I would take a human lifetime with Theresa over a lonely eternity as a goddess any day.

I asked for one wish, an instant of respite, before all my power vanished. In that blink of an eye, I reached down and touched Hunter, purifying his blood of all cravings. He might still be emotionally addicted to drugs, but physically he'd no longer need them, ever again.

I also touched Hakeem. I couldn't return all of his gift—it had been too freely given. But I returned what I could so that he would at the very least have a touch of grace while driving.

Then the last of my godhood flowed out of me. I stood, as a human, dwarfed by the All World tree. It hadn't taken everything I'd offered it; I still had my post-cog abilities. Seemed the tree believed I needed them.

Anubis still stood beside me. He'd shrunk down as well, going from a dog-headed man into merely a dog.

Mind you, a dog that was as big as a fucking horse. He had sharp, pointed ears, a long snout, and short black fur. He looked like a darker version of a pharaoh's hound. He raced up the side of the tree, climbing it effortlessly, then settled down in the Y of a branch.

Not only would the tree guard against all those who dared to use it to cross between the worlds, Anubis would be there as well.

I knew that wouldn't stop the gods forever. They were sneaky and were sure to find a hole in the gate.

But I was willing to bet that it would be later, rather than sooner. The human worlds would be free of the influence of the gods for a century or more. Free to screw it all up, or possibly to find their own way for once.

Hunter and I would still have weird shit in our lives. But there would be far fewer apocalypses on our watch.

I was okay with that.

Saving the world never paid worth shit.

15

Hunter and I met at a locally owned coffeeshop. It was a cozy place, with comfortable chairs and broad windows that faced south. It was still fucking cold—February in Minneapolis and all that—but the sunlight felt good.

We sat ourselves in the front of the shop, me with hot chocolate and extra whipped cream, Hunter with black coffee, and watched the midday downtown traffic.

It had been three days since we'd left Jacobsen Consortium with our former prisoners in tow, three days of constant news articles with hourly updates.

The announcement that Jacobsen Consortium had a secret prison in the bowels of its headquarters shook things up considerably. That at least half a dozen government officials had been compliant in the coverup was just icing on the cake. Josh and his whole crew of spies had also been exposed, and were facing charges.

Public opinion had swerved in favor of the *blessed* for once. It was a strange how people suddenly stopped being afraid of me, Hunter, and the others.

I didn't expect it to last long, but I sure as fuck was going to take advantage of it while it lasted. My phone was buzzing night and day, and we had more cases than we could handle.

Fortunately, Sam had her people already in place when the news hit. They were able to take over the conversation, pointing out that this would have never happened if the *blessed* had been in charge of themselves.

While I cynically didn't believe a word of that crap, particularly given how the *blessed* had left me out in the cold previously, at least publicly I supported the position.

It took some coordinating between me, Sam, and Theresa, but we finally got the timing down right.

All I had to do was to play my part to the hilt.

Hunter cleared his throat, bringing my attention back to the day. "So. Boss. Whatcha want to talk about?"

No one sat close to us. In the far corner a young woman banged away on her keyboard, typing so angrily I wondered what it had done to piss her off. The cute barista stood behind her counter at the back of the shop, reading something on her phone.

I took a sip of the blessed sweet chocolate before I spoke.

"How do you feel?" I asked instead of answering him.

Hunter shrugged. "Good." He paused, then stared hard at me. "Calm."

Huh. I hadn't expected that, but it made sense.

"As one of my last acts as a goddess, I cleaned your blood," I told him. "You're not addicted physically anymore. Can't be." That last was a stretch. If Hunter worked at it, he likely could get himself addicted again. But he'd have to seriously abuse himself in the process.

Hunter nodded. "I suspected that," he said. "Thank you."

"You're welcome," I said. "You realize that because the gates to the worlds are more closed than they have been, the *poisoned pearls* probably won't work as well as they once did."

"That's true. But because the gates are closed, we probably won't need the extra help as much, either," he said.

I smiled. God, it was good to have a partner who understood these sorts of things. But I still had to ask.

"Are you certain you still want to continue working with me?" I asked. I needed to check with him. I knew he liked it. But I wasn't sure it was good for him.

"Audrey and I talked about it," Hunter admitted. "About me quitting and going to work for her. She made a sweet case about how good I'd be working with the other vets."

"And?" I prompted when he didn't continue immediately. I had to admit my heart had started hammering. What would I do without him?

I'd survive. I knew that. But nothing would be the same.

"It doesn't make sense, not right now. Maybe in a year from now," Hunter said, giving me a sly grin.

"Asshole," I said. "Worrying me like that."

"You need my help," Hunter added, still grinning. "And I like working with you, boss. Yeah, the weird stuff will be a challenge sometimes. But how can you defeat your enemy unless you regularly engage with him?"

I snorted. "Truer words, man."

We sat in silence drinking our respective drinks, letting the afternoon sun bake us into our new shapes, leaving us pliable for the new form we were both taking.

Becoming was more than just about godhood, you know?

And I was finally becoming what I'd always been meant to be.

Wife. Daughter. Kick-ass investigator.

With a whole tray of sarcasm on the side.

I mean, I wasn't about to give up all my superpowers, right?

16

DEBRA COULDN'T HAVE BEEN MORE surprised when Cassandra came walking into her breakfast nook Friday morning, a week after the Jacobsen scandal had broken.

Cassandra knew better than to just arrive unannounced. She should have called and let Debra know she was visiting. Debra was frequently busy, or out.

Then again, Cassandra did know Debra's habit of spending her mornings alone. And at least had timed her visit to coincide with the end of Debra's alone time.

"Morning!" Cassandra said cheerily. She sat down in one of the guest chairs, swinging her black boots up onto another.

Debra merely had to glance at Cassandra's feet before she took them down and properly placed them under the table.

Good. Maybe her daughter wasn't spoiling for a fight. She was at least dressed nicely, in a cute purple blouse over a dark purple camisole. Of course, it was too tight, but Debra had given up fighting Cassie and her style choices years ago.

Cassandra helped herself to a cup of coffee as well as a slice of toast. She sat smiling and contently munching in the morning silence.

Debra finally had had enough. "While it's lovely to see you, especially at such an early hour, I'm certain you didn't come here just for coffee and toast."

Cassandra shrugged. "You do have really good coffee," she said, taking another sip.

After another long beat of quiet, Cassandra continued. "I'm here because I need a favor."

Debra sat back, blinking. She tried to cover her surprise by taking her own drink of (admittedly marvelous) coffee, but she knew she wasn't fooling her daughter. "Really?" Debra said, aware that her voice contained something of a purr.

"Really," Cassandra said. "I need you to come to brunch with me today. You don't have to eat anything, you just have to be there."

"Impossible," Debra said. The Jacobsen Consortium board of directors was holding a public meeting that morning. She *had* to be there. The new board was being verified today. She was already assured a seat. She had to make sure that certain undesirables weren't allowed onto the board.

"Mom, please," Cassandra pleaded. "I need you. Today."

Debra had never heard that tone in Cassandra's voice before, at least not since she'd been a child. Naked and raw with emotion, with pain.

Debra narrowed her eyes at Cassandra, really looking at her. Now she noticed the dark circles under Cassandra's eyes, as if she hadn't been sleeping well. Cassandra had also lost weight, which normally would have been a good thing, but she was on the verge of too much weight loss.

"Why?" Debra asked. She *had* to be at the board meeting. Maybe she could just make the tail end of it? Would that be enough?

"I asked Theresa to marry me," Cassandra said, her voice full of unshed tears. "I fucked it up."

"I'm sorry she turned you down," Debra said gently.

Cassandra nodded, her look growing determined. "She didn't believe me when I asked her. Didn't believe the proposal was *real*."

That surprised Debra. Cassandra was one of the most...well, *real* people she knew.

"So you need to be there, at brunch today. When I ask her again," Cassandra said.

At Debra obvious confusion, Cassandra continued. "Asking her to marry me in front of you, my mother, will show her that I mean it, that I'm serious about being with her."

Debra nodded slowly. That made more sense to her. Cassandra didn't care about the world's opinion of her.

But Mommy still mattered, as she should.

"Must it be today?" Debra asked, thinking about the rest of her schedule. "How about next Tuesday instead?"

Cassandra shook her head. "It's been a week. Any more, and she'd going to think I changed my mind." She paused, then added, "Please. Mom. I really need you today."

Debra opened her mouth, then shut it again.

It wasn't that her daughter was more important than the Jacobsen Consortium board meeting. No, there were thousands of lives at stake there, which weighed more than the single one sitting in front of her.

However, Cassandra had asked for a favor. Said *please*. Had practically begged for her mother's approval.

That meant something.

Plus, Cassandra would now owe her a favor in return.

If some of the seats on the board were filled by idiots, Debra would be able to oust them later. They wouldn't make any important decisions immediately, of that, she was certain.

She could be there for her daughter today.

THERESA WAITED NERVOUSLY at the restaurant. It was a high-end place, located north of downtown, in an old grain mill that had been revamped into retail on the lower floors with flats above. It overlooked the Minnesota river and all of downtown.

If it wasn't for this scheme of Cassie's, Theresa never would have agreed to eat here. This wasn't their type of place. Cassie was all for old dives and greasy spoons, not yuppified joints with heavy linen tablecloths and napkins, cut glass flutes for Champagne, the wait staff all in white shirts and black ties.

But Cassie had convinced her it was necessary. They'd already made up, and Theresa had privately already agreed to Cassie's marriage proposal.

This was part of the public play that would help them both in the long run.

Cassie showed up with Debra in tow just a few minutes later. "Good morning, my dear," Debra said, walking directly over to Theresa, taking her hands, then air-kissing both her cheeks. "How are you doing today?"

Theresa tried not to roll her eyes too hard. Of course, once Debra had agreed to have brunch with them, she would take over the entire operation, acting as if it had been *her* idea in the first place.

"I'm doing well," Theresa said truthfully.

Debra sat down beside her, her laser focus still on Theresa. "And how about your job?" Debra asked.

"There are rumors that we'll all be asked to quit, then reapply for our positions," Theresa admitted. "The NDAs we signed were pretty egregious. There's been some talk of a class-action lawsuit as well."

Debra nodded as if she was completely sympathetic to Theresa's plight. Cassie's hand found hers, giving it a warm, solid squeeze.

"We've been assured that the new employment contracts would be much more friendly," Theresa said. She shrugged. "We'll see."

She and Cassie had talked about that as well. Theresa would have to retrain if she wanted to work someplace else. She was willing to do it. They'd decided to wait, however, and see what the new contracts offered.

A lot of Theresa's upper management had already quietly left. Including Julie the evil H.R. person.

Theresa hoped that a lot of her upper management would still be sued, if not arrested, for enforcing such draconian measures on the rest of them.

"Let's talk of lighter things then, shall we?" Debra said. "Have you seen the plans for the new hockey stadium?"

Theresa brightened right up. She was aware that she was dominating the conversation, talking about the new stadium, what that would do for her team, as well as wandering into some stats about her favorite players, what they'd done after leaving the college team and joining "that other place"—the NHL, whom she'd never forgiven.

It gave Debra the opportunity to talk about the tax base necessary to support sport teams, how the voting needed to go, and some of the backroom politics that had gone on for the levy to be passed.

However, what else could they talk about? She and Cassie had agreed that it would be best if Theresa did most of the talking, as Cassie really didn't want to get into an argument with her mother and wasn't one hundred percent certain how to avoid it.

After they'd eaten (Theresa had had a divine omelet, whose fluffiness had defied gravity) and the final round of mimosas and coffee had been served, Theresa felt the air change.

She'd already said yes. Still, an almost familiar nervousness surrounded their table. At least Theresa knew what Cassie had planned to say this time.

"Theresa," Cassie said, standing. "Mom," she added, nodding at her mother.

Debra sat up and smiled proudly again, as if this had all been her idea.

"Yes?" Theresa asked, looking at her love. "What is it?"

Cassie got down on one knee, taking Theresa's cool hand in her warm ones.

"I love you," Cassie started off with. "I want to show that to you, every day. Be with you, every day. Prove it to you, every day. You mean the world to me. Being with you means changes, yes, but being without you would mean changes for the worst. I never want to lose you. I want to be with you to the end of my days. Please, please, believe me when I say that I love you and I want to marry you, to declare our bond as solid and sacred, in front of man and all the gods. Will you marry me?"

Theresa blinked away at the tears in her eyes. Damn it! She wasn't supposed to cry this time. "I will marry you, Cassandra, and be happy with you the rest of my days."

Theresa glanced over at Debra. She was still smiling, though she looked a touch impatient.

Had they delayed her enough?

Cassie got out the small box that still held the beautiful emerald ring. It was on a silver, platinum band, and fit Theresa's finger perfectly. Then Cassie surged up and kissed Theresa soundly.

Theresa didn't mind the PDA for once. How often was she going to get engaged? She rested her arms on Cassie's shoulders and returned the kiss, giving as good as she got.

She broke it off when Cassie reached up and started caressing her breasts. "That's enough," she said, laughing.

Cassie merely gave her a cocky grin before sitting back down on her chair, still holding Theresa's hand.

As planned, the maître d' came over with a new bottle of

Champagne just at that moment, pouring them all glasses, offering his hearty congratulations.

Debra stayed through the ensuing toasts, then finally said, "I'm so happy for the two of you! We'll have to do dinner, soon. Now, I must go."

Cassie nodded, smiling, as if nothing could diminish her happiness.

Theresa understood the feeling.

"Thank you," Cassie said to her mom. She even sounded sincere. "You want me to call Hakeem? He could get you to the meeting quickly. He's the best driver I know."

Debra seemed surprised by the suggestion, but she accepted quickly. "That's the man who drove us here? He is a very smooth driver," she said.

Seemed Hakeem was capable of charming even Debra Lewis. Not surprising, really. Had Debra not noticed that the drive to the restaurant had taken much longer than it should have?

Hopefully, she wouldn't notice how long Hakeem took to get her to the meeting, either.

Cassie was already texting Hakeem, who, it turned out, was just three minutes away.

"Thank you," Cassie said again to her mom as they all stood up to give each other air-kisses goodbye.

Properly mollified, Debra left the room in a controlled hurry.

"Think it was enough?" Theresa asked as Cassie sat down beside her.

Cassie shrugged. "Hope so. Now it's in Sam's hands."

Theresa nodded. "Thank you," she said.

"For what?" Cassie asked, looking adorably confused.

"For trying to make it all right," Theresa said. "Not just between us. But for everyone."

Cassie shrugged. "It's my job, you know?"

Theresa did know. In that way, Cassie and her mom were very

much alike. Both out to save the world, just in their own very special, unique ways.

Theresa also knew that it would take at least a lifetime for her to fully express her love to Cassie, her appreciation for the goddess who was still in her life.

She couldn't wait to start.

SAM STILL SAT at the head of the table in the small conference room. The newly elected board had decided to take a break after the last round of voting. There were only a few more things to be completed.

Most of the twenty people in the room gathered in groups of twos and threes, quietly chatting, though a couple of people still sat and went through their notes, like Sam.

The room was one of the smaller conference rooms at the Jacobsen Consortium headquarters. Another five people and the room would be overly full. Tall windows lined one long wall, showing the brilliant day outside. The smell of cheap coffee filled the small space. The donuts were long gone. If it had been warmer, Sam would have suggested opening at least a few of the windows and getting some fresh air in here. The room had a strange energy to it—both nervous as well as joyous. There was so much work ahead of all of them.

But they were almost finished that morning. Just a few more things to accomplish.

Cassie had already warned Sam that her mom was on her way.

For the first time, Sam felt up to the task of meeting Debra Lewis.

And finally thwarting her.

Dennis the telepath stood in one corner of the room. Though his expression was as bland as the plain beige shirt and brown tie that he wore, Sam still suspected that he was delighted. He'd been surprisingly easy to bring over to their side. All he wanted was a position of respect and power.

He had that now, in spades.

His counterpart, Sharleen, stood across from Dennis in another corner. She was the opposite of him in every way. While Dennis had the round figure of an office worker, Sharleen still looked like the lean, mean, killing machine that the army had made her into. She wore a bright fuchsia blouse that highlighted her black skin beautifully, and tight jeans that showed just how beautiful a woman's curves could be.

Sharleen had similar powers to Dennis, and the ability to influence people unaware. The pair of them could either work together to mold the opinions of an entire room, or they could run interference on one another, canceling out each other's powers.

Sam was aware that the chances of Dennis and Sharleen actually working together were generally about the same as a snowball's chance of surviving in hell.

Debra finally arrived. She looked around, controlling her surprise adequately when she realized that she only knew about half of the people in the room.

Her position on the board had been assured. Sam had seen to that.

What was the old saying? Keep your friends close and your enemies closer?

"It's been ten minutes," Sam finally said, raising her voice above the various conversations. "Let's begin."

It amused Sam to realize how the board seated themselves, with Debra in the middle of the lawyers and bankers along one side of the table, while the others sat opposite them.

The others all being members of the *blessed*.

Yup. She really would have her work cut out for her trying to bring this group cohesion.

"I'd like to welcome Debra Lewis," Sam said after the meeting was called to order. "She is the mother of Cassandra Lewis, a post-cog of some renown."

Of course, some of the smart alecks in the room replied with, "Hi, Debra!"

Sam nearly snorted at Debra's prim look. Obviously, that wasn't how a proper board meeting was supposed to be run.

She was in for quite a surprise.

"Since Debra missed the earlier introductions, and we are still getting to know each other, why don't we go around the table again? Give your name, your profession, and your position on the board," Sam said.

She looked over her shoulder at Dennis, nodding for him to start.

"Dennis McCutcheon," he stated proudly. "Telepath and Sergeant-at-Arms for the Jacobsen Consortium board of directors."

"That means he's one of the two telepaths in charge of mental security at the meetings," Sam explained to Debra. "No other telepath will be able to eavesdrop on board meetings. And no one will be able to influence other members of the board unduly. He's empowered to question any member coming in who radiates strong fear or other emotions. As is Sharleen."

Debra narrowed her eyes at Sharleen and her introduction, but didn't say anything.

The rest of the board introduced themselves, adding their position on the board, such as secretary or member-at-large. All the currently recognized branches of psychics were represented, though Sam was planning on broadening out their base as soon as it was feasible, bringing on the psychics who currently fell between the cracks, such as those who saw patterns or could make plants grow.

The mundanes started to introduce themselves. Samuel made the room laugh with his title of "Financial Wizard".

Debra was smart enough to go along with everyone, and introduced her role as, "private citizen and concerned parent."

Sam introduced herself last as the chairman of the board. She'd considered making her introduction more cute, adding something like "and chief bottle washer."

She didn't, however. The lawyers and bankers, as well as Debra Lewis, needed to respect that Sam was actually in charge.

Debra looked around the table after everyone had been introduced, finally seeming to realize that she was outnumbered. Fourteen members of the board were of the *blessed*, while merely seven members were mundane.

A ratio that was now codified in the newly updated bylaws for the corporation.

"Madam Secretary, what is the next item on the agenda?" Sam asked Linda, the Asian woman sitting just a few seats down. Her Chinese name was Lin Hua, but in formal occasions like this, she preferred going by her American name of Linda.

Lin Hua was just for friends and family, those who knew her better.

And Sam hoped that she'd have a chance to get to know Lin Hua a lot more intimately.

"Just three items, Madam Chairman," Linda said. "First, there's one last portion of the bylaws that needs to be verified, plus the director's statement, and then setting the time and date for the next meeting."

"Bylaws?" Debra asked. "You've already changed the bylaws? Don't you have to give notification before that meeting takes place?"

"We did," Sam said. "The email notification was sent to all members of the past board."

Debra's eyes narrowed.

"As their last act, the old board voted in the updated bylaws," Sam continued blithely. It was either that or face a class action lawsuit by all of the *blessed*. Criminal charges were still being placed. "At the start of this meeting, we sent out the notification that we'd be voting on the rest of the bylaw changes as we were all gathered here."

"I wasn't here," Debra said frostily.

"One hundred percent attendance isn't required. We just needed a quorum," Sam explained.

It had taken a while for Sam to work her way through all those business books, like *How To Incorporate Your Business,* as well as the various tutorials on YouTube. But Sam was smart, and she finally had a grasp on how a corporation really worked.

There was more for her to learn, she knew. Some of the lawyers and financial wizards on the board were sympathetic to her cause, though, and were happy to help educate her.

Sam knew she hadn't immobilized Debra. Nothing short of death would do that, and Sam suspected that Debra would set up her will such that she would still be able to pull strings from far beyond the grave.

However, Debra was defanged at the moment.

Sam couldn't help her triumphant smile when Debra finally realized that she no longer had a place of power. She still had a seat at the table, but not in a position of power.

Debra gave Sam a shrewd smile as well as a nod, as if saying, *well done.*

Sam could only nod in return.

Let the games begin.

She just hoped that she'd be up for the challenge of regularly fencing with Debra Lewis.

What was it that Hunter had said?

How can you defeat your enemy unless you regularly engage them?

ODIN STOOD on the Valhalla side of the Bifrost bridge, looking across the snowy chasm, in the place where Heimdall usually stood. The keeper of the bridge was in his warm house, probably carving.

Brilliant stars shone down from a velvet black sky. Clear winds flowed down from the mountains, making the snow whirl and dance in places. Behind Odin, across the valley, his men sang in his hall, toasting each other with the finest mead, ready to face the next day's battle.

The crisp air invigorated Odin, making his blood hum steadily. He'd recovered greatly since his "death"—as his heart had never really stopped beating, it was difficult to specify exactly what state he'd been in previously. His old strength flowed through his arms and legs, making him even more fierce when it came to war.

Odin and his men met on the glorious field of battle most days, aiming to win the prize of valor. Or they held contests, wrestling or drinking or even sprinting, constantly striving to be the best.

While Odin wouldn't admit it out loud, he did kind of miss Loki. Odin couldn't even go and visit the other god anymore; seemed that when Cassandra had killed Loki, the All Worlds tree had decided that the trickster had tied himself too firmly to the magical spell that had opened the planes to the gods.

Now, the spirit of Loki was imprisoned within Yggdrasil itself.

Had that been why Cassandra had given the All Worlds tree her power? To keep Loki in his place?

Odin would have liked to ask her, but he couldn't.

Perhaps Yggdrasil would have let Odin pass. They had been companions and were still tied together in some aspects.

However, then there was that damned dog to contend with.

Though it was too dark to see across the Bifrost bridge, Odin could still feel the presence of that foreign god at the other end. Sometimes during the day, the clouds would mist together just right and Odin would swear he'd even see the face of the dog staring back across the bridge at him.

Ah, well. Eventually that too would pass, Odin was certain of it. All things changed, ended, and were born anew.

In the meanwhile, perhaps Cassandra had been right in closing the gods off from all access to the human worlds. Odin was curious to see what humanity could do on its own, away from the influence of all the gods.

Perhaps they could bring their own heaven on earth, as he knew that Cassandra hoped.

They certainly could never bring about a place as wonderful as Valhalla.

Odin turned away from the bridge and started walking back across the valley of the gods, toward his hall and his men, singing mightily, his song echoing off the mountains on either side.

It was good to be home.

READ MORE!

Be sure to read all four kickass Cassie stories:

Poisoned Pearls
Tainted Waters
Spoiled Harvest
Bloodied Ice

ABOUT THE AUTHOR

Leah Cutter writes page-turning fiction in exotic locations, such as a magical New Orleans, the ancient Orient, Hungary, the Oregon coast, rural Kentucky, Seattle, Minneapolis, and many others.

She writes literary, fantasy, mystery, science fiction, and horror fiction. Her short fiction has been published in magazines like *Alfred Hitchcock's Mystery Magazine* and *Talebones*, anthologies like Fiction River, and on the web. Her long fiction has been published both by New York publishers as well as small presses.

Find Leah's books here.

Follow her blog at www.LeahCutter.com.

Reviews

It's true. Reviews help me sell more books. If you've enjoyed this story, please consider leaving a review of it on your favorite site.

Come someplace new…

Are you a traveler? Do you enjoy exploring strange new worlds, new cultures, new people?

Journey into the various lands envisioned by Leah Cutter.

Sign up for my newsletter and I'll start you on your travels with a free copy of my book, *The Island Sampler*.

I will never spam you or use your email for nefarious purposes. You can also unsubscribe at any time.

http://www.LeahCutter.com/newsletter/

ABOUT KNOTTED ROAD PRESS

Knotted Road Press fiction specializes in dynamic writing set in mysterious, exotic locations.

Knotted Road Press non-fiction publishes autobiographies, business books, cookbooks, and how-to books with unique voices.

Knotted Road Press creates DRM-free ebooks as well as high-quality print books for readers around the world.

With authors in a variety of genres including literary, poetry, mystery, fantasy, and science fiction, Knotted Road Press has something for everyone.

Knotted Road Press
www.KnottedRoadPress.com